GARDEN OF EDEN

GARDEN OF EDEN is a work of fiction. The events and characters that are described are imaginary and are not intended to refer to specific places or living persons.

GARDEN OF

EDEN

V.M. JACKSON

One

Unable to fully open her eyes, Eden blinked rapidly, shielding her face from the blinding light hovering over her. As the ringing in her ears faded out, youthful laughter could be heard in the distance. She felt a soft, warm breeze graze her skin, and a spearmint taste fill her mouth. One by one, her senses returned to her. Slowly lowering her arms, Eden squinted around as the beaming light began to dim away. It took her a minute to make out the outline of a large, familiar building in front of her.

"What in the world?" She furrowed, soon realizing she was standing in front of her old elementary school. She turned to her left, and then to her right, quickly scanning her surroundings, her self-awareness kicking in. She was in her old neighborhood, a place she hadn't seen since she was twelve-years-old. The buildings and grounds that looked large to her as a child now seemed strangely small. Eden began walking her old route home from school, the distance now shortened by her longer strides. The more she walked, the louder an innocent, familiar female voice grew, eventually stopping her in her tracks directly in front of her best friend Quinn's house.

Virginia Beach, Virginia. 1999

Mannequin Gray, the only daughter of the wealthy, honorable Judge Steven Gray, and his wife, Dr. Olivia Gray. Their large, four-story house sat alone at the top of the hill, surrounded by a white picket fence overlooking the lake. There were three levels of decks, four patios, a large fragrant garden, and, oh yes, no one could see their house from the road. Despite being born with a silver spoon in her mouth, Quinn was *never* rotten. She was graceful, poised, well-mannered, soft-spoken, and appreciative— everyone loved her, especially the boys.

Quinn was tall and curvy, dipped in baby smooth, rich caramel. She had mid-back length, cinnamon brown curls, a pair of breathtaking smoky gray eyes, and a smile that could make Satan himself return to righteousness. Quinn had a seamless, raw beauty, a spitting image of her mother. They both looked as if they were ripped straight from the pages of a magazine. Eden could see sixteen-year-old Quinn giggling on her front steps while her high school sweetheart, Andre, stood in the grass nearby proudly showing off the way he caught a winning touchdown pass to win the school championship.

"Mannequin?" Dr. Gray emerged from the back door, sticking her head out, as Quinn turned to face her.

"Hey. You're home early," Quinn glanced at her watch.

"I am. It's a slow day. No one is dying, giving birth, or having a heart attack, so I'm on call. Thought I'd come home and get dinner started," Dr. Gray pleasantly smiled, noticing Andre standing in the grass. "Well hello, Handsome."

"Hi Dr. Gray," Andre blushed.

"How's that leg doing? Is it healing properly?"

"Yes, ma'am. I feel as good as new. I always do after leaving your hospital," he winked with a smile.

Dr. Gray playfully laughed. "That's good to hear. Since you're doing better, I assume you wouldn't mind mowing the lawn you're standing on, would you?"

Andre's smile slowly shifted into a straight face. "Sure, I wouldn't mind at all." He replied, masking his annoyance.

Quinn discreetly giggled.

"Great," Dr. Gray beamed. "Oh, Mannequin, I brought a patient home with me. She was released from my care this morning, tonsil free."

She smiled just as Quinn's beautiful eyes lit up like a kid on Christmas morning, jumping up from the steps.

Eden watched her eleven-year-old self duck underneath Dr. Gray's arm to come out of the back door, smiling from ear to ear.

"Eden!" Quinn hollered as they both ran into each other's embrace. " Open your mouth, let me see what the back of your throat looks like," Quinn said in excitement. Dr. Gray leaned against the door frame, shaking her head with laughter.

Eden smiled gracefully, watching herself and Quinn in their innocent, youthful moment. Without warning, her visual memory faded to black, transforming the beautiful, bright sunny sky into a moonlit dark, chilly night. Eden looked around in fear, noticing that she was now standing in the middle of a dead-end road that led into the woods.

"Okay, I'm *definitely* dreaming now," she confirmed, studying the familiar road and the dark scenery. Her gaze quickly averted to the left just as a black Range Rover emerged out of nowhere, unable to stop. Startled, Eden attempted to dodge the moving vehicle, but she couldn't will her limbs out of entropy fast enough.

"Stop!" She hollered, stretching her hands in front of her. The black truck traveling at full speed drove directly through her like a ghost. Eden screamed in a panic, spinning around to face the car and frantically feeling her body.

"What on earth?!" The tires screeched quickly just before hitting a red *Do Not Enter* sign in front of it, finally coming to a halt. Eden watched as her other best friend, Pandora, emerged out of the driver's seat, clutching the bottom of her ruffled prom dress.

Joanna Wilson was a five foot three, extremely petite and pretty girl. Her skin was the color of a soft harvest moon, and her dark brown shoulder-length hair was always styled to perfection. The two dimples embedded in her cheeks were as deep as the ocean, and her full, dark pink lips had just the right amount of lip-gloss painted on them. Her slanted, mysterious chocolate-colored eyes always twinkled with a hint of mischief. Although just as equally gorgeous as Quinn, no one should be fooled by her beauty; *Pandora was a menace.*

Creek Manor, Virginia, 2001

"Anna, where are we? This doesn't look like CVS," Quinn hissed from the passenger seat, watching Pandora jump out of it.

"Your period didn't come on, and you didn't have us sneak out of prom to go with you to CVS for tampons, did you?" Quinn asked. Eden giggled in amusement, peaking her head between the front seats to see what was going on.

"No, I'm sorry. I lied," Pandora huffed, pulling a can of white spray paint from under her dress.

"What are you doing? What's that?" Quinn asked with widened eyes.

"An informal warning for Sheila Bradford," Pandora hissed, shaking the canister before opening it.

"Principal Bradford's daughter? The geeky president of the science club?" Quinn looked confused.

"Geeky my behind," Pandora fussed. "She's a thieving little skank, and I just caught her and Bobby all over each other in the janitor's closet."

"What?" Quinn gasped.

"The dark-skinned chick with the coke bottle glasses, right?" Eden asked. "I told my mom I saw a girl dodge security and run into the broom closet! She didn't believe me. She's a horrible chaperone; I don't know why they would invite her to watch someone else's kids. She brought me along as company and probably doesn't even realize I snuck off. Just like she didn't notice the football team spiking the punch earlier, or that Pandora stole Sheila's mother's car keys right from her purse while she was talking to her-" Eden caught herself.

"Eden!" Pandora sneered, causing Quinn to gasp in shock.

"Sorry," Eden replied, embarrassed for opening her big mouth.

"Oh my Goodness! This is Principal Bradford's car? I thought this was the car your parents rented for prom," Quinn yelled.

"No, ours is white. Anyway, I'm doing Principal Bradford a favor," Pandora stated, matter-of-factly.

"By stealing her car?" Quinn hollered.

"By letting her know that her daughter is a trashy whore." In big letters, Pandora boldly spray-painted the words *your daughter is a trashy whore,* on Principal Bradford's car. Quinn screamed in fright, quickly covering her mouth with her hands.

Eden's mouth fell open. "Wow, you guys are gonna get in *so* much trouble," she laughed in amazement.

"And then you brought Eden into this? Pandora, she's a kid who looks up to us," Quinn fussed.

"Quinn, stop being such a princess. We're about to graduate. Do something mischievous for once," Pandora stated in annoyance, throwing the spray paint can into the woods before running over to a nearby tree.

"Mischievous would've been putting gum in Sheila's hair, not stealing her mother— THE PRINCIPALS car and vandalizing it! That's a felony. You clean her car off right now and let's take it back to school before someone notices it's missing."

"You guys might wanna get out of the car," Pandora replied in a strained voice, walking back with a big cement block.

"No! I am not getting out of this car, what if someone sees—"

"Holy crap, she's got a brick," Eden cut through Quinn's words.

Before Quinn could react, she saw Pandora walk to the front of the truck, planting her feet in preparation to swing the cement. Quinn flung open the passenger door and jumped out, with Eden quickly following suit. Pandora used all of her strength to swing the cement into the air. It crashed right in the middle of Principal Bradford's windshield, shattering it completely.

"Come on! Let's get out of here. I know a shortcut back to school," Pandora whispered loudly before taking off into the woods. Eden followed behind with no questions asked. Quinn clutched the bottom of her prom dress, trotting behind in fear.

"We can kiss graduation goodbye…and college as well, because when my parents find out about this, I'm gonna be grounded for the next four years," Quinn cried, trying her best to keep up.

"If she's such a bad influence, why have you been friends with her for so long?" Eden asked, out of breath.

"I don't know. I've questioned my poor choices since middle school."

Eden laughed hysterically watching the three of them drift off into the woods. Suddenly, a brightly lit white path formed under her feet, and she found herself walking along it. As she walked, she reflected on the early experiences that contributed to the woman she'd grown into.

The clouds in the sky transformed into movie screens, displaying images of important times in her life. It was almost as if her brain was going through some kind of reboot. One of the screens showed Eden helping her mother, Ruby, in the downtown Virginia hair salon that she owned. Another screen replayed the year Ruby and Eden's father divorced after fifteen years of marriage, and Ruby went through a terrible depression. Eden was always a momma's girl, but that year they grew closer than ever.

A different screen showed Dr. Olivia Gray, one of the best doctors in the nation, shooting herself in the head the day of Quinn's high school graduation. Eden saw Ruby holding onto Quinn so tightly at her mother's funeral, while her younger self and Pandora sat beside them, face to face with a dead body for the first time. Quinn refused to go up to the casket or even look at it. She just stood there like a statue, robotically shaking hands. Ruby responded for her as people walked by repeating the same phrase. *"I'm sorry for your loss. I'm sorry for your loss. I'm sorry for your loss."*

Another screen showcased the day Pandora was rescued after being kidnapped by her neighbors and locked in their dungeon for almost nine months. Pandora's behavior shifted after that. She grew a hatred for her parents and lashed out in constant anger and rebellion. Ruby took her in and raised her alongside Eden, keeping her out of trouble. Other screens showed moments of companionship and rivalry between Eden and Pandora who, from living together, were more like sisters. Another screen showed Sunday outings to museums, the seashore with her friends, and visits to her grandmother's house, where Eden became someone extra special.

As Eden reached the end of the path, a final screen stretched out, taking over the entire sky. She saw a man that once looked familiar to her pointing a berretta in her face. His eyes were cold, demented, and full of revenge. Eden gasped at the man in her vision, clutching her chest in fear. He sneered, belting out a cold, chilling phrase just before unloading a bullet from his gun, straight into Eden's head. Eden jumped back at the horrible scene, screaming in terror.

Finally, an image of herself confined to a hospital bed, fighting for her life, surrounded her. Eden's eyes gaped open, staring at the horrible view. She could hear the breathing machine pumping air through her lungs. Her heart rate was slow but steady. She could see Quinn crying, begging her to hold on. An angry Pandora also stood close by, looking on in horror. With a face full of guilt, Jackson shook his head as he took in the ordeal. Lastly, she noticed Andre walking around the room praying.

"Oh no!" Eden screamed. Suddenly, she remembered the gun pointed at her face just before everything went black and she woke up to what she assumed was a dream. Her breathing sped up and her eyes frantically scanned the room. Though it felt like one, *this was no dream.*

"Am I dead?" She asked herself in fear.

"Not exactly," a soothing, familiar voice answered from behind. Eden spun around to see her mother walking toward her. Ruby wore a long white dress, white stockings, and white heels. Her hair was pulled into a side bun, secured with a white flower headpiece.

"Mom? Oh my goodness!" Eden's mouth opened wide as she ran toward Ruby, overjoyed to see her again.

"Of all the pretty white dresses in my closet, whose idea was it to bury me in *this one*?" She asked, playfully glaring at Eden. "This one makes my hips look huge, and now I'm stuck in it for eternity," Ruby laughed, welcoming Eden into her arms.

Eden squeezed her tightly. "I've missed you *so* much," Eden pulled back slightly, staring at her mother in awe. "Are you alright?"

"I'm doing just fine. It's *you* I'm concerned about," Ruby stared into her daughter's eyes with her arms folded across her chest. Eden's eyes immediately filled with guilt and dropped to the floor. "What happened to my sweet, humble baby girl, on fire for life?"

"Life…is what happened. Everything changed after you left."

"Why?"

"What do you mean, why?" Eden replied. Annoyed, she looked up at her mother. "My world changed. You died, mom. You left me— just like that, and then my baby died, followed by the death of all of my hopes and dreams, and then-"

"And then because of all the bad choices you made after that, now you're strapped to life support getting ready to die," Ruby said. "Was it worth it, Eden?"

Eden slowly shook her head no, looking at Ruby with a pained expression. "I regret all of this. I wish things were different and I could turn back the hands of time. I wish you'd be a reality again."

"After the horrible mess you've made of your life, you should be grateful the Good Lord snatched me away when he did. I am *not* someone you'd be happy to see in the flesh right now," Ruby scolded.

"What was I supposed to do, mom? The love of my life married my best friend. My daughter died...you died. I was left to fend for myself. It's not fair that in all of this, I'm *still* the bad guy."

"You always did have a horrible habit of blaming everyone else for *your* mistakes," Ruby shook her head. "You lost your mind and acted a fool in *my* name, using *my* death as an excuse to ruin *your* life."

"It wasn't an excuse—"

"Sweetheart, life happens to us all," Ruby interrupted, "the good, the bad, *and* the ugly. You aren't the first daughter to lose a mother. Quinn lost hers the day of her high school graduation, but with good friends and a good support system, she went on living. And look at Anna. She was stolen from her family and raped in a basement for nine months of her life. You don't see her using that as a crutch, do you?" Ruby pointed, boring her eyes into Eden's. "You lost me, and you lost your baby. Your friends tried to be there for you, and the things you did to them were horrible. I left you my beautiful home and lifelong financial stability from my insurance policy and look at what you did with it. Life can either make you or break you, depending on how you play the hand you're dealt. You had *plenty* of chances to turn your bad hand into a winning one."

Ruby's words caused more tears to stream down Eden's face. "What chances? I didn't realize what was happening in my life until it was too late. Reality happened, and I went with it," she cried in defense.

"The signs were all there, the chances were all there. You ignored them," Ruby replied softly.

"There were no signs!" Eden defended.

"Sure there were. Allow me to refresh your memory."

Two

"Weather the storm, don't let the storm weather you."

One year ago...

Eden was awakened by the deafening sound of her alarm on the other side of her room. Dragging herself out of bed, she staggered over to the alarm clock, repeatedly hitting the snooze button.

"Oh no," she peered at the clock through her heavy eyelids. "I set the wrong time *again.*" Scurrying across her bedroom, Eden snatched off her pajama shirt and walked out of her shorts before entering her bathroom to shower. A year had passed since the death of her mother and her daughter. To the public eye, Eden seemed to have adjusted to their deaths quite well. Ruby Grant was the Jewel of Virginia. She was best known for her coffee shop, "Brew'd Awakening," and her hair salon, "Head Office". She owned both businesses for nearly twenty years, making herself well-known and loved by many. Her sudden death was truly felt. Ruby always saw to it that her only daughter was well taken care of, even in death. She left Eden over two million dollars of cash and investments, along with both of her popular businesses. The condo Ruby purchased that now belonged to Eden was paid off as well. At twenty-eight-years-old with no husband, children, or financial limitations, Eden's possibilities were endless.

Just as she turned off the water and opened the shower door, she heard her cellphone ringing from her bedroom. Securing her towel around her body, she rushed into the bedroom to grab it.

"Good Morning, this is Eden," she spoke, pleasantly.

"Good morning, Miss Grant. This is Peter, the code officer for the state of Virginia."

"Good morning," she raised an eyebrow.

"We were supposed to meet two weeks ago to discuss some violations with your coffee shop. You never showed up, and we've reached out several times to reschedule."

"Oh no," Eden rubbed her temples, realizing she'd forgotten about the appointment. "I'm *so* sorry. I've had so much going on over the last month and it completely slipped my mind. Can we reschedule for some time next week?"

"I'm afraid we can't. Your coffee shop has some major safety concerns. The electrical system is faulty, and your sprinkler system failed inspection twice. There have also been complaints that you're not keeping the place sanitary, as there have been rodents spotted in the kitchen area. You're gonna have to pay some major fines, in addition to repair costs in order to be re-inspected."

"What?" Eden yelled into the phone, "what kind of fines and repair costs? How much are they?"

"About thirty-five forty thousand dollars," the inspector replied.

Eden almost jumped out of her skin. "This must be a joke. No way can repairs and a simple re-inspection cost me forty grand."

"It does when you neglect your place of business."

"*First* of all, go to hell," she spat, immediately offended. "I don't neglect my business. I'm sorry I have a life and can't spend every waking moment there. I'm not paying forty thousand dollars."

"So you'd rather have us shut the place down than pay for the repairs and inspection?"

"Do what you need to do. I don't care anymore," Eden fussed, ending the call and tossing her phone on her bed. "Ugh!" She shook her head in disgust, reaching into her desk drawer for her bottle of Xanax. She took two pills from the medicine bottle and threw them into her mouth, using the half-drunken cup of water on her nightstand to wash them down. To the untrained eye, Eden had a handle on life. But in reality, it was life that had a handle on Eden. She barely slept at night, and secretly abused Xanax and anti-depressants during the day to keep her on cloud nine and away from her harsh reality.

Ruby's hair salon was shut down a few weeks prior because Eden refused to pay the taxes on it, and now her beloved coffee shop was next in line. The once mild-mannered, humble girl that Ruby raised was now temperamental, lazy, selfish, impatient, and rebellious. Eden splurged her fortune on lavish trips out of the country, expensive jewelry, and designer clothes. She redecorated her mother's home with all of the latest electronics, modernized furniture, and expensive paintings. Eden hired a butler, a maid, her own personal hairstylist, makeup artist, and a cleaning crew. She owned a Lamborghini and a limousine, complete with a chauffeur to drive her anywhere she wanted to go. Everything about Eden screamed money, from her black Stewart Weitzman diamond stilettos, black distressed

Pierre Balmain jeans, and black Versace crop top she quickly dressed herself in for her first day of grad school— the only *good* thing she invested her money in. Walking into the kitchen, she flicked on the television and reached into her cabinet for a Pop-tart, quickly eyeing the screen when she heard the news mention Pandora's name.

"*And she's done it again, America. Another cold-blooded murderer back on the streets, thanks to Defense Attorney, Joanna Ford,*" the news reporter said just as all of the cameras flashed on Pandora. Dressed in a calf-length, figure-hugging, black dress that emphasized the contours of her curvy frame, Pandora paraded down the courtroom hallway, winking at the victim's angry lawyer. Eden could easily walk in heels, but she could never pull off Pandora's jaw-dropping stiletto strut.

Pandora walked with purpose, pride, and perfect posture. Her head was straight, and her eyes were forward as she minced past the reporters, putting one foot in front of the other, causing a swing in her hips, and a bounce to her derrière. She had a hypnotizing, melting glide that was seductive, yet graceful. Her husband, Jackson, followed a few feet behind like a bodyguard, making sure the news reporters or family members of the victims didn't get too close to her.

"*Barbara, that woman is a lioness!*" The news anchor laughed to his co-host, "*the kind that would eat her own young to survive if she needed to.*"

"*A lioness indeed,*" Barbara replied, amused, "*with her King of the Jungle not too far behind.*"

The cameras flashed on Jackson swatting away paparazzi with one hand, and securely gripping Pandora's arm with the other. He escorted her down the narrow steps of the courthouse. The minute she reached the bottom of the stairs, Jackson walked ahead of her, extending his arm to open the large courtroom doors. Pandora pranced past Jackson as he watched with a sparkle in his eye.

Jackson was an extremely busy accountant, but he always found time to personally escort his wife to and from court to ensure her safety during big trials. Pandora was his life, and the grin she gave him let the world know the feeling was mutual. They were on fire for one another…and so was Eden's stomach. She swore she would vomit if she watched another second of them.

Rolling her eyes in disgust, she pressed the power button on her remote. "An assassin just walked free because of her, and they're worried about her *stupid* marriage," Eden tossed the remote and grabbed her purse before opening her front door. The second she opened it, she reached down to pick up the pile of mail sticking out of the mail slot. As she walked over to her trashcan, shuffling through her letters, her eyebrows furrowed when she noticed Mannequin and Andre plastered on the cover of her Essence magazine subscription.

Eden flung the rest of the mail on the counter and flipped through the magazine. Essence ranked Andre as one of the most powerful men in America, and Quinn, among the most beautiful women in the world. The magazine praised them for being a power couple and displayed different photos of them doing ministry in their Megachurch and community outreach. Essence also bragged about being the first to capture photos of their 6-month-old daughter, Heaven, whom Andre and Quinn had successfully kept out of the public's eye, until now. Pictures of the beautiful infant sharing happy moments with the proud couple, took up three pages. Eden grumbled under her breath, tossing the magazine in the garbage.

"*Power couple*," she mocked. "Give me a break, who do they think they're fooling?"

Glancing at the clock on her stove, Eden gasped and headed out of the front door. Twenty minutes later she parked her car and walked onto Virginia State University's campus like an A-list celebrity. The diamonds in her ears, on her wrist, and her shoes sparkled in the bright sunlight as the gentle breeze from the beautiful spring morning flowed through her shoulder-length weave. Making her way across the large campus, Eden stopped traffic and turned heads with a sly grin plastered on her face, soaking up the attention. The second she stepped into her sociology class, she spotted Jade, a girl she met at orientation, sitting near the back. Glancing up from her phone, Jade's eyes lit up the second they landed on Eden.

At five foot eight, one hundred and twenty pounds, Jade had the body of a supermodel. Her Halle Berry short cut went perfectly against her strong facial features. Her skin was a soft almond brown, and her slanted, narrowed eyes gave her a sultry, seductive look.

"There you are, I looked all over for you last

week," Jade squealed, excited, as Eden made her way to the back, taking a seat next to her.

"Hi," Eden beamed, "I'm so sorry. I had to run to my car and when I came back, I couldn't find you to give you my number."

"It's fine. What a relief to see a familiar face on the first day of class," Jade replied with a worried look on her face. "I'm so nervous."

"I wouldn't be, it's just school" Eden laughed, "It's not like we're signing up for the army."

"Yeah, I guess. It's just nerve-wracking for me because everything's happening at once," Jade muttered with a somber glow, "a new state, a new school...I feel like such an outsider."

"That's right, you *did* say you just came here from Chicago," Eden pulled out her iPhone to silence her ringer.

"Yeah, I've been there my entire life. My dad is the chief of police there too, so it's hard for me to do anything without him up my behind all the time." Jade laughed, reaching into her purse for a stick of chewing gum. "I needed a change."

"I definitely understand. You'll love Virginia. I mean, it's not as lively and busy as Chicago, but it's a lot of fun if you know where to go."

"What about the guys?" Jade asked with a mischievous stare. "Any cute ones? Because all the ones I've seen so far are mediocre and boring."

"There's a cute one right there," Eden slyly grinned, gazing up at a guy a few rows ahead of them that had been eyeing her since she walked in. Jade looked over at him, jerking her head back into a wince.

"Ew, *Travis*?" Jade chuckled, putting the stick of

gum into her mouth before crumbling up the wrapper in her hands.

"You know him?"

"Yeah, he's from Chicago too. I grew up with him. He's like a brother to me. *Supposedly,* he came here with me to get away and try something new, but I actually think my dad paid him off to follow me and keep tabs on me," she laughed.

"He's sexy," Eden confirmed, just as Travis turned to look her way with a flirtatious smirk. He stood six feet tall with a medium basketball player's build. Travis was baked in deliciously chocolate tan with piercing brown eyes, and a sharply defined, close hair cut with more waves than an ocean. His neatly sculpted goatee defined his alluring, dark pink lips that glistened from the moisture of his tongue.

Eden's mouth slowly opened, mesmerized by him. The second his eyes locked with hers, she felt a swarm of butterflies fluttering around in her stomach. A guy hadn't caught her attention like that since Jackson.

"I'm pretty sure he's gay," Jade whispered, causing all the butterflies in Eden's stomach to wither up and die.

"Gay?" She winced, rubbing her temples to free her mind of the lewd thoughts she'd quickly formed of Travis.

"I mean, I've never *asked* him," Jade laughed at Eden's disappointment, pulling out a notebook from her bag, "but I've known him all my life and have only seen him with one girl; *10 years ago.*

"Right," Eden muttered, still disheveled. "Well, that was short-lived."

The professor rushed into the classroom. "Good

morning, everyone! I'm so sorry I'm running a bit late. Welcome to Sociology." He walked over to the chalkboard, introducing himself.

Eden's cellphone began vibrating loudly in her purse. Taking her attention away from the professor, she reached into her bag and glanced at the phone. Pandora's name flashed on the screen. Eden got up from her desk and quickly walked out of the classroom into the hallway before accepting the call.

"Hey, Anna, what's up?"

"Happy first day of school!" Pandora's big mouth echoed through the phone, causing a shy grin to immediately form on Eden's face.

"You remembered, thanks," she giggled.

"Of *course* I remembered," Pandora fussed. "Why would I forget something like that?"

"Well you were just on the news bombarded with a bunch of cameras and questions, so I assumed you were busy and forgot, that's all."

"I *am* busy," Pandora confirmed, slightly out of breath.

Eden could hear the clicking of her heels stampeding across a floor.

"I'm actually getting ready to walk into a press conference, but I would never forget something so important to you. I wanted to tell you how proud I am of you and tell you to come over tonight so we can celebrate. Joe just got a promotion at his job so I figured we could all have a few drinks."

"Yeah, sure. I'll come over around eight," Eden replied with a smile.

"Perfect! See you then. I have to go," Pandora stated quickly just before her voice trailed off and the call ended.

Eden locked her screen, attempting to place her phone back into her bag, as a text message from Quinn popped up.

"Thinking of you! Enjoy your first day of classes, grad student!"

A dozen smiles and kissy-face emojis followed the message. Eden's eyes filled with regret. She felt terrible for the bitter thoughts she had of her best friends earlier, and she hated that her hidden jealousy of them had gotten the best of her within the last year.

Pandora was ruthless and would give you her behind to kiss in a heartbeat, but she had a soft spot for her best friends— especially Eden. Regardless of how busy she was, she called and texted Eden every day to check on her, and always made time to hang out. Quinn constantly begged Eden to come to church or to come stay with her and Andre for a few weeks to spend time with Heaven. Both of her friends hated that she lived alone, and they were always concerned. It was Eden's envy of them that tainted her perception, causing her to be distant.

Tossing her phone into her bag, she turned to walk back in the classroom, accidentally bumping into a tall figure.

"Hi," Travis grinned.

"H-hi," Eden stuttered, her eyes looking everywhere but at him. Gay or not, the awe of him still made her blush.

"I'm Travis," he smiled, gazing at her beautiful face.

"Eden," she muttered back.

"That's a beautiful name for a beautiful girl," he

flirted. Eden slowly looked up at him.

"Thank you," she blushed, slightly furrowing her eyebrows at him.

"Let me guess…Jade thinks I'm gay?" He laughed.

"Well…" she scratched her neck with a pensive expression.

"I'm not gay," Travis smiled, showing all thirty-two of his perfect teeth.

"Oh, thank God," she sighed with a giggle.

"But if were gay, I'd certainly reconsider today," he bit his bottom lip, winking at Eden. Blushing, Eden folded her arms and looked away. Travis wanted to speak a second time, but Eden's beautiful face choked him up. Putting his hands into his pockets, he blushed as well.

"I'm not used to this at all, I'm sorry," he admitted. The bass in his voice raised all of Eden's hormones back from the dead.

"Not used to what?" She looked up at him.

"Approaching girls like this. I'm a laid-back kind of guy. I see a lot of beautiful women, but they all look the same to me. It's very rare that a girl would catch my attention to the point where I'd walk out of class to go looking for her."

"So, I'm guessing I caught your attention?"

"You did. I hope your boyfriend isn't offended…"

"I don't have a boyfriend," she smirked.

"Well…that's good to know…"

Three

"The thoughts of the righteous are just; the counsels of the wicked are deceitful" –Proverbs 12;5

Eden parked alongside Pandora's house and got out of her car. Gazing up at the beautiful home sitting on four acres of land, Eden's mouth fell open at the fancy sight in front of her. Pandora previously owned two homes: one in Maryland where her firm was, and one in Virginia where her friends and family were. Jackson lived in North Carolina and owned a home passed down to him from four generations. After arguing over who would live with whom for almost nine months, Pandora and Jackson both swallowed their pride, sold their homes and bought a place together, two months ago.

Eden had seen the place when they first moved in, but she hadn't been back since. Their home was immaculate and enormous, the kind most kids dreamed of growing up in. Secluded amongst trees on one of Virginia's most exclusive streets, it had turrets, gables, dormers, two balconies, a screened-in front porch, a freestanding garage, a gazebo, a pool, and formal gardens. It was indeed the American dream.

Eden walked across the large lawn, wired at each perimeter with cameras, security lighting, and motion sensors. The minute she stepped into the half-opened doorway, she was met with walls and ceilings covered in mirrors and a high-tech bordello. Eden wasted thousands of dollars renovating her mother's home in an attempt to measure up with her friend's way of living, and she almost had them beat, but not anymore. Pandora's fancy home was *way* above her pay grade.

Glowering at the place, Eden was immediately jealous.

"Amazing, tell the *whole* world how much money you guys make," she muttered under her breath.

"Oh my goodness! Hi Eden," Andrea squealed in shock before rushing over to her with a hug.

Eden quickly dismissed the rest of her envious thoughts as she turned to face Andrea. "Hey, Andrea," she smiled, accepting her hug before rubbing Andrea's nine-month pregnant belly.

Andrea was five foot five, one hundred and forty pounds. She had a smooth mocha complexion, and slanted, seductive eyes. No matter what hairstyle she chose, she always completed it with a bang that covered most of her forehead. Andrea had the body of a video vixen, complete with triple D breasts and the kind of behind that stuck out so far you could sit a cup on top of it. Although her appearance gave off a somewhat snobbish personality, Andrea was a sweetheart and the only girl that ever made it past Pandora to marry her brother Joseph, six years ago.

"Wow, your belly looks like a boulder," Eden chuckled.

"Girl, I *feel* like a freaking boulder," Andrea laughed, shaking her head, "I can't *wait* to get these babies out of me."

"You look beautiful though," Eden warmly smiled, looking at Andrea from head to toe, "when's your due date?"

"Next week...I hope I can make it until then. I

can barely see my feet."

"I remember those days," Eden laughed. "Hang in there."

"How've you been?" Andrea asked in a conflicted voice.

"I've been great," Eden hesitantly nodded back with a fake smile.

"That's good to hear. You look great. I'm so glad to see you moving in a positive direction considering everything that's happened."

"Me too. Feels good to be back to normal," Eden lied, knowing her emotional state had become anything *but* normal.

"Babe, who are you talking to?" Joseph's slurred, intoxicated voice sounded in the living room.

"It's Eden, sweetie," Andrea replied.

"Eden? Eden get in here and congratulate me!" Joseph playfully hollered.

Andrea rolled her eyes and smirked. Eden laughed, walking into the living room where Joseph stood anxiously with his hands on his hips, watching a football game.

"Hello, Mr. Promotion," Eden smiled, rushing over to him. Wrapping her arms around his neck, she planted a kiss on his cheek.

"Thank you, thank you," Joseph cheesed, accepting Eden's hug. "Where the heck have you been? I haven't seen you in over a month."

"I've been around," Eden shrugged, "preoccupied with things at home. I also just started school, so things have been pretty hectic," Eden forced a smile. If one more person asked her where or how she's been she swore she'd slap the taste out of their mouth.

"That's *right*," Joseph's eyes widened. "Anna did tell me you started grad school, congrats!"

Even in a drunken state, Joseph was still a sight for sore eyes. He had butter pecan skin, bright hazel eyes, and a head full of beach sand-colored curls to match. Joseph reminded you of the boy next door. Since grade school, all the girls had been crazy over him, but the only girl Joseph ever went crazy over, was Quinn. Finally, after college, Joseph realized it would be a chilly day in hell before Andre *ever* let Quinn go, so he gave up hope, fell in love, and married Andrea.

"Thanks so much," Eden looked around, "where's Anna?"

"Well, she said she was going upstairs to change her clothes. But then Jackson came home and now he's upstairs too," Andrea smirked. "She's been *changing her clothes* for the last forty-five minutes."

Joseph covered his ears, annoyed.

"*Come on,* Andrea, she's upstairs changing her clothes, okay? Just let me believe that," he huffed in denial, still refusing to accept that his little sister was grown and married.

"I'm sure that's totally all she's doing," Eden giggled, "I'll go up and check." She turned and walked across the polished wood floors until she reached a graceful banister that curved up toward what looked like a soaring, second-floor gallery.

As she made her way up the stairs, the sounds from the loud television in the living room faded out, and a masculine groan filled Eden's ears. She froze in her tracks, remembering that familiar voice all too well. *It was Jackson.* Almost immediately Eden's mind was filled with flashbacks of all the years he and Eden spent making love to one another, or so she *thought* it was love at the time. After seeing the way he was with Pandora, Eden realized Jackson was telling the truth when he was confronted. He never loved Eden, she was just what he said she was— *something to do after his deranged ex.* Jackson got comfortable, and Eden got pregnant. It took her some time, but after a while, Eden accepted Jackson and Pandora's marriage.

As far as Eden was concerned, Pandora could *have* Jackson's heartless, cutthroat, conniving behind, and because all of those traits fit Pandora's personality to a T, Eden decided they were meant for each other. However, as Eden stood on the staircase frozen solid, something felt different. *Enviously different.* The more intense Jackson's pleasure radiated through her ears, the more jealousy revved up inside of her. Eden considered herself to be great in bed, but she never made Jackson sound like *that*. She should've turned around and gone back downstairs, but her curious discontent urged her to continue up the steps to find out what was so great about Pandora.

Pandora's bedroom…

Pandora went down on her husband like she could put the porn star industry out of business. Jackson slumped against the door frame completely out of breath. Just as Pandora stood up, Jackson gripped Pandora by the waist forcing him into her.

"You're not having a heart attack on me, are you?" She giggled.

"Feels like it," Jackson smiled, his frowned face

returning to normal as their eyes met.

"I love seeing you so weak and helpless. Turns me on," Pandora traced his lower lip with her tongue, inhaling her panting breaths.

"Yeah?" Jackson muttered.

"Yeah," she smirked. The loud sound of her work phone interrupted their lustful moment.

"I have to take that," she declared, breaking free from Jackson's hold.

Jackson fixed his pants as Pandora walked over to the office connected to their bedroom.

"Babe, I gotta get going before I miss my flight. I'll check in with you when I get to the airport," Jackson declared.

"Alright, have fun," Pandora blew Jackson a quick kiss before answering her phone.

As Eden peered through the crack of their bedroom door, anger and anxiety poured off of her like venom. She always wanted to know Pandora's secret for having such radiant, glowing skin, and now she knew— *Jackson's protein shakes.* Jackson Ford was so stunningly virile, and powerful. His entire body was full of physical strength and grace and yet, Pandora could bring him to his knees. She was erotic. She was the real thing, and she was out of this world.

Eden watched Pandora standing in her office surrounded by all of her expensive toys. Pandora's beautiful face frowned, focusing on her client on the other end of the phone. Her mid-back length hair was pinned up into wild, exciting curls. Her knee-length, white dress stuck to her body like glue, showing off its tone.

The sight of Pandora in her element, wielding the power that built her empire, made Eden's knees buckle. Her breathing sped up and her eyes glowered. A strong hatred for Pandora began boiling under her skin just as Jackson swung open their bedroom door, causing Eden to jump back.

"Eden," Jackson's eye grew big, "hey."

"Hi," Eden smiled, masking her feelings, "I just came up to let Anna know I was here."

"No problem. She told me you were coming. How are you?" Jackson asked. Deep down, he still felt terrible for what he'd put her through. The uncomfortable energy emitting off of him let Eden know it.

"I'm great…thanks for asking," Eden responded, sweetly.

"Well…I'm gonna get going. I have a flight to catch." Jackson rubbed the back of his neck, moving around Eden to exit the room.

"Enjoy yourself. This is a really beautiful home, by the way."

"Thanks, I'm glad you like it. Take care, and hopefully, I'll see you around when I get back," Jackson stated before hurrying down the steps.

"Sure," she nodded with a smile, hoping so badly that Jackson would trip down the remainder of those stairs and break every bone in his body. That had to be the most awkward ten seconds of her life and she was *so* glad it was over. Eden walked into Pandora's room just as Pandora ended her work call.

"Oh, hey!" Pandora beamed, walking over to Eden with a hug. The second Eden felt Pandora's touch, she got angry again.

"Hey," Eden choked the words out.

"You weren't here long, were you? I got sidetracked with some stuff," Pandora replied.

Sidetracked with Jackson down your throat, Eden thought. "No, actually, I just got here."

"Great," Pandora smiled. "Well don't you look fancy for the first day of school," she laughed as her eyes traveled up and down Eden's attire.

"But of course," Eden smiled, "always dress like you're going to see your worst enemy. Isn't that what you taught me?"

"I sure did," Pandora laughed, walking over to her closet to retrieve a pair of shoes, "and you look beautiful," she winked at Eden before disappearing into the closet.

"You have some nerve talking about fancy. Look at this place," Eden walked around Pandora's bedroom.

"You like it?"

"Yeah, it's amazing what you've done with such a modest budget," Eden replied sarcastically causing Pandora to burst into laughter.

Without warning, Eden felt a surge of panic begin like a cluster of spark plugs in her stomach. Tension began to grow in her face and limbs. Her breathing became more rapid and shallow. She was having a panic attack.

"Where's the bathroom?" Eden blurted out quickly, trying to contain herself. The last thing she wanted was for Pandora to get an introduction to her chaotic down spiral over the last year.

"It's right over there," Pandora pointed behind her, studying Eden with a confused gaze, "are you alright?"

"I...I have to pee," she lied.

Eden rushed past Pandora, hurried into her bathroom and closed the door behind her. She quickly turned on the cold water from the faucet in an attempt to mask her heavy breathing. Gripping her temples with her hands, her thoughts accelerated in her head. She wished so badly for them to slow down so she could breathe, but they wouldn't. Her breaths came in gasps, making her feel like she would blackout at any moment. Her heart hammered in her chest as the room spun and she squatted on the floor, trying to make her reality slow to something her brain and body could cope with. *She hated having anxiety attacks.* They were always unannounced and broke free at the most inopportune times. A dryness formed in Eden's throat, as emotions pierced through her heart and tears fell from her face. Standing up, she reached into her purse, grabbed two Xanax pills and popped them into her mouth. In these moments she understood the drug addict, and the alcoholic...*anything to ease reality.*

"Breathe Eden," she coached herself. "Breathe easy, breathe sl——"

Before she could finish her sentence, Pandora swung open the bathroom door with a worried look plastered on her face.

"Eden?" Pandora furrowed, surveying her friend's face.

Eden used both hands to quickly dry her eyes, but it was useless, as more tears cascaded down her disheveled face.

"I'm okay," she sniffed, "I swear."

"Honey, what's the matter? Why are you

crying?" Pandora walked over to her.

"I'm okay, Anna," Eden assured, continuing to fix her flustered appearance, "it's just stress. School stuff...I'm fine."

"Oh, thank gosh," Pandora sighed, "I was worried. You looked like you were getting ready to faint back there. Don't let the first day of school rip you to pieces like that," Pandora grabbed a Kleenex from the tissue box on her vanity before wiping the remainder of Eden's tears, "save that for finals, you're gonna *need* it."

"You're right," Eden forced a smile, "I guess it's just a bit overwhelming trying to get back into the swing of things."

"I see. You'll do fine. Come on, let's go get you a drink," Pandora laughed.

"A drink would be perfect right about now," Eden chuckled. "Hey, where's Quinn? I didn't—"

The sound of glass breaking, followed by loud screams, cut through Eden's words. They both traded wide-eyed glances and hurried out of the bedroom.

Downstairs...

"I hate you, Joe!" Andrea yelled at the top of her lungs, grabbing another shot glass from the kitchen counter, throwing it in Joseph's direction. A drunken Joseph staggered out of the way as the glass broke against the kitchen door, just missing his face.

"Andrea, calm down, you're destroying my sister's house!"

Pandora and Eden rushed into the kitchen.

"Don't tell me what to do! I'm so *sick* of you. The past month, all you've been doing is drinking.

Every time you come home, you're drunk. I'm nine months pregnant with twins— *your* twins, and you have the nerve to tell me I let myself *go*?"

"I didn't say it like that!" Joseph yelled back. "That's the way your hormones took it. I said you should *consider* wearing more pregnant-appropriate clothing to accent your belly instead of stuffing yourself in your old clothes. When you were pregnant with David you looked amazing, so, I said don't let yourself go *now*."

Joseph could barely finish his sentence before a butcher knife from Pandora's cutting rack came flying in his direction.

Eden's eyes laced with fear. She had no idea Andrea was crazy. Maybe that's why Pandora liked her. "Andrea, stop!"

"I've had it up to here with you," Andrea glared. "You've been nothing but rude and ignorant to me this entire pregnancy. You've spent more time here with your sister than you do at home. It's like you can't stand to be around me."

"Maybe if you weren't so hormonal and argumentative, I'd be home more. I can't think straight with your annoying, whining *all* the ti—" Joseph's words were cut off by a steak knife soaring at him, grazing the side of his head. He hollered, gripping the cut.

"Alright, stop it!" Pandora demanded, angrily. Eden wanted to slap Pandora across her face. Andrea was doing just fine trying to chop Joseph into a million pieces. Now, her demented stare was on them.

"Anna, I can't take it anymore," Andrea began to cry, as Joseph rushed out of the kitchen toward the bathroom, blood trickling down his forehead.

"You and your twins must have a *death* wish!" The devil peered straight through Pandora's eyes, filling the entire kitchen with venom, "throw one more thing in my house."

Eden's eyebrows raised at the sight of Pandora's coldness. Pandora had been so nice and patient with Eden over the last year, that Eden almost forgot Pandora was the mother of merciless. The way Andrea quickly adjusted her attitude let Eden know Andrea remembered too.

"I'm— I'm sorry, okay," Andrea calmed her nerves, gazing up at Pandora, "I took it too far."

"I think you need to get out before I drag you out," Pandora scolded, roughly ushering Andrea to the front door.

"Wait, Anna," Andrea fussed, "Anna, I can't drive. My belly is too big. Joe drove us here. Can I just go see if he's okay?"

"Then I will drive you to a local *bus stop* and you can call him from your cellphone while you're waiting," Pandora stated, coldly. She turned to face Eden, "I'll be right back. Make sure he's okay."

Pandora shook her head in disgust as Eden nodded, holding in her laughter.

"Anna, Please just—"

"*No*," Pandora interrupted, "don't say another word to me until you pay me back for all the *crystal* you just shattered against my wall."

Joseph staggered back into the kitchen just as they left the house. He leaned against the wall, securing a wet paper towel over the side of his head.

"Are you cut bad?" Eden asked with a look of

concern. She approached him to assess the damage.

"She really cut me," Joseph said in disbelief, shaking his head, "I can't believe her."

"Let me see your head," Eden asked. Joseph leaned down and moved the paper towel, revealing a gash. "Ow," she winced, "I hope you don't need stitches."

"I can't take any more of this nonsense. Like, I can't say anything to her without her taking it overboard. I have to be drunk and living somewhere else in order to effectively function."

"Well, from experience, pregnant women are extremely emotional and over the top. I know I was, and I only carried one baby. She has *two*," Eden replied, walking over to the sink to wet another paper towel.

"So, what am I supposed to do, just walk on eggshells with her?"

"With certain things, yes, especially when it comes to weight." Eden walked over to Joseph and placed the paper towel over his head.

"I don't remember you being this over-the-top when you were pregnant. I remember you as this dainty, beautiful, pregnant woman. You wore a lot of dresses and it was just...amazing," he grinned, briefly reminiscing before his look averted to an annoyed glare. "Andrea makes me wanna *throw up* with the way she acts."

Eden stared back at Joseph while he talked. She had no idea that he paid attention to her like that.

"Well, thank you for the compliments," she smiled, "but I didn't feel anything like what you just described."

"Really?" Joseph asked, slightly shocked. "Well,

you were."

Eden bore into Joseph's drunken, dilated eyes and bit her lip. Being this close to him started to turn her on.

"Thanks," she seductively grinned, leaning in closer.

"Sure," Joseph responded back innocently, too drunk to realize Eden's changed demeanor.

Eden leaned in a little closer and kissed his juicy pink lips. The second their lips connected, Joseph's eyes bulged. He jerked her away in a frantic. The paper towel fell from his head onto the kitchen floor.

"Eden…" Joseph stared at her with his mouth open.

Eden knew what she was doing was wrong, but the forbidden feeling of touching something that didn't belong to her sent chills down her spine.

Joseph swallowed hard as his startled eyes locked on hers, trying to understand what was happening.

Eden stood back with a smirk, watching him recover. "Did I do something you didn't like?" She asked, boldly.

Joseph was speechless. He'd never thought of Eden in a sexual way…*until now.* The liquor in his system only added to his urge.

"No," he spoke in a faint voice, "you didn't."

That was the only cue she needed. Eden strutted over to Joseph like a cobra ready to attack. Leaning into him, she took his mouth into hers as they broke into a lustful kiss. Unzipping his jeans, she slid them down. Eden had only gone down on a man once and wasn't a fan of it, but after seeing Pandora in action, she was eager to compete in an attempt to see if she could make Joseph just as satisfied as Jackson was earlier. She let go of Joseph's lips and began kissing down his neck. Joseph's eyes followed Eden as she continued to travel down south, squatting in front of him.

"Eden, wait. This is wrong. I'm married," he replied with fear-filled eyes. Joseph attempted to move away from her, but before he could, Eden reached into his boxers, stopping him in his tracks.

"Jealousy…Envy…Betrayal…Deception," Ruby spoke in a stern whisper, shaking her head. Eden watched herself, embarrassed and ashamed. She watched her devious eyes glowing with satisfaction when it was all over.

"Okay, *so what*, I was wrong," Eden huffed, turning to face her mother, "what about Pandora? What about what she did to me? I don't see you giving her the third degree, and *she's* the one that caused me to act like that," she spat.

"*Pandora* is not on life support with a bullet in her head, now is she?" Ruby crossed her arms.

"Well, when people aren't held accountable for their actions, the ones they've screwed over are left to hold them accountable, so this is what happens," Eden pursed her lips together.

Ruby laughed, shaking her head. "It's funny how you can look into a mirror and see *everything* but yourself. Pandora didn't take anything from you. You *both* dated Jackson unknowingly. Unfortunately, he toyed with you but loved her. She followed her heart and was honest with you about her feelings. You both settled your differences and mended your friendship. *She* let it go, but *you* decided to hold on to it until it transpired into jealousy."

Eden shook her head in denial. Tears rushed to the cracks of her eyes. "I didn't hold on to it on purpose, I just didn't know how to let it go. It was never my intent to be jealous of either of my friends. I love them both, I just couldn't control myself.

"That's what happens when you operate in the spirit of jealousy for too long. It takes over and will slowly destroy you," Ruby responded. Her voice sent chills through Eden's body.

"But how could I have known this?" Eden asked, wiping the tears from her eyes, "I had nobody around to steer me in the right direction."

"You have a psychologist and a lawyer for best friends. You have one to tell you the truth, the whole truth, and nothing but the truth, and the other one to help you *deal* with the truth," Ruby's eyes bored into Eden's. "Instead, you started comparing yourself to them, using their development as a marker of your own. You became consumed with envy, unmotivated to change anything about *your* life because you're too busy using *their* lives as your reflection. You left your growth and potential to be successful unattended, and that's *nobody's* fault but your own."

"Whatever," Eden stated, her demeanor growing

flustered, "I didn't—"

"You abuse anxiety medication, anti-depressants, expensive clothes, and a flashy lifestyle, in an attempt to tell yourself you're still in control. You're performing sexual acts with a married man, not because you wanted to, but because you're willing to do whatever it takes to maintain your delusion of grandeur," Ruby bellowed, "you're trying to control it all, but just being controlled *by* it all."

"You'll never understand what it's like to be me," Eden fussed, "you had it all, mom. Quinn has it all…Anna has it all. I felt like I had something to prove to them. I didn't want them to see that I needed them. I felt pressured to—"

"Pressure!" Ruby shouted. "That's the word. The pressure to perform a certain way, look a certain way, dress a certain way- to put on the perfect mask, with the perfect smile. To be the perfect image of everything everybody else expects you to be. Pressure to keep up, pressure to keep going, pressure to stay ahead, stay afloat, stay relevant. Oh, and the pressure to not be the first one who cracks. *Under the pressure.*"

Four

Eden drove her black Lamborghini through her neighborhood en-route to pick up Jade. After scoping out the Virginia nightlife, Jade became a frequent visitor at a night club called *Dirty*. She invited Eden to come out with her for a girl's outing.

Eden had never been to Dirty before. Truth be told, she'd never been to any kind of nightclub. With friends like Quinn and Pandora, their girl's outings consisted of sleepovers at each other's houses, vacations across the country, and shopping trips to high-end stores. However, after Eden's rendezvous with Joseph, and her uncontrollable emotions running amuck, she felt like the change of scenery would be good for her. The second she drove across the train tracks a change of scenery is what she was met with. The beautiful trees, smooth streets, and flowery smelling night air she drove through on the way to Jade's had now turned into what looked like the projects. There were broken streetlights and graffiti everywhere. The air was thick with smog, the houses were meshed together into row homes, and a grim aura seemed to hang over them. There were shadows in odd places and strange-looking people in brightly lit areas. The streets Eden passed by had guys dressed in white t-shirts standing on corners, and young children on steps that looked as if they hadn't bathed in a while. Eden's eyebrows furrowed as she glanced over at the clock on her dashboard. *There are toddlers outside at 10:30?* She thought.

"*Make a left onto Divinity Street, and then the destination is on your right. 3254 Divinity Street,*" the GPS instructed. Eden slowly turned down Jade's street, immediately being met with wandering eyes. The music was disturbingly loud, and the air reeked of cheap sex, strong urine, and fried food. Eden stopped her car in front of Jade's address, observing her surroundings. People walked past her car in an attempt to see who she was. Girls in trashy clothing, old weave, and large hooped earrings rolled their eyes when they realized it was a woman behind the wheel.

Eden put her car in park and pulled out her phone to text Jade and let her know she was outside. The sound of unseen barking dogs caused her to jump. Her eyes quickly scanned the area around her car. Cats rummaged through the garbage spilled over in the nearby gutters, rats squeaked menacingly in the alleyways, and the roaches crawling in and out of people's homes appeared a bit too bold.

"This can't be right," she mumbled as she continued to look around the area, paranoid, "no way does she live here."

Just as she went to dial Jade's number, Jade emerged from her rundown apartment building.

"Okay…I guess she *does* live here," Eden muttered.

Jade noticed a black Lamborghini double-parked outside of her house. Her mouth fell open when the passenger side window rolled down and Eden's smiling face appeared.

"Hey!" Eden smiled.

"Good Lord," Jade quickly rushed down her

steps and over to Eden's car. "Whose car is *this*?"

"What do you mean whose car is this? Who's behind the wheel of it?" Eden responded, boisterously.

Jade opened the passenger door and got inside. "This is nice! What the *hell* type of work do you do to afford something like this?"

Jade's reaction reminded Eden of all the times she'd go to see Pandora or Quinn, and they'd always impress her with some fancy new gadget. *It felt good to be on the other side of things for a change.*

"I don't work. It was a gift from my mother," Eden replied, plugging the club's address into her GPS before she drove through the block.

"I need a mother like yours, then."

"Why does everyone keep looking at me like that?" Eden gazed out of her window at the many pairs of eyes following her car down the block.

"Well, first of all, look at what you're driving," Jade laughed, "secondly, goons around here pretty much know each other for good or bad, so they know when a stranger arrives."

"Goons?" Eden looked confused.

"People," Jade looked just as confused, "didn't you tell me you lived here all your life?"

"Yes, but I'm from across the train tracks. I've never been to this side before."

"*Oh*, you're from the bougie borough, with all those high-sadity republicans and stuck up rich people."

"If that's what you wanna call us," Eden shrugged.

"That's cool. This neighborhood reminds me of my own hood in Chicago, so I felt right at home here," Jade affirmed as she pulled out a small bag of weed and a Dutch from her purse.

Stopping at a red light, Eden tilted her posture forward to see what Jade was doing. After emptying the contents of the brown Dutch into her purse, Jade filled the paper with marijuana from the small bag. She rolled it carefully and quickly before reaching for her lighter. Eden's nose wrinkled, cutting her eyes at Jade, and then to her Dutch. A loud car horn broke their concentration.

"Drive, lady!" Hollered the angry driver behind them.

"I am!" Eden responded back. Facing forward, she stepped on the gas.

Jade snorted, shaking her head as she rolled down Eden's window and lit her Dutch. The smoke quickly filled the car and traveled straight down Eden's throat. Eden blinked her eyes, coughing loudly.

"You're coughing like you've never smoked before," Jade cackled, amused by Eden's hacking cough.

That's a horrible smell," Eden shielded her nose from the stench, "and no, I've never smoked before."

"Seriously?"

"Seriously. I'm sorry, I guess I'm a nerd compared to you."

"You *definitely* are," Jade nodded in agreement with a bemused smile, "but, I like you, so I'm going to keep you."

They both shared a laugh and continued on, sharing conversations about where they were from, and things they loved to do.

Twenty minutes later, Eden turned down a small strip where Dirty was located. She slowed down to find a parking spot.

The description of the club definitely lived up to

its name. The dim-lit area outside of the nightclub was littered with drug dealers profiling on top of their fancy cars. Trap music blasted from the car speakers while a few neighborhood groupies flirted, in hopes of getting a few dollars tossed their way. In the same area, gangbangers lurked for trouble, and boosters scanned the area for somebody to rob. Girls dressed in skin-tight, cheap clothing and low-class strippers could be seen making their way into the side entrance.

After Eden squeezed into a parking spot, she and Jade exited the car. Eden swallowed hard clutching her oversized Gucci bag, immediately feeling out-of-place.

"This club is so lit" Jade spoke with excitement as they crossed the street. "You'll love it here."

"Jade!" A male's voice made them turn their heads.

"Travis," Jade's face lit up.

Travis and a friend quickly approached them.

"What the heck are *you* doing here? I didn't know you left your cocoon," Jade laughed.

"Ha," Travis smiled, shaking his head, "only for a little bit. My roommate wanted to get out, and I opted to be the designated driver."

Jade glanced over at Travis's friend.

"This is Cameron," Travis introduced. "Cam, this is my friend, Jade, the one I told you about from Chicago."

Jade eyed him, flirtatiously. "Hello Travis's friend, Cameron."

"How are you?" Cameron smiled, extending his hand for Jade to shake.

Cameron was six foot three, with a husky build. His skin was the color of peanut butter, laced with caramel. He had faint splotches of acne on his face, and dark lips from smoking too much marijuana. He wasn't Eden's cup of tea, but Jade sure looked like she was ready to take him into the nearest alleyway and give him a formal introduction.

"Hi, Eden," Travis grinned.

"Hi Travis," she blushed in return.

"I'm surprised, I wouldn't expect to see you at a place like this."

"Jade invited me out, so I came," Eden stated. "This is my first time here."

"Well, I see you two have already met," Jade looked at Eden and Travis.

"That's a nice ride you got," Cameron said, admiring Eden's car.

Travis turned to examine it. "*Much* too nice for an area like this. You're *asking* to get jacked."

Cameron nodded. "I'd park on a different street if I were you."

"I think she'll be fine here, but if you feel more comfortable parking somewhere else, we can," Jade said.

"I'm gonna go stand in this line before it gets longer," Cameron looked on at the line beginning to form around the club.

"I know a safer spot to park. I was actually gonna take my car there. You can follow me if you want," Travis looked at Eden.

"Sure, I'll follow."

"You guys go ahead, I'm gonna go stand in line with Cameron. I need some male protection anyway, as good as I look," Jade smiled, winking at Cameron.

Jade hurried over to the line to join him.

"You look nice, by the way," Travis muttered. He admired Eden's beautiful figure through the purple fitted dress that ended just above her knees.

"Thank you," she watched Travis walk ahead and get into his car. *You don't look so bad yourself,* she thought.

The minute Eden got into her car, she pulled out her Xanax and popped three of them into her mouth to prevent another public panic attack. She was still on an anxious high from Joseph, and this new scenery coupled with a newfound friendship in Jade began to overwhelm her nerves. *This was definitely going to take some getting used to.*

Ten minutes later, she arrived at the top of a big hill. She looked around the area, but there were no other cars except Travis's. Still, she parked anyway. After checking her makeup in the rearview mirror, Eden climbed out of her car.

"So, this definitely doesn't look like a safer place to park," Eden watched Travis get out of his car.

"Yeah it is," he smirked mischievously, "you don't see all these cars and civilization around us?"

Eden folded her arms, "no, I do not. Where are we?"

"Does it matter? You stuck out in that area like a sore thumb. I could tell you really didn't wanna be there."

"Was it that obvious?"

"To me, it was," he shrugged, turning to walk over to the edge of the hill. "You don't strike me as someone who'd hang around this side of town. Am I wrong?"

His response caught Eden off guard. She usually

put on a good front of adapting to her surroundings. How come he wasn't buying into it? She briefly stared at him before walking over to the edge of the hill.

"So, what's this place?" She asked inquisitively, changing the subject.

"Nothing fancy, just a quiet area I found after I got lost one day looking for a Wawa. I've been coming here a lot at night just to get away from my noisy apartment and clear my head."

Eden looked over the top of the hill and saw nothing but a huge cornfield. Her eyes scanned the area, secluded by bushes and trees. There were no lights, no birds chirping or crickets croaking. It was quiet, alright— *deathly quiet.*

"This isn't the part where you rape me and bury my body in the cornfield, is it?" She asked, cutting a glance at Travis. If it weren't for the anxiety medicine kicking in, she would've freaked out by now.

"What?" He turned to her, sensing her fear. "No, my life isn't that exciting," he chuckled, "I'm literally just *this* lame."

As their eyes met, Eden got lost in his gaze. Her brief paranoia quickly disintegrated. The chocolate leather jacket he wore was just as dark as he was. His fitted khaki top, slim-cut jeans, and brown boots gave accent to his defined, slender frame. Traces of his Polo Black cologne wafted past Eden's nose. He was handsome. And she wanted him.

"I'm sorry," she replied, "it's just a bit storybook and very cliché, that's all," Eden paused for a second to gather her thoughts. "You don't see too much of that anymore."

"You're right...you don't," Travis walked over

to his car to retrieve a blanket from his back seat. He returned, spreading the blanket out on the ground. He took a seat and held his hand up for her. "You wanna hang out for a while?"

What Eden *really* wanted was for him to mount her against his truck and sex her brains out, but for the sake of her dignity, she innocently smiled and refuted her thoughts as she walked over to the blanket and took a seat.

"Where are you from?" he asked.

"Norfolk, originally, but I moved to Richmond when I was twelve, and I've been here ever since," Eden replied, putting her cellphone into her purse.

"Really?"

"Yes…why?"

"You appear so uncomfortable for this to be your home."

"Well, I've never really been to *this* side of Richmond before," she blushed, lowering her head, "this is all new to me."

"I've had my eye on you since orientation," Travis admitted. "You had this aura about you. I couldn't put my finger on it, but it was different from every other girl in the room, and it got my attention. You sat down two rows in front of me and your vibe sucked me in like a vacuum. I wanted to say something to you, but I couldn't muster up the courage. Then, you walked into my sociology class and I decided that was fate giving me a second chance. But now, I'm confused. You're dressed differently, and you're hanging out in the hood. Your energy doesn't seem to match the sweet girl I laid my eyes on before. It's like your pushing yourself to portray a different image. Why?"

Eden averted her stare to a nearby tree. *Was he some sort of psychic? How does he know this stuff?*

"Okay, you sound like a total weirdo," Eden laughed, brushing off Travis's words, "you haven't been around me for a whole twelve hours yet, and you're making assumptions, treading in places you shouldn't be."

Travis reached for her chin and gently shifted her face back towards his.

"My apologies," he replied, "I'll mind my business from here on out." He removed his hand from Eden's face, placing them in his jacket pocket.

There was a serenity and calmness about Travis that pulled at her. She felt so strangely comfortable around him.

"It's fine," Eden gathered her thoughts. "So, how do you like Virginia?"

"I like it a lot. It's more relaxed and laid back than Chicago. I feel like I can be myself here."

"Were you someone different in Chicago?" Eden chuckled, raising an eyebrow.

"Something like that."

"Something like what?" She asked, eager to find out, "Jade said you were quiet and standoff-ish. Those are usually the ones that turn out to be assassins and drug lords right under your nose," Eden laughed.

Travis grinned, retrieving a bag of weed and a Dutch Master from his pocket.

"You haven't been around me for a whole twelve hours yet, and look at you…making assumptions, treading in places you shouldn't be," he mocked, silencing Eden's laughter.

"Whatever," she playfully nudged him, "I didn't

mean to be rude. It's just, you dove into my world without a formal invitation I just met you yesterday, and today we're camped out in the middle of nowhere, and you're asking me personal questions, trying to figure me out. Took me by surprise."

"When I see something I like, I go for it. I'm too old to send out my representative anymore."

"I see…you sent the *Feds*," she laughed again, this time, Travis joined her.

"What the heck is that?" Eden asked with a wavering smile, watching him roll his Dutch before lacing it with a white substance.

"It's marijuana," he stated the obvious, "you don't smoke?"

"I know what the marijuana is, Eden rolled her eyes, "what's that white stuff you're putting in it?"

"Angel dust. It's just a little something extra to relax me and help me enjoy life's moments a bit more." Travis inhaled a puff of smoke, releasing the essence into the night air. "Have you ever found yourself just cruising through life without leaving anything imprinting? Like, you live day-to-day on autopilot? Your body is present, but your mind is so far gone, it's ridiculous."

"All the time," Eden answered in a low tone.

Travis turned to face her, trailing his blunt toward her. "Try it." The longer he held out the blunt, the more he could see the curiosity in her eyes. "I promise you it'll change your perspective on a lot of things."

Eden slowly examined Travis. There was something so mysteriously beautiful about him, and she was determined to find out what it was. Her eyes lowered to his blunt, before traveling back up at him. There was an intense connection building between them, one she hadn't felt since Jackson. Travis was interesting and comfortable, and, maybe it would be okay to dive into his world a little more. A devious smile formed across Eden's face. Reaching for his blunt, she took it and inhaled.

Five

"Oh, Jezebel!"

The next morning, Eden was awakened by a loud knock at her front door. Opening her eyes to a splitting headache, she winced, gripping her head in pain. She rubbed a hand down her face before restlessly fishing around her bed for her cellphone. Her eyes shot open when she realized it was almost twelve-thirty in the afternoon. She'd missed her morning class and was getting ready to be late for the next one.

"Shoot," she fussed, disappointed at herself as she tossed the covers off of her and got out of bed. Eden checked her phone to see thirteen missed calls from Jade and a text from Travis.

Call me back when you get this so I know you're okay.

Squinting at her phone in confusion, Eden tried her best to remember what happened last night, but the sound of an even louder bang at the door jolted her out of her foggy memory. She walked over to her closet and reached for her long robe, before hurrying over to the front door. Peering out the peephole, her eyes furrowed a bit when she noticed it was Jade. She quickly opened the door.

"Hey," Eden squinted.

"Girl!" Jade huffed, blowing out a long sigh of relief as she crossed her arms, "don't scare me like that, again."

"What do you mean?" Eden tilted her head to the side, moving out of the way to allow Jade in. "How did you know where I lived?"

"You told the whole club where you lived," Jade informed her. She walked inside Eden's home, shaking her head. "You and Travis came back to the club, high as the clouds, miss *I've never smoked before*," Jade pursed. "Then, you took shots at the bar for about an hour. After you were good and drunk, you got into an argument with some girl who said your bag was fake," Jade rolled her eyes. "And then, your snooty, rich behind decided to show her just how much money you had by buying the whole entire club shots of Burbon. You're *crazy*."

"Oh no," Eden's mouth fell open, "I did?"

"Yes, and you gave Travis about fifty lap dances before begging him to take you home and sleep with you." Jade tried to control her laughter. "I caught this innocent vibe from you on the way to the club, but now I see you were just blowing smoke up my behind."

"Wait, so did he bring me home and sleep with me?" Eden asked. Her enlarged, hopeful eyes made Jade burst into uncontrollable laughter.

"No! I drove his car here, while he drove yours. He dropped you and your hormones right off at the door, plugged his number in your phone and left. *Told* you he was gay."

"Whatever," Eden giggled. "He's far from it."

"This condo is *disrespectful*," Jade muttered, looking around Eden's home in awe. "Is this yours?"

"Yeah, it was a gift from my mom," Eden nodded, on her way into the bathroom to grab two Ibuprofen from her medicine cabinet.

"You are one lucky daughter," Jade said, continuing to walk around the home, "what kind of work does she do?"

"She's dead," Eden replied flatly, swallowing the pills and turning on the water to brush her teeth.

"Oh...I'm sorry," Jade responded, slumping her posture against the bathroom entrance.

Eden rinsed her mouth out, turned off the faucet, and grabbed a paper towel to wipe away the remaining moisture from her lips. "It's fine. Did I really buy shots for the *whole* club?" She asked, changing the subject.

"Uh, yeah. You had a five-thousand-dollar tab, and you paid it like it was lunch money," Jade shook her head, still in disbelief. "You're lucky we were there to escort you out, otherwise you would have gotten robbed doing something like that in the hood."

"Well, thank you," Eden shook her head at herself.

"You mind if I smoke in here?" Jade asked, walking into Eden's living room, placing her purse on her coffee table.

"Sure. Only if I can smoke with you," she winked. Eden hadn't had a full night sleep since her mother's funeral, but whatever Travis had her smoking last night kept her relaxed, calm, floating on air, and she slept like a baby the entire night. She wanted to try it again.

"You know how to roll?" Jade offered, taking out the contents she needed from her purse.

"No, but you can show me," Eden smiled. She watched intently as Jade showed her step by step how to do it.

A few minutes later, Jade lit the blunt and they

were laughing, talking and passing it between one another. That same blissful feeling Eden had last night had returned to her. The high she felt was better than any anxiety or sleeping pills her doctor prescribed. Those medications gave her a calm, but empty feeling. The blunt she smoked put her in tune with her true emotions. She hadn't laughed so hard or felt so free in a very long time.

After twenty minutes, Jade looked at her phone before staggering up from the couch. "I somehow have to find my way to my car to get to class," she laughed.

"Go ahead without me," Eden flagged her, "I have to shower and get dressed, so I'll be late. Thanks for coming over to check on me."

"Sure thing. Do you want to go to dinner or something, tonight? I know a spot on 5th, that everyone keeps raving about."

"Count me in," Eden gave Jade a thumbs up.

"Cool, see you in class…and don't forget to text Travis, he's been blowing up my phone all morning asking about you."

A smile formed across Eden's face as she hurried over to her phone. "I'll do it right now."

"Oh gosh," Jade playfully muttered before walking out the door, closing it behind her.

Eden stared down at Travis's text, gazing at his name and picture he took of the two of them for her address book. Taking a deep, liberating breath, Eden felt good about life again. After responding to Travis's message, she put her phone down and walked into her bathroom to shower.

Shortly after, Eden was wrapped in a towel standing in her closet trying to pick out an outfit when another knock at the door sounded. Dropping her towel, she replaced it with her robe and walked over to the peephole. Her heart almost stopped when she saw Andrea standing on the other side of it.

Why would she be at my door? Eden thought. Andrea and Eden were mainly associates, they never exchanged phone numbers, beauty tips, or the latest gossip. Andrea didn't even know where Eden lived...or so she assumed. Andrea had always just been Joseph's wife—that's it.

Joseph! Eden's eyes widened like two fifty-cent pieces as her mind traveled back to his erection down her throat in Pandora's kitchen. Eden's heart began beating like a kick drum in her chest. *Did she find out?*

"Eden, come on, open up. I can see your big eyeball through the peephole," Andrea fussed, crossing her arms.

Eden swallowed hard, opening the door, ready to accept whatever karma she had coming to her. "Hey, Andrea," she greeted, raising an eyebrow.

"I'm sorry. I remembered your address from your mom a few years ago when she did my hair. I need to talk to you about the other day," Andrea said, sternly. Without waiting for an invitation, Andrea waddled right pass Eden, entering her home.

"The other day?" Eden asked with a look of disdain. She quickly tried to think of a lie to tell in her defense about Joseph.

"Yes, about what transpired between Joe and I in Pandora's house," Andrea replied through a shaky voice.

"Ooh...okay..." Relieved, Eden sighed to herself.

Andrea took a seat on the couch, sniffing the air. "Was someone smoking pot?"

"Uh...no, no, that's the neighbors," Eden lied. "It comes through the vents at times."

"Smells hideous," Andrea scrunched her nose up. Eden tightened her robe and took a seat next to her. "Anyway, listen, I know we aren't close, and you probably think I'm weird for just popping up at your house at random, but I need help and..." Before the rest of her words could come out, tears filled Andrea's eyes and her face turned a light shade of red.

"What's the matter?" Eden asked with a look of concern, handing Andrea a Kleenex.

"Joe and I just had a big fight that ended with him telling me how much he regrets marrying me, and me wishing him dead before I took my keys and left the house.

"Wow," Eden responded.

"I kept a big secret from him involving my first son's father," Andrea admitted, using the tissue Eden handed her to wipe her face, "he hasn't been able to fully trust me since. He's done such a great job raising my son and he's always wanted children of his own, but it's almost like he regrets getting me pregnant, now. Of course, my hormones and mood swings only make things worse. He can barely stand the sight of me, he's always making any excuse to go over to Anna's. I just...I don't know what to do. I feel hopeless. You've been pregnant in the midst of chaos before, how did you get through it?"

Eden studied Andrea's disheveled, helpless face. Immediately, she could empathize with the pain of carrying a baby by someone who treated you like they didn't love you. Rubbing Andrea's back, Eden shook her head.

"I didn't deal with it at first, I just mentally removed myself from the situation," Eden responded, softly. "Everything around me came crashing down all at once, and I didn't know how to deal with it, so I retreated to a place in my head for survival and hid there until my problems worked themselves out."

"I wish I could do that, but I have a son, a career… and a husband," Andrea trained her vacant eyes on a nearby picture on Eden's wall.

"Sorry I'm not much help," Eden winced, feeling bad, "I can tell you that good sleep definitely clears your mind more, and you look like you haven't had any in a while."

"Tell me about it," Andrea replied, rubbing the bags under her tired eyes, "I'm used to sleeping in my husband's arms, but most nights, it's just me and the dog. My mind wanders and worries, trying to figure out ways to fix us. Next thing you know, it's 5 A.M.

Eden nodded in agreement. She knew exactly how Andrea felt.

"You're not supposed to be driving at this point in your pregnancy either," Eden stared at Andrea, "You need to be careful."

"I know, and that pissed him off even more, but I needed to get out of there. He actually followed me in his car for a while, beeping and threatening me to pull over. I eventually ditched him."

"You guys are nuts," Eden laughed, glancing at the clock again before getting up.

"You have *no* idea," Andrea yawned, laying her head back on Eden's couch.

"Sleepy?" Eden smirked, amused as she went into her bathroom to apply her makeup.

"Sleepy isn't the word to describe it," Andrea laughed. "This couch is so comfy."

"I know. During my pregnancy, it's the only place I could sleep." Eden stared at her reflection in the mirror while applying her eye and lip liner, "really though, it *may* just be your hormones making the situation worse than what it really is. I would just try to focus on your older son and your job. Give yourself some time to breathe from Joseph so you guys can think with clear heads," Eden stated, applying her lipstick. "Plus, your due date is next week. You're gonna stress yourself out."

As Eden put her makeup case back into her cabinet and reached for her hair straightener, she realized that she was talking to herself. She stepped out of her bathroom and peered into the living room to see Andrea knocked out cold with her mouth wide open. Eden smiled, shaking her head in amusement. "That couch will get you every time."

Turning around to go back into the bathroom, a soft knock sounded at her door, causing Eden to throw her hands up in frustration. "Oh my goodness, am I *ever* gonna get to school?" She sneered, storming over to her front door. She was so annoyed, she didn't even bother looking through her peephole this time. Eden angrily shuffled her top lock loose and swung her door open to see Joseph's disheveled face.

"Okay, now how did *you* get my address?" She huffed, "did my mom do your hair at some point too?"

"Actually," he stared down at his phone in confusion, "I was searching for my wife on the find my iPhone app, and the location brought me here." Joseph looked up, "this is your house? Why would she be at your house?"

"Trying to get away from you, I assume. Apparently, that was an epic fail," Eden joked. She stepped aside to allow him in. Joseph gave Eden a darting gaze, rocking back and forth as he bit down on his bottom lip.

"Relax, I'm not a homewrecker. She doesn't know anything," Eden whispered as her eyes led Joseph to her couch where Andrea slept, peacefully.

Joseph sighed in relief before walking in, silently thanking God for mercy.

"Soo...you wanna grab her and go?" Eden glanced at her watch, "I have class in twenty minutes."

"I need to talk to you for a second," Joseph replied, looking around her condo for an empty room. He spotted her bedroom and gently ushered her inside. Joseph glanced once more at his wife, before softly closing the door, leaving it cracked.

"What's up?" Eden asked.

"What happened between us has been eating away at me since the other day," Joseph whispered, staring into her eyes. Shame and regret were written all over his handsome face.

"What happened between us?" Eden asked nonchalantly.

"Listen, Eden, I was drunk, I...I...I didn't—"

Eden used her finger to silence Joseph's lips, rolling her eyes in annoyance. *Do I have to counsel this hormonal, pregnant lady, and her husband? Where is Quinn when you need her?* She thought. "Joseph, it's -,"

"I feel really guilty," Joseph cut her off. "It's just

that...she's pregnant, you know? I never thought I'd have the guts to betray her like that— and in my *sister's* house," Joseph winced, ashamed, "if Anna ever finds out, she's gonna—"

"Joe. Please," Eden stroked his shoulder, trying to calm his nerves, "you have my word."

Joseph's pleading eyes gazed into hers. Since they were kids, he was always a respectful, loving, trouble-free kind of person. He was the good guy; the kind you'd marry and grow old with. Eden had become the first woman in history to complicate his world. At that moment, she almost felt bad. *Almost.* She peered into her living room at a vulnerable Andrea. Staring at another broken woman made Eden feel powerful and superior. She craved the competition; it boosted her self-esteem and made her feel liberated. Eden turned her gaze toward Joseph as she bit her lip, watching his flustered demeanor. Moving in closer to him, she softy leaned into his ear.

"I won't tell," she whispered. Seductively, her hand trailed down the back of his neck.

Startled, Joseph backed up, accidentally hitting the front of Eden's closet door with the back of his foot. The sudden noise caused Andrea to shift positions on the couch, before trailing back to sleep.

A sly grin grew on Eden's face. She watched Joseph, with all of his strong morals and values, having trouble denying his carnal desires. It turned her on.

"I should go wake her up so we can go home and try to fix our fight," he muttered. His subtle, deep voice vibrated through Eden's body.

Licking her lips, she carefully closed her bedroom door a little more, leaving it cracked just enough for her to keep an eye on Andrea. Eden slowly untied her robe, revealing her gorgeous nude body for Joseph's viewing pleasure. The pulse in his neck became visible as his eyes slowly trailed up and down Eden's frame. With what felt like superhuman strength, Joseph forced his eyes shut, shaking his head in an attempt to ward off his growing temptation.

"Eden, that's my wife, my *pregnant* wife, sleeping on your couch," he hissed softly, opening his eyes to stare at her. "What's gotten into you?"

"You don't like my body?" Eden teased. Of course he liked her body, and with all the problems he and Andrea had been having, it had been a while since he'd gotten good sex from her.

Eden's condo was uncomfortably quiet. There were no televisions, no music, not even the random weird sounds you hear in a house at times. The silence seemed to amplify Andrea's calm, peaceful breaths as she napped fifteen feet away.

Eden stared at Joseph through her devious eyes, fully aware of the spell she'd put him under. Her hands meticulously slid his rigidness from the crotch of his boxers. For some reason, the food on someone else's plate looked tastier to her. It was illicit and forbidden— she *had* to have it. Jackson was the only man she'd ever slept with, and it was time for his long-lived memory to be replaced.

"My wife is in the next room," Joseph rubbed a hand down his terrified, horny face, reminding Eden, *and* himself.

"You say stop and I will," she muttered, her lustful, captivating eyes daring Joseph to break his vows. Fueled by control, rebellion, power, and triumph,

Eden did everything in her female power to make Joseph forget all about Andrea, *and it worked.*

Pretty soon, a warm passion of lust ignited against the closet door of Eden's bedroom. Restlessly, Joseph touched all over her body, sliding his hands down her thighs and over her backside, caressing her bare skin. The feeling of being touched so possessively sent euphoria spreading through Eden's body like strong liquor.

"Touch me here…Mark me there," she whispered in Joseph's ear as she seized her moment, taking what didn't belong to her.

"Eden?" Andrea called behind her bedroom door as Eden's eyes popped open and Joseph froze in fear. Eden licked her lips with a Grinch-like smile plastered across her face as she pressed her fingers to her lips and motioned for Joseph not to move. Joseph couldn't move if he wanted to because his face looked as if his soul had jumped out of his body and ran straight to hell. Using her free hand to open her bedroom door just wide enough for Andrea to see her face, she glanced up at her.

"Yeah?" Eden asked.

"I heard noises, are you alright?" Andrea looked concerned. As his wife's voice radiated through his ear canal, Joseph's brain felt like it would short circuit and explode at any second.

"Yeah, I'm just…" Eden seductively blushed.

Andrea's eyes widened, realizing what Eden was in the middle of. She *thought* she heard a man's heavy breathing.

"Oh," she whispered in a conflicted voice, taking a few steps back, "sorry. I'm just gonna—" she mouthed and pointed to the front door.

Eden slowly nodded.

Andrea spun around, grabbed her purse from the couch and quickly headed out the door. Uncomfortable wasn't the word to describe how she felt. She didn't know Eden could be so bold...*If she only knew how bold.*

Six

"Hell and destruction are never full; so the eyes of man are never satisfied."

After Eden's dangerous, forbidden encounter with Joseph, her mind began spiraling out of control. The drug rush she continuously chased with Jade made her feel alive and desired, filled with passion and vitality. Within three weeks, Eden had gone from an entire year of celibacy to being naked on the floor of Joseph's office in the middle of the afternoon. Her promiscuity and lack of integrity caused Joseph to fall prey, trapped by bad choices, poor boundaries, and the opportunity to act. They constantly emailed, sexted, and indulged in dirty chats on social media. They attacked each other every single day; in her living room, in Joseph's basement, on top of Pandora's kitchen table, and anywhere else the opportunity presented itself.

Eden began feeling more powerful and superior to Joseph's wife. The daring thrill of lust, notoriety, and debauchery boosted her self-esteem. She felt flawless as she shredded off a layer of dignity with each orgasmic round, just as she hoped.

In addition to her wicked games, her heart also began falling head over heels for Travis as they too, spent every day together. He would meet her in the parking lot, walk her to class, and see her back to her car when the school day ended. When he'd come to her house to relax, hang out, and smoke, he always made sure to leave before the sun went down, no matter how much Eden pouted and begged him to stay. His energy and the way he carefully handled her was electric and captured her full attention. Eden's heart was in one place, and her reckless soul was in another as she embraced the wild adventure.

With her arms around Joseph's neck, Eden seductively used her body to press his backward, forcing them into his bedroom. Her hands groped his erection through his jeans. Her lips trailed down his neck as she used her tongue to lick across his racing pulse.

Joseph blinked his eyes, desperately trying to fight the urge to sleep with Eden in the bed he shared with his wife. "My God. Not here, not now. Andrea's in labor. I have to get to the hospital," his protest sounded weak, even to him.

Eden snatched his belt off and roped it around his neck.

"It has to be here...It has to be now," Eden whispered like a vixen. Within five minutes, Eden was clutching Andrea's pillow, getting her wish.

The sexual trance they were in was so good, neither of them heard the front door open until the sound of a familiar voice filled their ears.

"That's because you don't *listen*, and you posting a three-million-dollar bail raised a bunch of red flags with the IRS. How are you gonna account for that?" Pandora asked sternly, standing in the front doorway of Joseph's house. P.J, one of the most dangerous Jamaican Posse Drug lords in Virginia stood at the bottom of the steps.

"Donations from my momma's church, of

course," PJ smirked with an affirming head nod.

"Please, they're not gonna buy that B.S," Pandora snorted. "What about your cars, and your house in Falls City? They're gonna want to know how you got from Berry Farms projects to Falls City with no job, *ever.*"

"Whatever, I don't know, Anna, you're my lawyer. Tell me what to do," PJ looked at Pandora with a pensive expression.

She sighed. "I cannot give you incriminating advice," Pandora quickly turned to look in Joseph's house, and then back at PJ. "But, as a friend, I can show you how to clean your cash. Meet me at 10 A.M. tomorrow in my office. I have to go take care of something real quick."

"Thank you, sweetheart. I owe you one," P.J grinned, turning to walk away. Pandora stepped fully inside Joseph's home, closing the door behind her.

"Now, where the heck is this man?" She asked, annoyed. "Joseph!" Pandora called just as she heard rumbling coming from upstairs. Shaking her head, Pandora made her way up the stairs and into Joseph's bedroom just as he fixed his jeans and his flustered demeanor.

"Hey, what's up?" He asked, trying to contain the anxiety spilling from his racing heart.

"What the hell are you doing? Your wife is in labor. The *whole* family is at the hospital, and you're not answering your phone," Pandora fussed with a slacked mouth.

"I know, I know," Joseph said quickly, brushing the beads of sweat that protruded from his forehead, "I fell asleep, and my phone was on silent. I'm headed to the hospital now," he fished around his room for his car keys. "Were you there?"

"No, it's eleven o'clock on a Monday morning. I'm at work…busy as ever, and mom keeps calling my cell and my office, nonstop, looking for you. I came to see if you were here."

"I'm sorry," Joseph replied, finally locating his keys on his dresser. He grabbed them and moved toward the door, looking everywhere but at her. Pandora leaned against the doorframe and crossed her arms, staring directly at him.

"What?" Joseph asked, cutting his eyes at her before quickly averting them to the floor.

"Look at me," Pandora demanded softly. Joseph peered up at her with guilt-filled eyes. "What's going on with you? Your energy has been off lately. You're not yourself."

"I know, it's just…there's a lot going on right now—" Joseph stared into his sister's eyes, her stern demeanor causing his voice to trail off.

"Could it have anything to do with the skank under your bed that's jacked up your world and made you useless?" She hissed.

Joseph's eyes gaped open in fear. "Anna, I'm—"

"Listen, as lethal and addictive as the kitten can be to a man, be careful when it's attached to a cold, cunning, ruthless, careless woman, who, I'm *sure* knows you're married, and about an hour away from being a father," she muttered, coldly. Joseph's face might as well have cracked and shattered to the bedroom floor. "If you do not take charge of the situation," she pointed to Eden's toe faintly protruding from under the bed, "the situation will take charge of you. You will find yourself heartbroken, divorced, and in financial ruin. Pick your poison."

Pandora turned to walk out of his room, down the steps and out the front door, leaving Joseph speechless. Eden hid under the bed in pure and utter disbelief. Part of her was relieved that Pandora had no idea it was her. The other part of her was pissed because she knew her crazy carnival ride with Joseph had officially come to a stop.

An hour later…

Eden wasn't sure if her aggravated frustration stemmed from being forced out of Joseph's house through a basement window, with a clear warning that they could never see each other that way again, hearing Pandora speak the cold-hard truth about her or the feeling of losing the control and power she briefly held. Whatever it was, she needed to get high in order to clear her flustered mind.

After going home to shower off the stench of smoke and sex, Eden walked into the Olive Garden restaurant for her lunch date with Pandora and Quinn, forty-five minutes late. Honestly, she wasn't in the mood to see either of them, but after ducking Quinn for so long, she knew Quinn would start to worry if she failed to show up. The second she walked through the doors, she spotted Quinn walking back to their table from the bathroom. Essence magazine certainly didn't exaggerate her beauty. She was stunningly gorgeous—like a painted picture of an angel brought to life. As Quinn walked to the table, her leaf brown curls bounced flawlessly, spilling over her shoulders. Her dazzling white teeth and elegant smile were to die for. The black eyeliner she applied bought her exotic, stone gray eyes to life. Locking eyes with her was like entering into another world. She had a confident simplicity and a classic beauty that would *never* go out of style. Her curvy body was the picturesque feminine ideal. Her Amazonian figure sat well on her size eight frame, beautifully sculpted and poured into her black, figure-hugging jumpsuit. Quinn was humble, modest, understanding and spoke with a soft, sensual voice that you couldn't help but love. She was the poster of perfection. Quinn had never done anything to Eden. In fact, Quinn had never done anything wrong to anyone. However, her natural impeccable beauty served notice to Eden that while *she* went through extreme measures to be noticed, all authenticity had to do was show up.

"Hey, sorry I'm late," Eden lied approaching her friends. A fake smile replaced her scowling grimace.

Pandora looked at her watch while Quinn jumped up from her chair. Her face bursting with excitement.

"Lazarus has arisen!" Quinn beamed, squeezing Eden almost to death.

"Hey Quinn," Eden laughed. "Happy to see me?"

"Are you kidding? Yes! Where in the world have you been?"

"Late as ever," Pandora rolled her eyes, shaking her head as Eden sat down.

"Sorry, I was late getting out of class," she lied, again, "and I've been good, just keeping busy."

"I see," Quinn chuckled. "You never answer my calls or texts. I was starting to worry."

"No worries. I'm here now, and you look sexy, *First Lady,*" Eden smirked, biting her lip at Quinn.

"Fine as wine," Pandora chimed in, taking a bite of her breadstick.

"You're showing off with all that body," Eden teased, masking her envy. "I've *never* seen a first lady dress this way."

"What's wrong with the way I dress?" Quinn asked, jerking her head back.

"Nothing. It's just," Eden laughed, "you look extremely attractive and distracting. Most Pastor's wives don't dress that bold."

"Well, that's on them. I will not be dressing like I'm on the mother's board," Quinn answered softly. Pandora burst into laughter. "I believe it's okay to be stylish and sexy without being vulgar and trashy."

"That's my girl," Pandora nodded with a laugh just as her phone vibrated, "raising the bar for Pastor's wives *everywhere*."

"And crotches," Eden laughed.

"Stop it," Quinn pursed her lips into an unforced laugh.

"Oh my goodness! Look…" Pandora squealed, perking her body posture up. "Andrea had the babies." She held her phone out so Quinn and Eden could see.

Quinn gasped, clutching her chest. "They're gorgeous."

"Cute," Eden muttered in a flat monotone voice. She glared at the photo of Joseph planting a kiss on Andrea's cheek, while she posed with their new set of twin boys. He looked so happy—as if his lips weren't just between Eden's legs less than two hours ago.

"I'm so happy for Joseph," Quinn smiled. "Babies are such a blessing, and he's got a double portion."

"Me too. But I'll be even happier when he gets his life together," Pandora squinted at the picture one last time before closing her phone and shaking her head.

"What's going on with him?" Quinn asked, taking a sip from her cup.

"He's cheating on Andrea," Pandora fussed, "she was in labor earlier, and he was at home with some trashy whore in his bed." Eden's hands balled into fists under the table at the sound of her being called a trashy whore.

"Not *Joe*," Quinn gasped, "that doesn't even sound like something he would do."

"That's the same thing I said," Pandora nodded, "other than you, I've never even seen him show interest in anyone else. He's not into whores or one-night stands, and he barely has any female friends. I don't know who she is or where she came from."

"How can you be sure of the type of women he's around?" Eden asked with an offensive tone. "He's a grown man. You think he tells you *everything*?"

"Eden's right," Quinn agreed. "And, you said he and Andrea were having some problems. Who knows who he could have reached out too in that kind of vulnerable state."

"I feel so bad for Andrea," Pandora shook her head with a somber glow.

"Ditto," Quinn nodded sternly, "there's nothing more distasteful than a home-wrecking woman."

"Have you ever thought about how the other woman may feel?" Eden interjected, resting her back against the seat.

"What?" Pandora and Quinn asked in unison with identical blank stares on their faces.

"Seriously, try to look at the situation from her vantage point. I mean, yes, she was a mistress, but I reckon that her emotions were invested as well," Eden gestured with her hands. "The *nerve* of him to just drop her like a bad habit and pretend like the last, however long they spent together, never happened. I imagine she brought vitality back to his dying heart and made the most of the crumbs of his time she was probably given. Looking at it from her perspective, she should be praised for resurrecting him from the dead."

A long silence filled the table as Pandora and Quinn both stared at Eden with raised eyebrows and slacked mouths.

"Fuck- that- *bitch*," Pandora winced with an attitude, breaking through the silence. "She should be *stabbed* for trying to ruin his life. She didn't bring vitality back to his dying heart. She bought him a quick escape from his reality, and *probably* an STD. She's a fantasy—a lunch break, and if Andrea ever finds out, she'll be gutted like a *fish*."

"For the sake of her heart, and just having twin babies, it may be in her best interest not to find out right now, at least until things cool down," Quinn spoke.

Eden deviously thought of going to the hospital and dropping a bomb in Andrea's lap, in an attempt to ruin her fake little family. However, she chewed her breadstick with a mischievous grin and digressed, just as the waitress approached the table.

"Is everything okay over here, ladies?" She asked politely.

"Did anyone order anything?" Eden asked, picking up her menu.

"No, we were waiting for you, and you took too

long, so I don't have time," Pandora replied.

"Me either," Quinn agreed, "I have to get going soon, my lunch break is almost over. I'll just have another water with lemon."

"Make that two glasses of water then," Eden told the waitress.

"Sure thing," the waitress smiled with a head nod before walking away.

"How's Heaven doing?" Eden asked, changing the subject.

"She's great! Crawling all over the place, and pulling up on everything, scaring the crap out of me," Quinn shook her head.

Eden and Pandora chuckled.

"I'm serious, she's like lightning. I put her down in my bedroom, turned my back for two seconds, and she was out the door teetering on the staircase."

"Aww, I miss my baby," Pandora pouted, "I don't have any plans this weekend, and Jackson is out of town until Monday. Can I have her Friday night?"

"Sure," Quinn agreed, "Andre and I have a dinner party to go to, anyhow. I was going to call the sitter for a few hours, but you can take her for the night if you'd like."

"Great," Pandora's eyes lit up. "Jackson and I are almost finished her room, we just need to find the right curtain pattern to match the carpet. "

"Room?" Eden laughed, "you act like she's *your* baby."

"Well, she's my Goddaughter. That's the closest I'll ever get to having a baby, so I'm enjoying it," Pandora replied.

"Oh stop," Quinn shook her head, "I give you

and Jackson about two years before you end up pregnant."

"That's not gonna happen," Pandora stated.

"*Please*, as active as you two are," Eden snorted, "the only way you can steer clear of pregnancy, is if you physically can't have kids."

"Actually…I can't," Pandora's eyes dropped to the table, ashamed.

"Joanna?" Quinn was shocked, "you never told us that."

"The incident that happened when I was younger," Pandora looked up to face her friends, her eyes were filled with hurt. "My neighbor…he destroyed my reproductive system, so…" her voice trailed off.

"Jesus…" Quinn exclaimed.

"Does Jackson know?" Eden asked, with a complete lack of empathy for Pandora's confession, "because the last time I checked, he loved children and wanted three of them."

"No, he does not," Pandora answered in a regretful tone, "when the time is right, I'll tell him."

"That sucks," Eden muttered, emotionless. "Do you ever feel like you've *failed* as a woman? I know I would."

"Eden!" Quinn shot her a threatening stare.

"What?" Eden's eyes widened. She knew she was treading on thin ice, but in her mind, Pandora deserved it. "I'm asking an honest question."

"No, it's…it's okay," Pandora stated, softly, "I do at times," she chuckled to keep herself from bursting into tears. "But, in other news, I bought a new car." Pandora quickly got herself together and beamed. She opened up her phone toward her friends to show off a photo of a brand new, black Aston Martin. The bottom of Quinn's mouth almost hit the table, and Eden stared at the screen with raised eyebrows, boiling like lava on the inside.

" Wow,'" Quinn gazed at her phone screen in disbelief. "It's breathtaking."

"Thanks," Pandora smiled, before closing her phone, "I purchased it the other day. It was a gift to myself for winning my last case."

"Very much deserved," Quinn shook her head in disbelief. "I don't know how you pulled off convincing a jury that an international sniper suffered from schizophrenia."

"He *did* suffer from schizophrenia," Pandora mischievously grinned.

"Um, *no*, his psychiatrist took the stand and said he suffered from mild depression when he was ten-years-old after his parents divorced. I saw the hearing on TV," Quinn rebutted.

"No, what his psychiatrist *did* was give me an inch, and I took a mile," Pandora winked. "That poor, defenseless man was schizophrenic and bipolar, it just wasn't diagnosed yet.

"Defenseless?" Quinn reared her head back, "Pandora, the man beheaded half an army base with a machete and shot up the rest with an AK47."

"Now, now, let's not judge. He is a free man with a second chance," Pandora giggled.

"Your car color is a bit boring if you ask me," Eden interjected, purposely refusing to indulge in her friend's accolades, "I mean, it's an Aston Martin, they're prettier in white."

Quinn looked over and winced, giving Eden a

puzzled stare.

"They are *very* pretty in white, but I like black," Pandora snapped back, "it's the color of my soul."

"Everything okay, sweetie?" Quinn sensed Eden's frustration, "you look like something is bothering you."

"I'm fine," Eden replied dryly, pulling out her cellphone, refusing to look up at Quinn.

"Are you sure? Because—"

"I *said*, I'm fine," Eden said sternly. The darting gaze she gave Quinn caused Pandora to raise an eyebrow.

"What in the world, Eden? She's just concerned," Pandora defended. "Why are you so jumpy?"

"I'm sorry. I'm just sick of people asking me that," Eden admitted, forcing a smile.

"Well, I'm not people," Quinn replied, softly. "I'm your best friend, and there's something bothering you. I felt it when you first walked up."

"*I* felt it when you freaked out in my bathroom a couple weeks ago," Pandora admitted, "and I didn't believe your ridiculous lie about it being from school, either."

Since Eden couldn't get up and run out of the restaurant like she wanted to, she looked down and began texting on her phone. She was frustrated at herself, thinking she could fool a professional psychologist and a lawyer. The FBI used Quinn's expertise from time to time when they needed to get into the minds of criminals. Quinn could profile a potential multistate, serial killer in a heartbeat, so there was nothing Eden could say to throw her off.

Pandora could spot a liar and feel bad energy from a mile away. There was no getting past her either. Eden hated that they knew her like the backs of their hands, and she hated that their presence made her feel as small as an ant. So desperately, she wished she could disappear and wake up in front of Travis, Jade, and a blunt. Eden always had the upper hand with them. She was always in control. The more she felt Pandora and Quinn's eyes gazing at her, the faster her pulse raced.

"You know, it's okay to not be okay," Pandora softly spoke, reaching out to touch Eden's hand. "You've been through a lot in the last year, and there's no time frame on when you're supposed to get over it. But, pretending to be—"

Eden snatched her hand back and snapped her head up. "Listen, I'm a strong, independent, woman. I don't need help. I don't need fixing. I don't need a handout, and I *don't* need anybody feeling sorry for me because of everything that's happened. I'm in school, I have my car, I have money, a home, I'm good," she affirmed, "I am happy. I lead a busy life with a full schedule, just like you guys. The past is the past, and I am past it. I'm not weak like most women who've been in my position, I got this."

Quinn's eyes locked onto Eden's with a magnetic pull that wouldn't allow her to look away. Quinn was *very* sharp and could see right through her boldface lie. She could see the pain etched into Eden's soul. She could see depression and denial. She could also see her dilated pupils caused by whatever controlled substance she was influenced by.

"Strong, doesn't mean a woman never cries or isn't allowed bad days," Quinn said, "in fact, bad days only make her stronger because she drops her pride long enough to learn what life is trying to teach her. A strong woman doesn't pretend to be strong, she actually *is* strong. She lives a life of balance, not a busy life and a full schedule to keep her occupied. She's capable of doing a lot, but not foolish enough to do more than she is able. And, being an independent woman does not mean a woman doesn't need love or help. She can stand on her own two feet if need be, but she doesn't boast about it, or make others feel small just because they can't."

By the time Quinn finished talking, Eden's mind was on the verge of derailing. Her heart raced as if it were running a marathon, and her eyes glistened like a puddle of water. Part of her wanted to lash out in anger, and the other part wanted to crawl into a fetal position and cry. Unable to take another second of being in either of her friend's presence, Eden jumped up from the table and grabbed her purse.

"Where are you going?" Pandora asked.

"To the bathroom. I'll be right back," Eden replied in a huff, trying to mask her anger. The minute she turned to walk away, she bumped into the waitress who was on the way back to their table with their drinks. Both of the waters they ordered spilled all over Eden's shirt.

"Oh no, I'm so, so—"

Before the waitress could finish, Eden's temper uncontrollably surfaced. Baring her teeth, she gripped the waitress by the collar and raised her fist to knock her out. Quinn's eyes widened in horror, as she jumped up from her seat. Placing herself between Eden and the waitress, Quinn grabbed her arm before she took a swing. Pandora watched in shock with her mouth wide open. Customers began staring at the scene just as the waitress hurried off in fear. Eden's chest heaved up and down before snatching away from Quinn and storming out of the restaurant.

Quinn and Pandora looked at one another like two deer in headlights, wondering what in the world had gotten into Eden.

Seven

"If it doesn't open, it's not your door"

Eden sat in the back corner of her statistics class, watching her professor pace the floor while he lectured. Her classmates listened attentively, focusing on every word, their eyes following him like a hawk. Everyone appeared interested except Eden. Dragging her hands through her hair in frustration, her gaze bounced from place to place. After missing so many days of class, or being too high to concentrate, she had no idea what was going on. She felt as if she was in the twilight zone.

Eden's friendship with Travis continued to transpire in her favor, but after being deprived of the emotional security that casual sex with Joseph had given her, she felt empty. Her body now yearned for sexual attention. It didn't matter that Travis came over every day, bought her flowers, took her out, called and texted her on a regular basis, and gave her his undivided attention, his refusal to sleep with her made Eden feel rejected. There was something so beautifully different about him, and Eden wanted him...*badly*. Travis stayed on her mind around the clock, as she patiently waited for the day that he would ask her to be his girlfriend. That day seemed like it never would come. The way he looked at her and held her in his arms as they made out, Eden knew Travis felt the same way about her, but the minute their make-out session got heated, he would get up and go home. After he'd leave, Eden would cry, get high, and then cry some more until she fell asleep.

After the stunt she pulled at the Olive Garden last month, Pandora and Quinn were extremely worried and tried reaching out in every way possible, but Eden ignored their efforts. She knew she had a lot of explaining to do, but with her mind being caught in a tornado, she wasn't in the right emotional state to do it anytime soon. The more her professor talked, the more unfocused Eden became until finally, she got up from her seat, grabbed her purse and walked out the door.

"I figured I'd run into you," said a laughter-filled, familiar voice, causing Eden to turn around in the campus parking lot. Her eyes lit up the second she spotted Jade on the hood of her car, smoking a joint.

"We had the same idea I see," Eden laughed, parading over to Jade's car.

"Girl," Jade rolled her eyes, "I was in child psych looking like a deer in headlights. I'm so far behind, I just said to heck with it, and came out here to smoke."

"My sentiments exactly," Eden agreed just as Jade passed her the blunt. She inhaled a long puff, blowing out a deep sigh of relief. "I'm not sure this college thing is for me anymore."

"Touché," Jade agreed. "I've been feeling that way since last week. I think I'm gonna drop out and just go home."

"No, don't leave!" Eden replied with wide eyes.

"Girl, I can't take failing another class. I'm wasting my parent's money, and I don't wanna disappoint them any longer."

Eden shook her head. She really liked Jade and their friendship was just starting to take off. She didn't want her to leave. "I understand. Do what you feel is best...I guess. Lucky for me, I don't have any parents to disappoint," she passed Jade the blunt.

"Nope, you got nothing but luck on your side. You got the house, the car, the money, and those bomb Jimmy Choo's," Jade said staring at Eden's pink Jimmy Choo, leather boots.

"Thanks," she smiled, lifting her foot up to allow Jade a better view. "These aren't even out yet. I got an early release."

"I see. I saw those in the magazine," Jade replied, "they said they wouldn't be out until next month," she blew out a puff of smoke before passing her blunt back to Eden, "not that I could ever afford a pair, anyway."

"Let's go to the mall. I know a guy, I'll get you an early release," Eden responded, boisterously. Jade nearly fell off the hood of her car. She rapidly blinked her eyes before opening them wide, looking at Eden in disbelief. "I beg your pardon?"

"Come on, let's go. As a matter of fact, let's go on a shopping spree. My treat," Eden smiled, reaching into her purse for her car keys.

"Eden, don't play with my emotions like that. Are you *serious*?"

Eden was serious as a heart attack. She was willing to do *anything* to hoist herself back into the spotlight of love and attention.

"I'm serious," Eden giggled, "let's go splurge a little. Also, you're pretty popular around town now. Invite some of your friends over. Let's throw you a big, going away party at my house on Saturday."

Jade looked at Eden like she was crazy. "You

want me to invite my friends from the hood, to *your* house?"

"Yeah," Eden shrugged. "It'll be fun. Besides, it'll be a great way for me to mingle and meet some people, seeing that I'll be alone after you leave," she rolled her eyes.

"O- okay," Jade replied hesitantly, "if you say so." She jumped down from her car, taking another puff from her blunt before throwing it in a nearby grass patch. "Oh, wait a minute. I can't go to the mall right now, I have to pick Travis up at four. His car broke down last week, and I promised I'd drive him to class."

"What do you mean it's broken down?" Eden asked, taken aback, "he's been at my apartment since this morning. He's there now on my computer. How did he get there then?"

"He's been on the bus since last week," Jade informed.

Eden looked confused. "Why would he catch a *bus* to my house? I didn't know his car wasn't working. Why wouldn't he just ask me to come get him?"

"Eden, if I were him, I wouldn't tell my Lambo pushing girlfriend that my hooptie was broken down either."

"I'm not his girlfriend," Eden responded with an attitude, instantly annoyed again by the fact that she wasn't. "Still, that's a silly reason not to ask me for help."

"Don't take it personally. Travis has always been like that. He slept in his car for a whole month before my dad found out he was homeless. That's just how he is. He's extremely private. Very rarely will he ask anyone for anything."

In that moment, Eden felt terrible. She thought of all the times within the last week that she'd asked him to come over, and he showed up with no questions asked. She had no idea that he was catching the bus the entire time.

Eden paused, briefly thinking. "You know what...Let's meet up around three to go shopping downtown. For now, start planning this party."

"What about Travis? I told him I'd—"

"I'll take care of him," Eden replied quickly, getting into her car. "I'll text you when I'm leaving."

"Alrighty," Jade smiled. "I'll see you then."

"See you then!" Eden yelled back as she started her engine and sped out of the lot. Over the last couple of months, Eden felt like Travis treated her as if she wasn't worthy enough to be pursued as anything other than a romantic friendship. Since her personality wasn't good enough, maybe her money would do the trick.

After twenty minutes of driving, Eden pulled up in front of the Mercedes-Benz car dealership with a warm smile, and an erroneous belief that if she canceled out Travis's car problems, he'd finally see how serious she was and want to be with her. She shopped around until she spotted a buttercream, 2019 Mercedes-Benz, S-Class. After filling out the paperwork and paying the one hundred and thirty-nine thousand dollars to purchase it in full, Eden had the salesman follow her home in the brand new beauty. The price was a stretch for her pockets, especially since she had no more income coming in, but as she unlocked her front door and saw Travis smiling back at her, Eden felt like every dime was worth it.

"Hey," Eden beamed, closing her front door,

walking over to him with a hug.

"Hey you," he replied back, glancing at his watch, "I thought you had class until five-thirty?"

"I did, but I left. I couldn't focus."

"Eden," Travis darted his eyes at her, "this is the third time this week, what are you doing?"

"I'm not doing *anything*, that's the whole point," she insisted, dropping her purse on her couch before taking a seat. "Anyway, I have a sur—"

"No," Travis cut her off, taking a seat next to her with a concerned look on his face. "Listen, maybe introducing you to pot wasn't the brightest idea. You're overdoing it, and it's messing up your focus with classes."

"It has nothing to do with being high, Travis, I just—"

"You're lit right now, I can smell it. At two o'clock in the afternoon," Travis shook his head. "You've gotta slow down a little bit. I don't wanna be the reason you turn into a pothead."

"I don't understand," Eden winced, "you smoke just as much as I do if not more. What's the problem?"

"The problem is, I'm not missing classes or not showing up when I'm supposed to. I smoke on the regular, yes, but I don't allow it to interfere with my life. I had this same talk with Jade. Don't let this stuff jack up your future."

"You're about a year too late with that," Eden spat in a sarcastic tone, getting up from the couch, annoyed. She had every intention of coming home, showering Travis with his new gift, and watching the expression on his face while he slammed her against a wall and sexed her brains out. She didn't expect to be met with a lecture.

Getting up from the couch, Travis grabbed Eden's hand. "Look, I'm not judging you, just promise me you'll focus on school more?"

He intently ogled her. If she was ever unsure about his feelings, he made it clear now. Travis really cared about her. No man had ever concerned himself with her future.

"I promise," she declared, "as long as you promise to be honest with me when you need help."

"Help with...?" He narrowed his eyes.

"Here," she replied, humbly retrieving the Mercedes-Benz key from her back pocket before reaching out to hand it to him.

"What's that?"

"It's a key to your new Mercedes. I heard all about your car problems, so I figured I'd solve them for you," she smirked, placing the key into his hands.

Travis's eyes nearly distended out of their sockets. The look on his face caused Eden to laugh.

"Eden," Travis stared down at the key and then back up at Eden.

"Don't tell me you can't take it, or it's too much," Eden responded, playfully cutting her eyes at him.

"Wow," Travis replied, completely dumbfounded. He slowly took the key from her hand.

Eden moved in closer to him and wrapped her arms around his neck. "Listen, Jade told me how private you are, and I understand, but I wanna believe that I mean more to you than just some casual friendship. When I found out you needed help, I wanted to be the one to help you."

Travis looked into her eyes, floundering for the

words that could express the shock coursing through him, but his mind felt completely frozen. "I...don't know what to say."

"A simple *thank you* would suffice. I paid for it in full, so it's yours," she replied with an affectionate kiss as he wrapped his arms around her waist.

"You *do* mean a lot more to me than just some casual friendship," he admitted. "But you could've just given me a ride or lent me the eight hundred bucks to get a new engine. You didn't have to buy me a Benz."

"Well, I wanted too, so I did. Enjoy it. Now you don't have to catch the bus to my party on Saturday." She turned to walk into Ruby's old bedroom.

"What party?" Travis asked. He followed Eden into her mother's room as he slipped the key into his jeans pocket.

"This Saturday," she repeated, opening Ruby's walk-in closet door in search of her strobe light. "Jade told me she was going back to Chicago, so I asked her to invite all of her friends over for some drinks and laughs."

Travis raised his eyebrows. "You're gonna invite Jade's friends into *this* type of community?"

"Yeah..." Eden placed the large strobe light box on the bed. "I don't have a lot of friends or a social life for that matter. I need to step my game up."

"Eden, I don't think that's a good idea to invite a bunch of people you don't know into your house, especially not the kind of people she surrounds herself with."

"That's rude," Eden looked up at him, slightly offended. "You act like you don't even care that she's leaving. I thought she was your friend."

"Not at all, I care about her a lot," Travis defended. "Jade has been my friend since I was eighteen-years-old. She's like family to me. It annoys me that she's giving up on school so easily, but you can have that kind of luxury when you're a spoiled brat. She was raised differently. You don't fit in with her kind of energy."

"Well gee, thanks *Dad*," Eden shook her head as she pulled the light from the box, "I can handle myself though, I promise."

"O...kay," Travis warned.

"I got this strobe light for my sixteenth birthday. I finally get to put it to use again," Eden replied with excitement, blowing the dust from the light.

"Whose room is this?" Travis asked, turning his attention to the pictures on the dresser. Out of all the renovations Eden had done to her home, her mother's bedroom remained untouched. It was exactly how Ruby left it the morning she was killed.

"It's my mother's room," Eden replied in a low tone, taking a seat on Ruby's bed.

"I didn't know you lived with your mother," Travis turned to face her. "She's never here."

"Yeah, I know," she muttered, shifting her eyes to the large picture above the television of her and Ruby at Eden's college graduation. Immediately, the hurt she felt from not having Ruby around gripped her heart like an angry fist.

"I see where you get your nonchalant, facial expressions from," Travis chuckled, looking at a picture of Ruby, "will she ever be home when I'm around so I can meet her?"

"I wish," Eden's voice shook. "She died last

year."

Travis flinched. "Wow, I'm sorry."

"It's okay," she lied, quickly wiping away the tears that filled the crack of her eyes.

Travis walked over and sat down next to Eden, wrapping his arms around her. "You never told me that."

"I don't really tell anyone," Eden admitted, her face turning bright red the more she held her emotions in. "She was killed by an inmate who escaped from prison. We were supposed to meet for lunch that afternoon, but I went into

early labor that morning. I couldn't get in touch with her to tell her. Later on, I found out why."

"Labor?" Travis's head tilted to the side.

"Yes," Eden bit her lip remorsefully. "I fell in love for the first time ever with this guy I met in college. My mom couldn't stand him," Eden choked out a laugh as tears trailed her face. "After six years of dating, I got pregnant and then dumped for my best friend. I went into labor unexpectedly and had to get a C-section because my daughter's heart rate was too slow. By the time they took her out, she was dead."

"What?" Travis gazed at Eden with a long, pained stare, periodically wiping away her uncontrollable tears. He would have never guessed something like that to be a part of her past.

"So, that's my life...my mom left me rich and alone. My ex is married to my best friend, and my other best friend just had a baby girl a few months ago. I'm surrounded by pure hell, so—"

"So that's why you're trying to make friends, pretending to be someone you're not," Travis nodded in confirmation.

"I'm not pretending to be anything, I'm just trying to be happy and live my life as best as I can," she turned to look at him.

"But you're going about it the wrong way."

"You wouldn't understand," Eden shook her head, wiping her remaining tears. "Nobody does, that's why I don't talk about it."

"You're right, I don't know how *you* feel, but I understand how *it* feels," Travis declared. "I grew up with both of my parents. Four years ago, I went skiing in the mountains with some friends and fell off a slope. I broke both arms and had a really bad concussion. My mom and my girlfriend who I'd been dating for over three years, drove up to get me. They ended up sliding off a narrow highway because of the crazy weather. They both died..." His voice trailed off, filled with regret. Speechless, Eden's stomach tightened as she grabbed her chest.

"I was so broken after that and wanted so badly to be healed, that I let anyone in. I crammed them into what small space I had left and hoped that they had good intentions. They didn't. Don't be like me."

Eden stared into his eyes for a long moment before responding. "I won't..."

At that moment, the strong connection she felt for Travis over the last month began to make sense. He had officially stolen her heart with no intentions of returning it anytime soon. Leaning into her, he softly pressed his lips into hers as she exhaled, basking in the glorious moment of being understood—finally.

Travis stood up, bringing Eden up by her hands before wrapping his arms around her waist and taking her mouth into his. The minute his lips touched hers, she was breathless. She had been waiting for this moment since the first day she met him, and it had finally come.

Without warning, Travis forced himself to push away from her. "I should get going."

"What's wrong?"

"Nothing," Travis tightly shut his eyes, rubbing a hand down his face. "I just...I should get to class."

"Forget class, I'll be your teacher," Eden bit her lip into a seductive grin, trailing her hands down her curves.

"Eden, you're not ready to commit to me yet," he expressed, backing away from her.

"Travis, please," she begged, feeling her heart sink into her stomach at the sound of his rejection. "Stop torturing me like this. I wanna be with you. I *want* you."

"I like you a lot, and I want you too—," he reached for her face and gently stroked her cheek. "But I also don't wanna be used, nor do I want you to do yourself an injustice."

"I'm confused.

"Eden, you don't want me because you think I'm a good guy. You want me because you think I can fill a void in your life, and that's a recipe for disaster. Don't seek someone else out for the sake of being healed."

"That's not true," she defended, shaking her head frantically.

"So why do you want to have sex with me so bad?" He darted his eyes at her. "I can't read minds, but I can feel energy. Since day one, you've been trying to jump on me without even knowing who I was."

Eden flung her hands into the air, painfully staring back at Travis. "What in the world...what kind of guy gets turned off by a woman who wants to sleep with him? Shoot, maybe Jade was right. Maybe you *are* gay," she hissed in frustration.

"Oh yeah?" His eyebrows rose in offense, roughly retrieving the Mercedes-Benz key from his pocket before flinging it on the dresser. "What kind of woman buys a guy a Benz in exchange for sex?"

Eden's jaw dropped open.

"That's right," he continued, "I'm not stupid, and I'm *not* gay. I'm also not looking for a friend with benefits. I need to know that your heart is in the right place and that you *really* know what it is that you want because once you're mine, I'm not letting you go."

"Excuse me?" She spat, jerking her neck back, "What are you, some kind of God? You're asking me to prove myself to you?"

"I'm telling you that you're broken and insecure, and I can't be with you until you fix it."

His boldness made her nostrils flare and every hair on her neck raise. "You know what," Eden's eyes tightened in anger, as she stormed to her front door and pulled it open. "Leave."

"Why? Because you don't wanna face the truth?"

"No, because you've just diminished my honest heartfelt feelings for you into being some confused skank looking for sex," she hissed, feeling insulted.

"That's not what I meant. I—"

"Leave," she repeated, coldly.

"Really?" He huffed, shaking his head. "So much for being honest and real."

"No, you're a douchebag just like the rest of them. Get out."

"Whatever," he quickly retrieved his backpack from the floor and stormed out. He barely made it through the doorway before Eden slammed the door shut. She collapsed against the door and crossed her arms in frustration. After Jackson, she'd vowed to never get close to another man, but after seeing something different in Travis, she gave it a try. Eden invested much time and effort into getting to know him. She couldn't believe the way he hurt her feelings and embarrassed her heart. She knew she had issues. She expected they would work themselves out with the right man and convinced herself that Travis would be the one. Jerking her body back against the door, she began to cry.

Ruby tilted her chin down, frowning at Eden with a stony expression.

"What?" Eden rolled her eyes, watching her emotionally broken self-crumble to pieces in her living room. "What kind of lesson is God trying to teach me *now,* instead of showing up back then when I needed it?"

"This isn't a lesson from God, sweetheart. This is a lesson from a recovering doormat," Ruby replied, calmly. "Actually, this is a repeated lesson, because you watched me suffer through some of the same emotions during my marriage with your deceased father many years ago."

Eden's eyes enlarged, staring at Ruby in terror. "Dad's dead?"

"He sure is," Ruby shook her head, remorsefully.

"How!" Eden yelled as tears flooded her eyes. "When? I've been writing him letters and never got a response. Was that why?"

"The white woman he left me for, shot him to death about four years ago, isn't that something?" Ruby sarcastically gasped in shock, clutching her hand to her chest. "Nobody's even realized he's dead yet. His remains are buried under the vegetable garden in their backyard— the same garden he threw me into and kicked me until I passed out after I found out where his mistress lived."

"Daddy…" Eden shook her head and cried, her voice filled with guilt.

"Poor thing. God rest his *burning* soul," Ruby beamed, energetically. "Anyhow, you watched me suffer with that man, and I schooled you *then* about self-respect and not feeling like your life needed to be validated by others," she preached, shuffling through papers attached to the clipboard she held. "And here I am in the afterlife, schooling you again. A mother's work is *never* done."

"It's easy for you to sit here and judge my mistakes without considering the type of mindset I was in," Eden defended. "I felt stuck, so I opened up and made new friends, how was I—"

"Correction," Ruby pointed at Eden, "You tried to *buy* new friends. There's a big difference. Love, friendship, and respect are not sale items. Love is not a product like shoes or lemons, yet people-pleasers try to buy it with favors and being agreeable. I don't get it," Ruby declared with a wince, shaking her head with crossed arms. "Money doesn't buy people's love, money *borrows* people's love."

"I'm sorry, was there a positive route somewhere that I could have taken?" Eden sarcastically hissed, her face withering with anger. "Was there another way out that I missed?"

"There is always a way out for those who are

clever enough to find it," Ruby proclaimed, "but you weren't looking for a way out. Your selfish greed and need to be acknowledged, mirrored, and validated was all *you* cared about. You were starving for attention, and willing to pay any price to get it."

Eight

Gone Girl

After tossing the remainder of her smoked blunt over the balcony, Eden stepped back inside her dimly-lit, overly crowded condo, instantly being met with a sweaty concoction of alcohol, cigarettes, and the stench of marijuana. Word traveled quickly about her party, via social media. More people showed up than she had room for. There were guys clustered in groups in her living room engaging in conversation and smoking weed, and girls parading around with red Solo cups showing off their skimpy attire. The playlist full of Trap and R&B music from Jade's iPod blared loudly through her subwoofers, as Eden watched her guests thrusting and grinding to the beat. There were lesbians making out against her wall, and thugs stretched out on her couch, receiving lap dances from strippers.

Eden walked through her living room dressed in a skintight, black dress, ending just inches below her backside. She could feel the lustful stares of the guys watching her body like a hawk, along with the envious glares from some of the girls who'd come to the party just to see what her house looked like. Much to some of the hater's dismay, Eden's party turned out better than expected, making her an instant neighborhood celebrity. She began getting all of the praise and attention she craved, however, after the horrible fight she had with Travis the night before, it didn't seem to phase her. She moved about her house with a fake smile and a somber glow, watching the clock, anticipating when it would be over so she could wallow in her self-pity and broken heart.

"Eden!" Jade hollered over the music from down the hall, motioning for Eden to come to her. Eden shuffled down the hallway to meet her friend, trying her best not to brush up against people as they stumbled around, drunk and disoriented.

"Hey, what's up?"

"Where you been? I've been looking all over for you?" Jade asked, taking a sip from her cup of vodka and cranberry juice.

"I was on the balcony smoking, what's wrong?"

"Nothing's wrong with *me*, I'm having a blast. What's up with you? You seem sad."

"I'm great," Eden lied, forcing out a fake chuckle, "I'm just high as a kite."

"Me too," Jade laughed. "This party is great! You should see my Facebook timeline. All of VA is tagging me right now."

"Awesome, I'm glad everyone's having a good time," Eden responded, emotionless. Just then, Cameron stumbled over to Jade, wrapping his arms around her waist from behind.

"So, I just lost twelve straight games of beer pong," he slurred, bursting into uncontrollable laughter.

"Really? We can't tell," Jade laughed, catching wind of his rosy red cheeks and unfocused stare.

"Come on, come dance with me," he replied, burying his face into Jade's neck. He pressed himself against her while leading her down the hall.

"Oh my gosh, your breath is so hot and funky right now," Jade laughed, "and I'm so high, I probably won't even remember to tease you about it tomorrow."

Eden giggled, shaking her head as Jade and Cameron disappeared into the living room.

"You're Eden, right?" A masculine voice spoke loudly over the music from behind her.

Eden turned around. "That's me," she responded.

"I'm Mike. I think we have sociology together," he extended his hand. Eden accepted his hand, giving him a brief staredown. Mike was tall, brown skin, and athletically built, with a long, neatly sculpted beard.

"I don't know how I missed *you* in class," she grinned at him, flirtatiously, "but, hello."

"Yeah, I sit a couple rows across from you. I've been eyeing you for a while now," he smirked, rubbing the back of his neck, making Eden blush. "You wanna dance?"

"Maybe later," she smiled, pointing to the direction of the living room, "I'm gonna go to the balcony and smoke real quick."

"Oh wow," Mike jerked his head back, partly shocked, "you don't look like someone who smokes."

"Looks can be very deceiving," she winked.

"Mind if I join you?"

"Sure, why not?" She giggled, turning to walk down the hallway. Mike stuffed his hands in his pockets and followed behind her, locking his eyes on the back of her figure.

Eden's legs nearly gave way when she entered her living room and saw Travis. Knots formed in the pit of her stomach as she watched him leaning up against her living room wall with a red cup in one hand, attentively focused on his iPhone in his other hand. You would have thought Eden was star struck the way her chest heaved up and down, drinking in his gorgeous reflection. It was as if the whole room had faded to black with tunnel vision, and she could only see him.

Did he come here to change his mind, or is he here to be smart and flaunt himself in my face? She thought, her eyes becoming glossy as she remembered her harsh words to him the other night. Suddenly, a girl dressed in a tight spandex skirt stumbled her way over and practically threw herself on him. Travis looked up from his phone, gripping the girl by her waist with one arm to keep her from falling. The girl laughed, wildly hooking her arms around Travis's neck, nearly spilling his drink. Eden watched bitterly, crossing her arms over her chest. It was evident that the girl was drunk, but Eden didn't care. The more she watched her fondle and grope all over Travis, the more pissed off she became.

"Two can play that game," she mumbled to herself, spinning around to face Mike. She wrapped her arms around his neck. "You know what? I think I *will* take you up on that dance," she stated with a sullen look. "We can smoke after."

"Your call, baby girl," Mike obliged, sliding an arm around her waist to pull her closer. Eden smiled, mischievously. She strutted around, leading Mike to a corner of the living room. Without further ado, she dropped her body like she was dodging a bullet, and swept the floor like a seductress, giving Mike the business with her backside on the way up. She dipped left, and he dipped along with her, moistening his lips as their bodies moved in sync. Mike leaned against the wall, catching everything she threw his way.

　　With her back to him, Eden pressed herself against his body, linking an arm around his neck. Mike used both his hands to glide down her curves, smiling like a kid on Christmas. Eden's eyes trailed over in Travis's direction to see if he noticed, and the staredown he was giving them sent immediate chills down her spine. Travis's face was tight, and his lips sneered in disgust, unable to contain his emotion. Eden smirked at him deviously just as Mike began rubbing his hands down her thighs, lowering his head to kiss her neck. Travis's eyes widened, as veins appeared on his neck. He was pissed, and Eden knew it. She pursed her lips and glowered, loving every bit of it. Since *he* didn't want her, he could stand on the sidelines and suffer, watching someone else who did. Suddenly, Travis's entire aura shifted into something Eden had never seen on a human being before. His eyes became shrewd and assessing, almost appearing as if a veil had slid away from them. They bore into Eden's, revealing a scorching force of jealousy that made her feel uncomfortable. The more she danced with Mike, the more the intense magnetism that Travis exuded grew, until Eden unintentionally stopped dancing, and froze. The devious smirk on her face slowly wavered into a pensive expression as she watched him clench his teeth and ball one of his fists. Biting his bottom lip, Travis gave Eden a slow, disbelieving head shake, before dropping his cup of liquor and storming off down the hall. Eden watched him walk away, immediately feeling bad. She wanted to go after him, but she felt as if she was rooted in place and couldn't move a muscle. Her heartbeat grew sluggish and her eyes prickled with tears. Her intent was to make Travis jealous, not to hurt him.

"Why did you stop dancing?' Mike whispered in Eden's ear.

"I'll be right back," Eden muttered, finally pulling away from Mike and rushing down the hall after Travis. Her thoughts spun like a whirlwind. *One day he likes me, the next day he doesn't. Now today, I'm the devil for showing someone else attention*, Eden shook her head, stopping in front of Ruby's door while she glanced down the rest of the crowded hallway in search of Travis. Without warning, she found herself being yanked into Ruby's dark bedroom and thrown against the nearest wall, as the door slammed shut. An angry Travis fused her forearms to the wall with his strong grip.

"Don't play with me," he scowled.

"Don't throw me like I'm some rag doll! What's wrong with you?" She fussed. Eden frantically tried snatching her arms from Travis's grasp, but he was too strong.

"Who *was* that guy?" He yelled, the edge in his voice setting off all kinds of alarms.

"Why do you care?" She spat back.

Travis's face tightened the more Eden continued answering his questions with questions of her own. "I'm serious, Eden," he snarled, tightening his grip on her wrists.

"What the heck? Are you some kind of schizophrenic? Do you *not* remember yesterday?" She stared at him, partly confused, "and let go of my arms Travis, you're hurting me." The deep crimson moon shined through the curtains of Ruby's window, exposing Travis's reflection. The demented look he gave her lay somewhere between sanity and madness. "Travis!" She wiggled, furrowing her eyebrows into a pained stare.

"Can you handle being my girl? Are you ready to fall in love with someone like me?" He panted in an authoritative tone, refusing to loosen his grip as he moved in closer to Eden.

"No…I cannot!" She hissed. "You don't know *what* you want from me."

Travis took her mouth with his, silencing her frustration with a kiss that literally made Eden stop breathing. Freeing her arms, Travis clutched her face with his hand, creating the belief of ownership. He passionately explored Eden's mouth with his own. His lips were warm and soft, the suction fast and greedy.

"I told you, once I make you mine, I'm never letting you go," he declared, boldly. "Tell me, is this what you want?"

The sound of Travis's voice filled Eden with an edgy restless energy. If good things come to those who wait, then great things must come to those that waited the longest. Eden stared back at Travis with a raging lust. The awareness of him prickled across her skin, spreading desire through her body like the plague.

"Yes," she whispered in desperation.

"It's settled then. You're mine," he whispered, trailing his tongue down her cheek. "From now on, your body belongs to me. I'm the only one allowed to see it. I need you humble, too. I don't like a showoff. Understand?" Travis continued touching her, building her need.

Air hissed from between her teeth. "Yes," she moaned.

"Secondly, I'm a private man, and I don't like the world in my business. So, no gossiping to Jade about the way I'm making you feel right now." As a shadow crossed Eden's face, Travis could see vulnerability in her eyes.

" I'm also very possessive, Eden," Travis leaned in closer to her, erasing the remaining space between them. He smelled sinfully good, and the intense trance he had her mind in, drove her crazy. His control over Eden was absolute, and his seduction was wickedly accurate. He claimed her mouth again, exploring it erotically, as Eden kissed him back as if she could eat him alive. Before she knew it, she found herself face up at the top of Ruby's bed, being drilled like a black and decker.

Every cell in her body screamed, and her mouth flew open to draw in desperate breaths of air. It was almost as if Travis was designed to sex a woman right out of her mind, and he did just that. He knew all of her spots and took her to limits beyond her wildest imagination. He pounded ecstasy into her until her head nearly went through Ruby's headboard. Time and everything else in her world ceased to exist as he took her body on a journey that had an unknown destination... At that moment, Eden knew she would *never* be the same again.

"Talk about making someone roll over in their grave," Ruby pursed her lips and shook her head. "On *my* bed."

"How was——" Eden's words were cut short by the sound of a train, rushing loudly down train tracks. She looked around in fear. "What's that?"

"That was the last train headed to your

freedom...*and you missed it,*" Ruby crossed her arms.

"Why didn't it wait for me?" Eden asked, innocently.

"It's *been* waiting, Eden. If you weren't so tangled up in Mr. *Dark & Dangerous,* you would have realized it."

"How? He seemed like a nice guy. He was everything I needed, everything I wanted, and everything I didn't have," her voice trailed off as tears filled in her eyes.

"Dressed like the devil himself," Ruby chuckled.

"Mom look at him," Eden cried, pointing at Travis. He held Eden in his arms, kissing her softly, grateful that they were finally a couple. "Does that look like the devil to you?"

"Were you expecting pointy horns and a red cape?" Ruby tilted her head to the side. "Satan is the Prince of Illusion, that's Mr. Incognito. He comes looking like a manifestation of everything you've ever wanted."

Tears fell from Eden's face as she bit her lip and looked at Ruby with eyes full of regret.

"But you were warned yet again, baby," Ruby shook her head, pacing the floor. "There is great gratitude owed to God when he intercedes to close a door on your behalf. You never know what he's trying to protect you from, but you refused to walk away. You kept kicking it, screaming at it, trying to buy your way into it, banging on it—you keep knocking on the devil's door and eventually, *he will answer you.*"

Nine

Over the next two months, Eden and Travis's relationship took off rather quickly. The indestructible walls she once built after being hurt by Jackson, started to crumble right before her very eyes. Travis appreciated Eden's quirkiness, her short attention span, and her outlook on life. He didn't mind that she asked too many questions, and he didn't judge her for not having her life figured out yet. Travis made her feel interesting and always took inventory of the little things no one else ever noticed. As the weeks passed, Eden became so strongly drawn to him that when they were together, nothing else mattered. They had the best conversations and thrived off of each other's energy. After giving him a key, and free reign over her condo, Travis fired all of Eden's staff. He saw no need for a butler or a maid because he cooked and cleaned every day. When she came home for the evening from classes, there was always dinner, flowers, and a bubble bath waiting for her. Travis informed Eden that he was the only man she'd ever need for *anything*, so he got rid of her limousine driver as well. He opened all of her doors, did the grocery shopping, and took her back and forth to classes. Eden couldn't even remember the last time she got to drive her car by herself or go somewhere alone. With him by her side, around the clock, he made sure she studied for her exams and got good grades. He also used her money to buy her a whole new wardrobe, a much more modest one, free of designer labels, tight jeans, and cleavage-revealing tops. Finally, having a man that cared so deeply made Eden feel like she was on top of the world. Things she once worried about were no longer problems, and it felt refreshing not to be consumed by unnecessary details because Travis handled them all. There was never any pressure or stress when she was with him, only a natural sense of comfort and a real appreciation for each other. Eden never felt like she needed to put on a show to impress him anymore because he only seemed infatuated with the real her. Time spent with him was effortless, peaceful, intimate and playful all at the same time.

The one thing she did miss, however, were her friends. After the stories Eden shared with Travis about Quinn and Pandora, he informed her to stay away from them and saw to it that she did. At his request, she cut off all communication with them, but after two months, her conscious began bothering her. Now that she was in a much better place emotionally, Eden felt extremely guilty and embarrassed for the way she treated her best friends. Quinn and Pandora weren't just some failed friendships that she could ignore and forget, they meant a lot to her. Their bond was important to her, and she wanted to make things right. She wanted them to know how well she was doing in school, and she wanted to introduce them to Travis and Jade.

Since Eden was a little girl, she had never gone more than a week without a text, phone call, or visit from them. Eden was grateful that Travis was so protective of her, but ignoring her friends made her feel empty, as if she were missing something. Unwilling to let another day go by without seeing them, she decided to pay Quinn a visit. Knowing that Travis would try to talk her out of it, she decided to drive on her own while he was out grocery shopping. She was just in time because Quinn was on her way out to a function with Andre.

"Thanks so much for agreeing to drop Heaven off at Anna's for me," Quinn said, disappearing into her closet. "Andre and I are running ridiculously late for this gala."

Andre rushed into the bedroom, adjusting his blazer. "Baby, they changed the colors from red to black," he looked frustrated. He peered into the closet at Quinn who was already dressed in a red, calf-length dress. Quinn dropped her shoulders, allowing the red and gold Louboutin's she held in her hand to drop to the floor. "They waited until the last minute to tell me, thank God we didn't leave yet."

"*Okay*...Black, it is then," she shook her head and laughed, rummaging through her clothes for something black to change into.

"I'm sorry, sweetheart. You look beautiful, still." He confirmed, staring at her attire.

"Thanks. Just give me five minutes, and I'll be down," Quinn ensured.

"Great," he nodded, turning to walk out of the room. He was too much in a rush to even realize Eden's presence.

"Sheesh," Eden cringed, "I would be so mad if I took all that time to get dressed just to have to change," she shook her head, "that red dress was pretty, too."

"I'm used to it," Quinn replied, rushing to change her clothes.

"Used to being inconvenienced like that?" Eden cocked her head back. "You're the First Lady. That's like royalty, basically. As much as you and Andre sacrifice for the state of Virginia, and all the other surrounding areas, you should be entitled to perfection wherever you go. I'm sure your presence at whomever's gala you're attending, makes them look more important. The nerve of them to wait until the last minute to tell you about a wardrobe change."

"Sweetie, you're in for a rude awakening with that type of thinking," Quinn giggled, just as her red dress came flying out of the closet. "In life period, you have to learn to be *realistic* rather than *idealistic*. If you grasp the idea in your head that everything concerning you and your circumstances, even your relationships, should always be perfect —no inconveniences, no hindrances, no unlovely people to deal with—then you're setting yourself up to fail."

"So you operate in a negative mindset to prevent disappointment?   Is that what you're saying, *First Lady*?" Eden teased, scooping Quinn's red dress off the floor, neatly placing it on her bed.

"No," Quinn sneered, walking out of her closet, "I'm just realistic enough to understand ahead of time, that very few things in real life are ever perfect. For example, Andre and I have traveled almost every weekend for the last six years to a different city, to hold seminars. We would rent out hotel ballrooms and convention centers, and the moment something went wrong, I would get upset and frustrated," she gestured with her hands, walking over to her jewelry box to retrieve her pearls. "Things like the air conditioner not working right, or not working at all, insufficient lighting in the conference room, chairs that were stained and ripped...we paid good money for the use of those rooms and rented them in good faith expecting them to be in a decent condition, so I was irritated when that wasn't case."

"That *sounds* irritating, especially for someone who's a perfectionist like you," Eden chuckled.

"Precisely, and I did everything I could to try to ensure that the places we rented were clean and comfortable, and yet, in about eighty-five percent of them, something did not live up to our expectations. There were times when we had been promised an early check-in for our travel team, yet, we'd arrive and be told there'd be no rooms available for several hours. Hotel employees would give out wrong information concerning the times of our meetings, even though we had told them repeatedly, and even sent printed material to them, showing the *exact* dates and times. Frequently, hotel and banquet employees were rude and lazy," Quinn adjusted her pearls and walked over to her mirror as Eden watched her. "Actually, I remember one time in particular when the dessert served to our *Christian* women's ministry, approximately eight hundred of them, was laced with rum. The kitchen got the dishes mixed up with what was being served at a wedding reception. It was so embarrassing when the women started coming to us telling us the dessert tasted like it had liquor in it." Eden gasped, amused as Quinn pursed her lips and shook her head, turning to face Eden. "I could go on and on, but the point is simply this: occasionally, but very rarely, we ended up with a perfect place, perfect people, and a perfect seminar. We rarely get upset anymore about the imperfections of our journeys, because we know it's a part of everyday life. Our job is not to control our circumstances, but to respond toward them," she winked.

Eden nodded in agreement, she'd never thought about things that way, but it made sense. As she stared at Quinn, her eyes went into a daze. Dressed in an ankle-length black gown that elegantly hugged her coke bottle figure, Quinn sat at her vanity chair to put her stilettos on.

"You look amazing," Eden smiled.

"Why thank you. You sure it's not too *skanky* for a First Lady?" Quinn teased, raising an eyebrow at Eden before standing up to take one last glance in the mirror.

Eden blushed, averting her gaze to the floor. "I'm sorry, Mannequin."

"I'm just joking, it's okay," Quinn giggled.

"No, really," Eden replied, getting up to walk closer to her, "I've been mean, and distant, and just…everything but a friend, and I'm sorry."

Quinn turned to her. "I accept your apology, and I'm happy to see you're doing better. I've really been worried about you."

"I know you were. You and Anna both, and I pushed you guys away," Eden responded as guilt filled her eyes. "I don't know what happened, I guess I—" Quinn walked up closely to Eden, softly placing her hands into hers. "Sometimes, when our lives need to be rebuilt, they will fall apart. The things you went through last year would have put Satan himself in a straitjacket. It was a lot, baby, and you didn't give yourself time to heal."

A lump formed in Eden's throat as she listened to Quinn talk. "When we don't learn to heal the wounds of our past, we will continue to bleed. You can bandage your bleeding with food, alcohol, drugs, sex, work, or whatever, but it will still seep through and stain your life. You have to find the strength to open the wounds, put your hand inside, pull out the core of the pain holding you prisoner, and make peace with it."

Tears fell from Eden's eyes and rolled down her cheeks as Quinn let go of Eden's hands and used her thumbs to gently wipe them away. Being in Quinn's presence was almost like standing toe to toe with God himself. She was always so peaceful and positive. Her words of wisdom were always strategic and precise. Her gentleness and compassion could shift an atmosphere and unthaw a frozen heart. Quinn stared into Eden's eyes as if she were looking into her soul. It was almost like she knew what was going on, without Eden having to explain it.

"I love you, alright?" Quinn bought Eden's chin up to face her, "and I'm always here for you, don't ever forget that."

"I love you, too," Eden replied. She reached out to hug Quinn, but the ringing of her phone vibrating in her pocket stopped her. When she pulled it out and saw that it was Travis, a big smile formed on her face. "Hang on, this is my friend I wanted to tell you about."

"I doubt it's a friend with *that* kind of smile," Quinn crossed her arms and smiled.

"I'll tell you about him later," she cheesed.

"Mmh," Quinn smirked, "I'm gonna go load the baby's things in your car. We have to get going, like now." She quickly turned and rushed out of the room.

"Okay, I'll be down in a second," Eden replied before accepting the call.

"Hel—"

"Where are you?" Travis fussed into the phone,

impatiently.

"You were out shopping so I came over to see my friend," Eden said, slightly furrowing her eyebrows at his tone of voice.

"What friend?"

"Quinn. I came over to talk. I missed her."

"The same Quinn and Pandora you told me about, that we promised to steer clear of?" Travis asked with a rude undertone in his voice.

"Actually, *we* didn't promise. It was your idea, but I missed them and- listen, I'll talk to you about it when I get home."

"Which will be?"

"Well, I'm headed to Pandora's house to drop off Quinn's daughter, and I wanted to hang out with her, maybe stay the night or something."

Travis almost jumped out of his skin. "Stay the *night*?"

"Is that a problem?" Eden winced, sensing his growing anger.

"We'll talk about it when you get home, but I need you here as soon as you can."

"Why? Do we have something to—"

"Eden!" Travis burst into anger, causing Eden to jump.

"Travis?" She replied, blinking her eyes in confusion.

"I don't wanna repeat myself." A long pause clutched Eden's voice before she hesitantly responded. "I'll. I'll be there shortly."

The phone disconnected in her ear before she could even say goodbye. Eden stared at her phone completely dumbfounded for a split second, before placing it back into her pocket. This was the first time he had ever spoken to her like that.

Maybe something upset him on the way back from the grocery store, she thought, walking out of Quinn's house just in time to see Andre securing Heaven in the car seat.

"Hey, Eden, long time no see," Andre said, as he kissed Heaven on the forehead and closed the car door.

"Ditto, I missed you guys a lot."

"Glad to see you're doing okay. You look great," he smiled. "Will we see you in church on Sunday?"

"I'm not sure, *Pastor.*" She laughed, getting into her car. "Maybe."

"I texted Anna and told her you're on the way. Drive safely," Quinn called, as Andre opened her car door and she disappeared inside.

"Yes, you drive *under* the speed limit with my baby girl in your car," he joked, rushing over to the driver's side of his car.

"Yeah, yeah, don't worry. I'll take care of the precious cargo."

"See you soon," Andre waved.

Eden chuckled, starting her car before pulling off. As she peered into her rearview mirror for oncoming traffic, she noticed Heaven, cheerfully looking at her. She was a spitting image of Quinn with her sandy skin and identical, captivating gray eyes. Eden knew how much Quinn and Andre loved one another, and she was so excited that after all these years, they were finally able to start a family. Eden smiled at the beautiful baby, reminiscing about the day Quinn went into labor.

One year ago...

Eden and Quinn sat on the barstool of Pandora's kitchen island playing Uno, while Pandora stood at her stove attempting to cook dinner.

"Anna, do you know what you're doing?" Quinn asked, shuffling the deck of cards.

"Of course I know what I'm doing," Pandora replied in offense, stirring the red sauce in the pot, "I know how to cook."

"Alright, I was just asking because the chicken has been in the oven for over an hour, and I don't smell anything," Quinn replied sweetly.

"What?" Pandora muttered in confusion, leaning down to peer into the oven. Her mouth slightly opened when she realized her food was still raw. "I just upgraded this stove last month, why isn't it working properly?"

"Well, unless it's a magic stove, I think you'll need to turn it on first," Eden responded, shaking her head. Pandora glanced at the off button on the oven and pressed it, causing it to light up and request that she set the baking temperature. "Oh..." She replied, dumbfounded.

Eden turned to the side, burying her face into her jacket to muffle her laugh as Quinn lowered her face, using some of the cards to hide her growing humor. Pandora turned to face them with one hand on her hip.

"Whatever, that was an honest mistake. I can cook," she laughed.

"Okay, Betty Crocker," Eden teased.

"I'm serious. Jackson loves my cooking. He eats it all the time. Here, taste my sauce," Pandora defended, spinning around to put some of the sauce from

her pot onto the large spoon she held.

"I'm sure it's delicious, but why don't we spare you the dishes and just order a pizza?" Quinn replied, getting up to waddle over to Pandora's drawer in search of Menus.

"That's reverse psychology for hell no," Eden burst into an even harder laughter, causing Quinn to drop her head and laugh along.

"You guys, I'm serious. Taste it, it's good," Pandora begged, walking over to Quinn.

"Don't do it, Quinn," Eden playfully warned in amusement.

"I'll taste it," Quinn giggled, hesitantly allowing Pandora to feed her the sauce from her spoon. Eden stared at Quinn with widened eyes and a slacked mouth as she and Pandora patiently waited for Quinn's reaction.

"It's actually good," Quinn affirmed with a head nod causing Pandora to purse her lips at Eden.

"Ha!"

"She's just being nice," Eden chuckled, "at any minute, Heaven is gonna send her into an early labor so she can pop out and slap you for poisoning her mother."

Pandora's mouth dropped open. "You know what," Pandora hissed, grabbing a knife from her chopping blade and rushing over to Eden.

Eden jumped up from the chair with a laugh, running around the kitchen island to get away from Pandora. "Leave me alone, Pandora, because I believe you'd really stab me," she giggled.

"You owe me an apology, and you have to taste my sau-" Pandora's words were cut short by Quinn's painful squeal, as she clutched her pregnant belly.

"Quinn," Pandora stared at her with a growing look of concern.

Before Quinn could respond, a surge of pain, unlike anything she had ever felt in her life, ripped through her uterus. She leaned over and hollered in agony, using the countertop to support her balance.

" Are you in labor? " Eden asked.

Quinn rapidly nodded, her face turning bright red from the pain, leaving her speechless.

"She's in labor!" Eden confirmed in an excited panic, running over to grab her cellphone.

"Quinn, if this is a joke, it's not funny," Pandora's eyes stretched open as she dropped her knife and hurried over to her.

"I'm calling an ambulance, and then Andre," Eden said, trying to control her trembling hands long enough to unlock her iPhone. "But, sit her down and prop her up just in case."

Pandora snapped her head toward Eden, raising her eyebrows. "In case of what?"

"In case they don't get here in time and we have to deliver the baby, duh!"

Pandora's heart began racing as she turned to frantically rub Quinn's back. Looking like a deer in headlights, she was unsure of what else to do.

Eden rolled her eyes and shook her head just as the dispatcher answered her call. Quinn began breathing the way they taught her in Lamaze class, as tears flooded her face and her legs nearly gave away from the pressure.

Pandora stood behind her, helping to lower her to the floor. "This woman is not going into labor on my three-thousand-dollar, Macassar ebony, wooden floors," Pandora assured herself, shaking her head in denial. Her assurance was short when she saw a gush of liquid rushing down Quinn's leg, splattering her floors and her shoes.

Eden bit her lip and smirked, thinking of how instinctively she knew just what to do to help Quinn. Andre raced down the highway, being followed by the police for his reckless speeding, but he refused to stop. By the time he pulled up to the emergency room entrance, four police cars had him surrounded. They let him go when they realized what was going on, and he made it to the delivery room just in time to see Heaven's head crowning. Eden smiled, remembering the way she and Pandora watched in amazement as Andre coached his wife to assist God in a miracle of birthing their daughter. She remembered the tears of joy throughout the room when everyone heard Heaven's voice for the first time. It was one of the most beautiful, momentous occasions she'd ever witnessed. As she continued driving in silence, listening to the innocent sounds of baby babble, a tear involuntarily fell from her eye when she remembered her *own* experience.

She remembered going into labor alone, unable to reach anyone. Pandora and Quinn didn't have their phones, and Ruby was in Babies-R-Us, unknowingly getting ready to be killed. She remembered the C-section she had to have to deliver her dead baby, and moments after her stillbirth, a silent delivery room. There were no tears of joy and no happy doctors. The Labor and Delivery floor turned into torture. Eden heard crying babies, sounds of happiness, doctors congratulating new parents; she heard everything but her own baby. Eden's nostrils flared, her chin began to tremble, and her eyes protruded at the road as uncontrollable tears fell from her eyes. She'd failed at her education and failed her mother when she got pregnant. She failed at trying to fall in love, and she failed at becoming a success like her best friends. The one thing she thought she'd be good at, was motherhood. Hell, teenage girls and dogs were successful at having babies, and she couldn't even handle *that*.

Eden pulled over and double-parked, reaching into her glove box for her blunt she rolled earlier. She snatched it out, lit it up and inhaled, leaning her head against the headrest. Eden had been doing well, refraining from bad emotions and was upset that her thoughts got the best of her, but glad she was able to smoke until she felt better.

Fifteen minutes later, Eden was high as a kite, not realizing she'd never even opened the windows to let out the smoke until Heaven started to cough, wailing her arms in her car seat.

"Oh, Heaven! Auntie's sorry, sweetie," Eden rolled the windows down, put her gear in drive and pulled off just as a woman on crutches was making her way across the street. Eden looked up and gasped, slamming on the breaks.

"Look where you're going, idiot!" The woman hollered, swinging a crutch in the air.

"If you weren't jaywalking you would've been fine," Eden fussed back.

"And if you weren't about to go through the red light, it wouldn't have mattered if I were jaywalking!"

Eden glanced up at the traffic light ahead, too

high to even focus on what color it was. "Whatever! Just cross the street, Lady."

"I hope you don't talk to your mother like that," The woman shook her head as she continued crossing the street.

Eden's eyes widened like a deranged psychopath. She was already upset thinking about her daughter, and this woman wanted to bring her dead mother into this? Eden balled her hands into fists and crouched forward, daring the woman to repeat what she had just said.

"You heard me!" The woman responded.

Eden jumped out of her car and darted at the woman like a stampede of Elephants. The woman swung her crutch, hitting Eden in the face, but Eden was so high and filled with rage, she didn't even feel it. She ran into the woman, shoving her so hard she almost knocked the wind out of her own self. The woman fell into the street and Eden ran over and began stomping her. Her hair swung wildly, her eyes glinted with anger, and drool seeped through the crack of her mouth.

"Hey! Cut it out!" Yelled a police officer, just walking out of a Rite Aid with his partner. They both ran over to the chaotic scene to break up the fight. One of them grabbed Eden around her waist and swung her off of the woman, while the other cop knelt down to help her. Eden kicked, screamed, and cursed in the police officer's grasp. He took her over to her car and slammed her against it.

"If you don't calm down, I'm gonna taser you!" He threatened.

"What is going on over here?" The other police officer asked, helping the woman off the ground.

"She nearly ran a red light and almost hit me. I told her to watch where she was going, and she cursed me out, jumped out of the car, and attacked me," the woman rubbed the dripping blood away from her busted lip.

"You need to watch your mouth, talking about my mother!" Eden snarled, attempting to charge at the woman a second time before the police officer pulled out his Taser.

"You take one more step, and I will electrocute the hell out of you," he warned. All of the hollering startled Heaven, and she began crying at the top of her lungs.

"What a disgrace! Acting like an animal with a child in your back seat. You should be ashamed!" The woman shook her head. The police officer opened the car door, and the excess smoke from Eden's laced marijuana hit him right in the face.

"Someone smoking pot?" He sarcastically cut his eyes at Eden.

"No, I wasn't," she lied, with pupils so dilated they looked like hockey pucks.

"Call Child Services about the baby," the police officer nodded to his partner.

"What!" Eden yelled, her eyes nearly bulging out of her sockets.

"You're under the influence, you're fighting in the middle of the street, and you have an infant in your car. That's aggravated assault and child endangerment," he reached for his handcuffs, walking over to Eden, "put your hands behind your back."

"Are you crazy? You can't arrest me, I'm on my way to take my niece somewhere," Eden started to walk toward the police, but he grabbed her arm and spun her around toward her car.

"I asked you to put your hands behind your back!" Eden jerked out of his grasp, turned around and spit at him, causing the officer to grab his Taser. Eden could hear Heaven's frantic screams, the woman with the crutches, hollering at the police to shoot Eden, and the other police officer on his walkie-talkie phoning for backup and Child Services. Without warning, everything began drowning out, and her vision faded to black.

Ten

*"And there is a friend that sticketh
closer than a brother" –Proverbs 18; 24*

With her elbows resting on her thighs and her face buried into her hands, Eden sat on the paper-thin, springy mattress in a holding cell at the Richmond Virginia Police Station. As she came down from her high, vaguely remembering the scene she caused that landed her in jail, her stomach growled as if she hadn't eaten in days. Fluorescent lights hummed and buzzed over her head, and quiet voices of private conversations could be heard outside of her cell door. Eden lifted her face, wiping the tears from her eyes as she looked around the cold, musty, damp cell.

"Why didn't I just listen to Travis?" She muttered. Travis told her that her bad habit would one day get her into trouble, and here it was. She promised him that she would stop smoking, and she did— when he was around. Every day on the school balcony, however, she would sneak there to get high. Eden didn't see it as a problem, but now, there was definitely a huge one.

How am I going to explain this to Travis? Her mind began. *How am I supposed to explain this to Quinn? Quinn would never speak to me again, for sure, and somebody would probably have to pull Andre off of me. Would the cop I spit on, charge me? What about the woman I attacked, is she going to press charges? Where was Heaven? How long will I be in this God-forsaken mess? What time is it?* Shaking her head in regret, Eden let out a long sigh and slumped her shoulders, as more tears began trailing from her pitiful eyes. She proceeded to lower her head again, but the sound of keys jingling in the lock of her cell door stopped her.

"Grant? You're free to go," said the overweight, Caucasian police officer standing in the doorway.

With raised eyebrows and a slacked mouth, Eden stood straight up and stared at the cop. "I am?"

"Count your blessings, sweetheart. If you weren't in such good company with the law, you'd be processed, charged, and on your way upstate right now," he pointed, stepping aside so Eden could walk through the door.

"Thank you," Eden said, hesitantly. She followed the police officer to the front of the station. She had no idea what he was talking about, but she was beyond grateful to have whatever charges brought against her, dropped. Eden followed the police officer to the front of the station to retrieve her belongings. She stopped dead in her tracks when she saw Pandora standing at the front window dressed in sweatpants, boots, and a backward baseball cap with Heaven in her arms, laughing with the police officers. Suddenly, Eden remembered the disoriented phone call to Pandora when she had arrived at the station. She was so high, she didn't remember what exactly she said, but she was relieved to see Pandora bailing her out.

"What a cute kid," one of the guards beamed at Heaven, playing with her cheeks, "you be safe on the way home."

"Absolutely, thank you so much for dropping everything," Pandora smiled gracefully, extending her free arm to hug the female guard.

"I *did* tell you I owed you one," the guard winked, accepting the hug. "You saved my husband's life, so I saved your friend's. Consider us even now."

"You bet," Pandora affirmed as Eden walked up to them.

"You've been touched by an angel, girl. Take care of yourself," the guard warned, staring at Eden. Pandora turned and walked out of the police station, not even acknowledging Eden's presence.

"Thank you, I will. I promise," Eden nodded, turning to catch up with Pandora. When she got out the front door, she could see Pandora already at her car strapping Heaven in her car seat. Eden lowered her head and took her time walking to the car, being slapped in the face by the trail of anger Pandora left behind along the way.

Pandora got into her car, slammed the door and slapped on her seatbelt, roughly unlocking the doors to allow Eden in. The second Eden got inside, Pandora sped off like a bat out of hell. Eden didn't even close her door all the way. Eden shook her head in remorse, turning to face Pandora in an attempt to apologize. Pandora's clenched jaws and flushed cheeks threatened her not to say a word, so she didn't. Eden sat back, pulled her phone out and played Candy Crush to help her endure the uncomfortable ride.

Occasionally, Eden cut her eyes at Pandora to see if she was calm enough to talk. She knew she'd messed up, and she wanted so badly to burst into tears and apologize, but the way Pandora glared angrily at the road and clutched her steering wheel like she could rip it off the dash Eden knew it was best if she held her emotions in and kept quiet. When they pulled up to Pandora's house thirty minutes later, Eden's eyes nearly bulged out of their sockets when she saw Andre's Range Rover parked on the side street. Her mouth gaped open in fear and she immediately began hyperventilating to herself. The thought of what she could possibly walk into made her heartbeat so fast she thought it would give away at any second. Her surroundings started spinning and her hands started to tremble.

"He would park his car in front of the garage," Pandora muttered, shaking her head at Jackson's car blocking the garage entrance. Instead of calling him and asking him to move it, Pandora decided to park behind Andre's truck, instead. The minute she turned her car off, she got out, slammed her door, grabbed Heaven, and made her way inside her house, leaving Eden in the car by herself.

The torturing silent treatment from Pandora, the fear of not knowing what Andre and Quinn would say or do to her when she walked inside the house, and her phone vibrating for the third time with Travis's name blinking across the screen sent Eden into a full-blown anxiety attack. Fear clutched her heart, her mind, and her limbs, as tears streamed down her face while she desperately gasped for air. She fanned herself wildly, slightly opening up the car door to get some fresh air. She didn't have her Xanax, and all of the weed she had stashed away from Travis was in her glove compartment, probably confiscated by the police already. Eden had no choice but to sit there and suffer. Butterflies swarmed in her stomach to the point where she grew nauseous and dizzy, as beads of sweat protruded from her forehead.

"Oh God, please make it stop," she begged to herself, trying to catch her breath and clear her thoughts. After fifteen minutes, her attack had finally ended, and Eden got out of the car, headed for Pandora's front door. At that moment, she regretted walking out of that holding cell at the police station. Being sentenced and sent upstate seemed like a much better punishment than this. After taking a long, deep breath, Eden walked up to the front door and opened it. There was no way to defend herself, and no way to get out of it, the only thing she could do was tell the truth. She walked inside Pandora's house, instantly being met with bright lights and the smell of food on the stove.

"Hey," Quinn walked up to her with a concerned look, rocking a sleeping Heaven on her chest. "I was just getting ready to come out and get you."

"H...hey," Eden hesitated with a glossy stare.

"You okay?" Quinn asked softly. Eden's soul almost jumped out of her body when she heard the bass from Andre and Jackson's big mouth, cheering at the television, as they watched highlights from the football game they missed.

"Um," Eden furrowed her eyebrows at Andre, and then back at Quinn who, by now had sensed something was wrong.

"Is everything okay?"

"Yeah," Eden slid her hands into her back pocket and stared at the floor. "I just didn't expect to see you guys here."

"We got to the gala extremely late, it was basically over. We came by to grab the baby, but I know

Anna would've had a fit if we'd just taken her and left. Andre and I just decided to stay for the night and turn it into a couples gathering," Quinn replied, patting Heaven's back.

"Oh…okay."

"I ransacked her fridge and found some stuff to cook so we wouldn't have to order out. Emphasis on *I found some stuff to cook*." Quinn laughed, amused.

"Cool, is she upstairs?"

"Yeah, on the ph—"

Eden hightailed it pass Quinn and made her way up the steps as fast as she could, blowing out a sigh of relief. She walked into the bedroom to see Pandora sitting at her desk, supporting her head with her elbows. She stared at the wall, expressionless, nervously tapping her foot.

Eden swallowed hard, closing the door behind her. "Listen, I can ex—"

"What the hell has happened to you?" Pandora bellowed, popping up from her seat. "You were high? Off what? *You smoke?*"

"No," Eden lied, "Yes…some—"

"You broke a woman's nose with your foot, over a petty confrontation? You *spit* on a *white* police officer?" Pandora looked at Eden with an open mouth and wide eyes as if she had no idea who she was anymore. "Black people are being unfairly profiled and killed in police custody by racist cops, and you had the balls to *spit* on one?" Pandora rubbed a hand down her face, pacing the floor while she shook her head, before locking Eden in place with her demented stare. Pandora's face was bright red, and Eden swore she could see steam flying out of her ears.

Eden leaned against the door speechless, staring back at Pandora with a shameful glare as if she had just been called down to the principal's office.

"And you did it all with the *baby* in the backseat of your car!" Pandora continued, closing the gap between them, wanting so badly to choke the life out of Eden. "Shoot, forget that she's your best friend's baby, a*nd* your niece, *and* my goddaughter, how about that baby belongs to a world-renowned Pastor and his wife," Pandora pointed at her door, "do you have *any* idea of the negative media coverage that—" Pandora wanted to say more, but her emotions snatched away her voice as tears dripped down her face. She bit her lip and turned her back. She was angry and confused, but most of all, she couldn't figure out what happened to her best friend.

Eden saw the look of disappointment and disgust written all over Pandora's face. At that moment, she wished she could crawl under a rock and disappear. "Anna, I messed up and I'm *sorry*," Eden replied in remorse.

Pandora wiped her tears and turned back around to stare at Eden. "I don't even know how to begin explaining this to Quinn."

Eden's eyes widened like two fifty-cent pieces. "No...No, please don't tell her," she shook her head in denial, causing Pandora to wince. "Anna, *please*? She'll never want anything else to do with me if she knew I'd messed up like that, and—"

"Oh, that would *bother* you?" Pandora tilted her head, crossing her arms. "After the way you've treated us over the last six months or so, you actually *care* about our friendship? Eden, you treat me like I mean absolutely nothing to you anymore. I have tried so hard to be there for you, and you shove me away every time," Pandora shook her head as uncontrollable tears poured from her eyes. "You ignore text messages, decline my phone calls, and reject any invitation to hang out with me. I have been worried sick about you— me and Quinn both. You've treated us like we're gum underneath your shoe. You know, the other week, I didn't sleep for almost two days because I was so concerned about you. I got up out of my bed at 3 AM and came to your house. I tried to use my key and found out you had the locks changed."

Eden stared back at Pandora with a face full of regret. In all the years they'd known one another, Eden had never seen her so disheveled and heartbroken. Pandora had such a soft spot for Eden, and the realization of how Eden had treated her gripped her heart until she burst into tears.

"I'm sorry, I swear to God," Eden cried, walking over to Pandora, her words barely audible.

"I heard yelling, what's going on in here?" Quinn asked, curiously walking through the door. She paused to examine Pandora and Eden's distraught, tear-filled faces and knew everything was far from okay.

"Quinn, everything that could ever be wrong at this point has happened," Eden admitted, "things have been wrong all year, and I'm sorry," Eden choked on her sob. Quinn softly shut the bedroom door, focusing her gaze at Eden.

"Listen, I've always looked up to you guys. I've always wanted to be just like you both, but it didn't happen that way," Eden shifted her stare between both of her friends. "Pandora, you're the world's greatest lawyer, and Quinn, you're like the world's savior. You guys have the money, the careers, the husbands, the homes, the baby....me?" Eden pointed to herself, "I feel like I got the short end of the stick. I got pregnant out of college, and chose love over my education, just to have it backfire on me." She turned to face Pandora, "Anna, I'm not jealous or angry about you and Jackson, but it did mess with my self-esteem. Made me feel like I wasn't worthy of love, like I wasn't smart enough or pretty enough. I don't know any fifty-dollar words or have people groveling under my mercy. All I have is a Bachelor's Degree in Human Services that I don't even care about because truth be told, I never had a passion to go to college anyway."

Pandora pressed her hand against her breastbone as a painful tightness formed in her throat, listening to Eden.

"Quinn," Eden turned to her, "God gave me a daughter, and then snatched her away from me before she could even take a breath, and now you have Heaven. Every time I look at her, I think, does God not love *me*? Did he think I wouldn't make a good mother?" Eden shook her head, attempting to wipe the tears from her face as more streamed down like a waterfall. Quinn leaned against the door with watery eyes, taking in every word.

"While you guys were out embarking on some of the greatest moments of your lives, I was at home, laying in my dead mother's bed, surrounded by money, her home, and the businesses she left me. I felt alone...empty. I felt so low to the ground, that I just stayed there. I lost sleep, my mind, and a larger part of myself. I started having anxiety attacks and constant thoughts of suicide to the point where I was evaluated by a psychiatrist, and they put me on pills," Eden's voice began to shake. "Pills to get up in the morning, and pills to go to bed at night. I didn't wanna tell you guys because I didn't wanna seem like the *weak* friend, the one that always needed something. I spent so much unnecessary money trying to compete and validate myself, that I'm basically broke. I got bitter and started to resent you both because being around you was a reminder of how much I'd failed. I met some friends at school that introduced me to angel dust and pot. I tried it once, and the level of high it put me on seemed to put an end to all of my misery. It temporarily cured my crappy reality, and poor choices, so I started to make a habit out of it."

Quinn and Pandora both opened their mouths in unison. Neither of them could believe what they were hearing.

"My mom's businesses have been shut down because I failed at maintaining them. All I have is my boyfriend, and two *very* close friendships that I desperately regret trying to destroy," Eden slumped her shoulders and lowered her head in defeat. All the pain she tried to bury in the back of her mind, retreated to her reality. Her breathing grew tense as she looked up and stared at her best friends, biting her lip in an attempt to stifle the cry that wanted out of her. Holding in her demons wasn't working anymore. The colorful world around her began melting to gray. Her emotions swirled like deep, strong, ocean currents. Eden was terrified to dive in, for fear that she might not make it out alive, but in that moment, she couldn't help it.

As her masks of make-believe and rebellion fell off, Eden's butterscotch eyes filled with all the hurt and pain life had put her through. Her face spelled devastation. It was the look of someone who had suffered for way too long and couldn't go through another second of it. A single tear slid down her soft cheek, followed by another one, and another, until soon, a steady stream of salty warm tears opened like a broken water dam.

Eden clasped onto Pandora's dresser for support as a raw, gut-wrenching cry escaped her. Her wails echoed through Pandora and Quinn's ears. They immediately rushed to wrap their arms around her. Her body shook, as they consoled their friend, holding onto her for dear life. They, too, couldn't hold back their own waterworks.

For a long time, all three of them just stood there, entangled within one another. Not one word needed to be spoken, and no questions needed to be asked. There wasn't a single ounce of judgment in the room, and no pressure for Eden to justify anything else. She didn't have to weigh her thoughts or measure her words. *That moment of silence was the best conversation they'd ever had.*

"I'm sorry," she cried mercifully, over and over again.

"Shh," Quinn rubbed her back

"It's okay," Pandora assured, wiping away Eden's tears.

After ten minutes, Eden was finally able to calm herself down. She felt as if a weight had finally been lifted off of her.

"I love you both *so* much," she said.

"We love you, too," Quinn replied, "more than you know, and we're here for you. Don't ever allow the enemy to take you through the exhausting emotions of jealousy, bitterness, and envy," Quinn shook her head, taking a seat on Pandora's bed, "none of that is needed with us."

"How much money do you have left?" Pandora asked, walking over to her vanity to fix her flustered face and dry her eyes.

"I'm not sure…Travis handles all of my money. Last time I checked, I had about fifteen thousand left," Eden muttered, taking a seat on the bed next to Quinn.

"Travis?" Pandora turned to look at Eden.

"Is this the boyfriend you were talking about earlier?" Quinn asked.

"Yeah," Eden replied with a warm smile, wiping the access tear stains from her cheeks, "we met the first day of school, and have been talking ever since. He's an *amazing* guy. I can't wait for you guys to meet him."

"But wait, school has only been going on for a couple of months, right?" Quinn raised her eyebrows. "You let him control your money after such a short period of dating?"

"He suggested it. He came into my life when I really needed him," Eden affirmed with a head nod, "I had over a million dollars, and now I'm down to chump change, almost. He's been helping me be smarter with it, and I trust him. He's helped me to focus on my studies more, and I've been getting good grades. When I first laid eyes on him, I'm not gonna lie, I really just wanted to sleep with him," Eden smirked, "but he actually was a nice guy and wanted to get to know me. Even when we started talking, he would never stay the night, or touch me inappropriately. He was a perfect gentleman. He still is."

"Wow. Very rare," Quinn nodded, impressed.

"He sounds like a great guy. Let's see him," Pandora walked over and pounced on her bed with them. Eden took her phone out and showed them a picture.

"Dear God, he's *chocolate*," Quinn stared in awe with a sly grin, "welcome to the dark side," she winked, causing Eden and Pandora to laugh.

"He's *really* sexy. Great choice," Pandora nodded, staring at Travis's picture.

"Thanks. You better not sleep with him either," Eden pursed her lips and cut her eyes at Pandora, closing her phone.

Snapping her head back, Pandora gasped.

Quinn playfully threw her body back onto Pandora's bed with her mouth wide open in disbelief, trying everything she could not to laugh.

"Whatever!" Pandora chuckled, shaking her head, "*anyway*, I'm gonna pay for the rest of your grad school education, if that's okay. As long as you're *serious* about it."

"Really?" Eden's eyebrows raised.

"You don't have a job, and I want you to save the rest of your money. I have an accountant that can show you different ways to invest and flip it," Pandora smiled.

"I'd love that, thank you so much."

"I know the chief inspectors of Richmond. I'll talk to them and find out what needs to be done to get Ruby's hair salon and coffee shop up and running," Quinn sat up, "and I'll pay for whatever it costs. I need my hair done, and my morning latte in rotation, and on the regular again."

"Wait, so are you gonna get it up and running for

Eden, or for your own convenience?" Pandora laughed.

"Both," Quinn smirked. All three of them shared a laugh just as Eden's cellphone rang. She smiled when she saw it was Travis, and answered it, hoping that he was in a better mood.

"Hey," she beamed.

"Seventeen times," Travis answered, taking slow breaths to control his boiling rage. Eden's smile slowly faded, sensing he was still in a funk.

"I'm sorry, it's been a long, *long* evening. I saw that you called earlier, but—"

"SEVENTEEN TIMES, EDEN!" He roared. His voice was so loud, it vibrated throughout the bedroom.

Eden's eyes widened in fear. Quinn and Pandora stopped talking amongst themselves and stared in concern.

"You told me you would be home soon. It's been almost six hours, and you've ignored every last one of my calls! What's going on?"

"Nothing is going on," Eden defended, "I'm hanging out with my friends, that's all," she hissed.

"You need to come home, now," he maliciously ordered.

"I can't. I don't have my—" she caught herself, careful not to let Travis know she didn't have her car. That conversation was for another day. "Listen, what is your problem? You've been—"

"You know what, goodbye, I'm done with you!" He yelled into the phone, hanging up on her.

"Hello?" Eden's voice cracked, partly shocked. She pulled her phone from her ear and look at it in disbelief.

"Who in the devil was *that*?" Quinn asked,

annoyed.

"Travis…" Eden hesitated. First impressions were everything, and he just ruined it.

"Yelling at you like that?" Pandora asked.

"He's been like this since I left earlier," Eden said, confused, "it came out of nowhere. Maybe he's having a bad day or something."

"I don't care if he's lost a limb," Pandora crossed her arms, glaring at Eden, "he would have my foot up his behind, talking to *me* like that."

"Yeah, that wasn't respectful at all," Quinn agreed.

Eden sat her phone on the bed and stood up to face her friends. "I know. Look, I don't understand what's going on with him either, but I'm pretty sure there's a good explanation for it. Travis is as respectful and gentle as they come," she defended, "this is a man that does my laundry, cooks my dinner, does my shopping, drives me to and from school, sends me flowers, and runs my bubble bath on a regular."

"Like I said, it doesn't matter. There is never a good explanation to speak to anyone like that, bad day or not," Pandora furrowed.

Eden sighed. She wanted so badly to convince them that Travis was a great guy. She glanced over at Quinn who looked as if she wanted to ask her a million questions.

"What?" Eden huffed.

"You said he got upset when you left earlier. Did you leave without telling him?"

"Yeah, he was at the supermarket and I was bored in the house, why?"

"I was just asking," Quinn replied with an

unfocused stare, putting all the pieces together in her head.

Eden saw the disapproving look on Pandora's face and shook her head. "You guys find something wrong with *everyone* I date," Eden spat, aggravated. "Please just give him a chance. He's a really good guy, and I like him a lot," Eden walked toward the door. "My charger is in my purse, in your car. I'm gonna run get it and charge my phone. Then, I'm gonna call him back and see what's going on."

"Keys are on the table," Pandora muttered, as Eden walked out and closed the door behind her.

"*Good guy*," Pandora replied sarcastically, slumping down on the bed next to Quinn, "I don't believe it. First of all, he even *looks* too good to be true."

"That's because he is," Quinn confirmed, deep in thought. Before Pandora could reply, Eden's phone rang again. This time, Pandora picked it up.

"Hello," she answered, pleasantly.

"You know what, you selfish little bitch!" He screamed, manically. Quinn's eyes widened in shock. Travis had just dropped the final piece to the puzzle right into her lap. Pandora gasped, clutching her chest.

"After all I've done for you, this is how you repay me? I've been nothing but good to you, and—"

Pandora stood straight up, her forehead wrinkling in anger. "Listen to me, I will rip your tongue out of your mouth if you don't watch your disrespectful—"

Quinn quickly tussled with Pandora for the phone, hanging it up and turning it off as soon as she got it.

"Don't get involved, please," she begged, "this is not the right time."

"Has she lost her *mind?* Quinn, what type of relationship—" Pandora fussed in a high-pitched tone, unable to finish her sentence.

"I know," Quinn agreed, "but considering all of her emotions, if we're not careful of what we say and how we say it, she'll shut down, and we'll lose her again—Maybe even for good."

Pandora let out a long, frustrated sigh, sitting back down on the bed next to Quinn. "No way does a temper like that stem from just a *bad day*. He sounded like a complete maniac— like it's in his blood. In two months, he's made Eden feel like the brightest star has fallen by her side, but in two minutes he's made me feel like I could put a bullet straight through his head." Pandora stared at Quinn in confusion. "What does that sound like?"

"Sounds like the DNA of a psychologically abusive man, and what she's misconstrued as bliss, is actually the beginning of domestic abuse…"

Eleven

"Better the devil you know, than the one you don't."

Eden was sound asleep in Pandora's guest bedroom just before the constant vibration of her cellphone woke her out of it. She glanced at the oversized clock on the wall, noticing that it was just after 1 AM. Using her hands to sift through the covers, she found her phone and put it up to her face, squinting her eyes at the bright light.

"Hey baby," she answered, her voice cracking.

"Hey, were you sleeping?" Travis asked in a calm tone.

"I was," Eden rubbed her eyes and sat up, "I called you back about four times and your phone kept going to voicemail."

"Yeah, I shut it off and got myself together. Listen, I'm deeply sorry for calling you out like that. I was stressed out, so I ended up drinking with Cam, and drunk dialed you."

Eden turned up her nose. Travis had no idea that it was Pandora he'd cursed out, not Eden. "Huh?"

"Can we start over? The way I acted was uncalled for. I've never in my life been so overprotective of someone in this way. I just got so upset after you left and didn't say anything. You didn't call, text, or anything," Travis replied with remorse, "then you tell me you're over at your so-called friend's house. After all the horrible things you've told me about them," Travis said sternly, "I don't want you surrounded by people who hurt you."

"It's okay, I understand," Eden turned the lamp on beside her. She knew there was a good explanation for Travis's behavior. However, she'd have to make up a different excuse to tell Quinn and Pandora. She didn't want them to know she had been bad-mouthing them. "A lot of things I told you about them came from a very bitter, and angry place. That's not who I am anymore, partly because of you. I came here to make up with them. We all talked, we cried, we laughed— it felt like old times."

"Baby, I don't want you to get hurt."

"I won't. They're not like that. Once you meet them, it—"

"I don't care to meet them. I just want you home, by my side. Where are you right now?"

"I'm still at Anna's. I'll be there tomorrow, I promise," Eden confirmed.

"I'm kind of in a bind right now, and I need you."

"What's wrong?" Eden slid back the covers and got out of bed.

"I came out to the bar and gambled on a game of pool. I lost a six-hundred-dollar bet. I only bought forty dollars with me for drinks. So now, these guys are getting pissed, and if I don't give them their money, something bad might go down."

"Why would you gamble with money you don't have?" Eden asked, immediately upset, "and so what if you lost. Just go to your car and leave. Forget them."

"First of all, one of them goes to school with us, and the other three look like bodybuilders," he laughed. "Secondly, I drove with Cameron, and he's more wasted than I am. I don't know how to drive a stick shift. Listen, just meet me here and bring the money. I'll find a way to pay you back."

"I don't have—" Eden caught herself for the second time, remembering she didn't have her car.

"You don't have what?" He asked.

Eden thought for a minute before answering. "Nothing, I'll be there shortly," she sighed.

"You're amazing, thank you," he replied in excitement.

Eden ended the call and quickly put on her clothes. She made her way down the steps, making sure to not make a sound. Eden didn't want to give Travis a reason to be upset with her anymore. Her plan was to borrow Pandora's car to meet him, give him the money, and be back within the hour without anyone realizing she'd left. The second she got into the kitchen and grabbed Pandora's keys, she slapped her forehead and cringed. Her purse was in Pandora and Jackson's bedroom. There was no way she could sneak in their room without waking them up. She looked on the counter and saw Pandora's purse sitting beside her keys. She walked over, looking inside for her wallet. Pandora usually never kept cash unless she needed to do something with it, so Eden sighed in relief when she found it flooded with at least eight, one-hundred-dollar bills. She took six of them and stuffed them into her pocket, making a mental note to stop by an ATM whenever she got her purse, to put it back.

Eden walked out of the house and drove off quietly. Twenty minutes later, she slowly pulled up on the other side of town at the address Travis texted her. Lucky Stacks Sports Bar was alive and bright, flooded with people inside and out at 2 o'clock in the morning.

People always did things backward in the hood, Eden thought. During the day, that side of town looked deserted, but at night, it was lit up like Vegas. As Eden turned down the small street, heads turned with her. Mouths dropped open and suspicious eyes watched. Eden stared back, momentarily confused until she realized she was driving a two hundred-thousand-dollar Aston Martin, in the hood. Eden laughed a little, soaking in the attention. She turned to the right to look through her side mirror. Her eyes almost popped out their sockets. There was Travis, standing against a light pole, entertaining a half-dressed girl who had her arms wrapped around his neck. Eden slammed on the brakes in the middle of the already compacted street and got out of the car.

"Come on, live a little," the girl said with a mischievous grin on her face, rubbing her body against his."

Travis smiled, gently backing her away from him. "I'm alright, thank—"

"Yes, he's *quite* alright," Eden hissed angrily, storming toward them.

The girl let go of him and turned around, annoyed.

"Eden," Travis looked up, partly confused. Since she was driving a different car, he didn't see her when she drove up.

"So *this* is Eden?" The girl replied, enviously eyeing Eden up and down.

"Eden, this is Amber…an old friend. Amber, this is my girlfriend, Eden."

"Pleasure to meet you," the girl rolled her eyes

with a sarcastic smirk.

"I can't say the same about you. Watch where you put your hands next time, or I'll break them," Eden threatened.

A few people standing around started to look in their direction when they heard the anger in Eden's voice. Travis leaned up from the pole and walked into her.

"Eden, come on, don't cause a scene, I hate that," he whispered in her ear.

"Then don't let random girls touch all over you in public like that!" She spat back with an attitude. Amber chuckled and strutted over to her Honda parked along the sidewalk.

"Honey, relax. Insecurity is *not* pretty," she winked, causing some of the onlookers to chuckle.

Eden's face turned red, as she tried to walk around Travis to punch Amber right in her throat. Luckily for Amber, Travis grabbed Eden around her waist and refused to allow it.

"Eden," he warned in a threatening whisper.

"Neither is that beat-up hooptie you're driving," Eden mocked, "why is it that those Fendi pumps you have on, look more expensive than your car?"

People started to laugh, as Amber pursed her lips in embarrassment. She tried to open her car door, careful not to hit Pandora's car.

"Whatever girl. Can you move your car? Please and thank you," Amber said.

"Oh, you want me to move my Aston Martin to make way for your hooptie?" She laughed, causing Travis to grit his teeth. *He hated a showoff.*

"Did you bring the money?" He cut through

impatiently before she could get another word out.

"Oh, you want *my* money? Why didn't you get it from the hooker with the Honda?" She responded, jealously lacing her tone.

"Eden," Travis darted his eyes at her, his remaining patience hanging on by a thread.

Eden rolled her eyes and reached into her pocket, slapping the money in his hand. Travis turned around to face the three guys standing behind them. He quickly counted the money and handed it to one of them.

"Good game, man," one of the men nodded, accepting the money, "thought you were trying to snake us."

"Good game," Travis said in a rush. He grabbed Eden's arm, quickly leading her to Pandora's car. "Move the car so she can get out of her parking spot," he ordered.

Eden wanted to reply with another smart remark, but she could see the veins protruding from Travis's neck. He was pissed. He couldn't stand bringing unwanted attention and drama to himself.

Eden got into the car, followed by Travis, who got in on the passenger side and waved goodbye to Amber. She poked out her lips and blew him a kiss, giving Eden a quick glance to make sure she noticed. If it weren't for Travis, Eden would have jumped through the passenger side window and knocked every one of Amber's teeth loose. Instead, she put the car in drive and sped down the street in a rage.

"You seriously think this is okay, and I don't have a right to be mad?" She asked, releasing her anger.

"Whose car is this?" He ignored her, looking straight ahead.

"Don't ignore me, Travis. I'm serious!"

"No," he replied as calmly as his flustered demeanor would allow him. "You don't have the right to ask me anything. She's an old friend, and she's drunk. I was handling the situation before you decided to walk up and make a big deal out of it."

"Whatever," Eden flung her hand in the air, instantly irked, "but it was okay for you to throw a whole tantrum because I left *my* house to go see *my* friends?"

"Whose car do you have, and where is your car?" He asked a second time, ignoring her smart remark.

"It's Anna's. Mine is parked on South Street. She had an emergency, so she picked me up from there, and I left my car," Eden lied.

"We're going to get it, and then we're going home to talk," he ordered.

"No, we're not. I'm gonna let you out by your car, and I'm going back to Anna's. I have nothing to say to you right now."

Travis rubbed both of his hands down his face. He was getting fed up with her smart mouth. "You know what, this isn't gonna work!" He bellowed, "I didn't sign up to date a loudmouth, abusive, wannabe ghetto girl!"

Eden jerked her head back, nearly crashing into the car in front of her that stopped at a red light. She slammed on the brakes just inches away from the vehicle.

"Abusive and ghetto? Really?"

"Take me to my car! As a matter of fact, take me to a bus stop! I'm going back to your house, getting all of my things, and I'm going home. I'll walk if I have to. I just wanna get the heck away from you, *forever*!"

Travis's words instantly struck a nerve, putting fear into Eden's heart. The chilling, familiar sound of rejection rushed through her body. Her hands grew cold and clammy, clutching the steering wheel.

He couldn't have meant that, she thought. The traffic light had already turned green, but Eden was so stuck on Travis's threats that she couldn't move. Angry drivers blew their horns and yelled all kinds of obscenities, as they swerved around her.

"Is that how you really feel about me?" She asked calmly, gazing over at him.

"Yes! Because you're changing up on me, and I'm not feeling it," Travis turned to face her. "I'm falling in love with you. I wanna marry you someday, but it's like you don't see it. All I've ever done for you was respect you, and you don't give me that same respect back."

The thought of falling in love and getting married made Eden smile inside, especially hearing it come from Travis's mouth. Maybe she did need to tone down her attitude a bit. The last thing she wanted was for Travis to dump her.

"You're right. I'm sorry," Eden nodded her head. Slumping her back against the driver's seat, she began regretting her actions.

"I don't think you are," he shook his head. "All of this is happening because of you. If you had stayed in the house and waited for me, I wouldn't have been in a position to lose a bet and see Amber. It's your fault I lost a bet, and it's your fault another female saw me and gave me her attention. Had my girlfriend been with me, instead of off with her fake friends, none of this would have happened."

Eden drove in silence, feeling terrible. Travis was right. *I should have been there*. She thought, as the recent events she'd gotten into came rushing to the forefront of her mind. *Had I been home, I wouldn't have gotten in trouble with the police.*

"It won't happen again," she told him. "I swear on my mother's grave. I'm gonna get my car, and then we'll drive Pandora's back and go home. I'll call her in the morning and tell her I had an emergency, okay?"

"As long as this doesn't happen again, cool," he nodded.

"It won't, baby," Eden said.

She drove the thirty minutes to her car, which had been left along the sidewalk where she'd gotten pulled over. Travis got into Eden's car and followed her while she drove back to Pandora's house. Another half-hour later, Eden pulled up at Pandora's house. She looked around at the windows and everything was still pitch black.

"Good, they're still asleep. Eden briefly thought of convincing Travis to stay the night so she could introduce him to everyone in the morning, but she knew he really just wanted to go home. She didn't want to have to make up a lie to Pandora about how he got there. Eden parked the car back on the street, ran in the house, and placed Pandora's keys back on the counter. When she noticed Pandora's purse, she quickly realized that she hadn't had the chance to replace her money. *I'll have to come back tomorrow to get my purse*, she thought, *I'll put the money back then.*

Eden crept back out of the house, locking the

door behind her. She hurried over to her car and got in on the passenger side, quietly closing the door. Travis stepped on the gas and pulled off, causing Eden to jump in fear.

"Travis!" she said, clutching her chest. "Sheesh, the point was to sneak off."

"Why? I'm not a kid," he chuckled.

"I snuck out and borrowed her car while everyone was still sleeping," she admitted.

"What? That's ridiculous. Real friends wouldn't mind you borrowing their car. I would never have to tiptoe around Jade and Cam."

"Well, my friends are different," she replied, slightly offended.

"You keep referring to them as your friends, but you seem more like their flunky to me," he teased, knowing he was stepping on her self-esteem, "they make you leave your car on a random street to come to their aid? Then, you're tiptoeing out of their house like you're playing hide-and-seek."

Eden crossed her arms, even more, offended. She wasn't a flunky. She had expressed her honest, sensitive feelings about them to him. He knew how insecure she was, why would he mock her and throw it back in her face? She turned to stare out the window, ignoring Travis's remarks.

"Anyway, do we have plans tomorrow? Because I have to come back to get my purse."

"Can't she just mail it?"

Eden turned to face him, her mouth gaping open at his audacity. "Are you serious?"

"Eden, we're not coming back here. It's because of *them* your acting like a bitch now. Tell them to mail it, or we'll just get you a new one," he stated boldly, his voice portraying a coldness she'd never heard before.

"Excuse me? What did you call me?"

"You heard me. Look, I'm not getting ready to argue with you anymore," Travis rolled his eyes.

Eden snatched her seatbelt off and roughly put her phone in her jacket pocket. "Stop the car. I'm getting out," she announced, still in disbelief that he'd speak to her that way.

Travis's eyebrows pulled together. He pressed the child lock button and continued to drive. "Eden, put your seatbelt back on," he demanded.

"No. I'll walk back to Pandora's. Let me out of the car. You must have lost your mind, talking to me like that," she huffed, glaring at him as if he was crazy.

Travis's blood pressure began to increase as his heart rate elevated. "I'm gonna tell you one more time. Put...your...seat—"

"NO!" Eden roared, her face florid red with anger.

Travis slammed on the brakes and jammed the gear in park. *Hell hath no fury or contempt as a narcissist you dare disagree with.* His eyes widened, glowering in anger, and his lips sneered in disgust. Before Eden could open up her mouth to continue her protest, she was met with a hard, backhand across her face. He hit her so hard, her entire body caved into the passenger seat.

Eden cupped her nose, and mouth just as a thin trickle of blood ran down her nose. He jumped into the passenger seat, straddling her, and began wailing on her like a Mike Tyson fight. Suddenly, it felt as if everything were moving in slow motion and she was having an out of body experience. Her vision tunneled in like a telescope. The unnerving agony from each blow to her head, face, neck, and chest kept bringing her back to reality. She could feel each individual cell, and blood vessel, bruising. As her heart thumped loudly through her ears, Travis continued to go nuclear on her. Her subconscious screamed for him to stop, but she couldn't get the words out.

Travis yanked her by her hair. Eden's vision started to become blurry. Through her smudged sight, she could see Travis's demented eyes sneering at her in disgust, and her mouth filled with the bitter taste of blood. As her head spun faster, and her heartbeat seemed to be running a marathon, Eden could no longer fight the unconsciousness beckoning to her. Finally giving in, she passed out.

30 minutes later…

"Talk to me baby," a deep whisper filled Eden's ears, as her eyes shifted under her eyelids, attempting to wake herself up, "I'm so sorry, please wake up and talk to me," the voice begged, fighting back tears.

As her awareness started to kick in, dull, pulsating aches began surfacing through her head, neck, chest, and arms. Slowly opening her eyes, Eden's vision grew dim around the edges and faded in slowly. It was as if someone had hit a reset button in her brain. She could make out a fuzzy image of what looked like her living room, but she wasn't sure. Wincing in pain, Eden used her hand to massage her head.

"Oh my God," the voice said repeatedly, as the texture of moist lips graced her cheeks.

When Eden's vision became solid, she realized

she was lying face-up on her living room couch with Travis straddling her. His eyes were full of tears, fear, and regret, as his trembling hands rubbed through her hair. Suddenly, her jogged memory returned to her. Staring into his eyes, she immediately became frightened, as her breathing grew heavy and her pulse quickened. She remembered the argument they had, just before he beat her down like a man on the street. She wanted to get up and run away, but her legs felt paralyzed.

Is this really happening? Did he really hit me like that? Why? Where did it come from? Tears rushed to her eyes.

"Eden please don't cry, baby, I'm sorry," Travis pleaded with a look of regret, wiping away her onset of tears.

"You told me you were here to protect me, and you put your hands on me?" Eden shook her head in fear. "We're done," she tried pushing Travis off of her, but her weak body wouldn't comply.

"Eden, no, no," Travis formed praying hands with tears rushing down his face, "please don't leave me."

"Travis, get off of me, *please*," she begged, using what little strength she had to try and wiggle him off.

Travis stood, allowing her to get up. It took her a few seconds to get her equilibrium together, but once she got her balance, she walked furiously to her bedroom, grabbed Travis's overnight bag and threw it at her front door.

"Wait, can I tell you something first?" Travis asked with a look of desperation.

"Get out, now! Before I call the police," she threatened, pointing at the door.

"I *will* leave, but please just hear me out, okay?" He requested, locking Eden in place with his sad, pleading eyes.

"Travis, no! You're crazy—"

Travis rushed over to her, invading her personal space as he gripped her waist and pulled her into him. "You're the first woman that's ever made me feel like this, and I don't want to lose you because of my past," he held on to her and cried, "I watched my dad abuse my mother for fifteen years. He beat my sister, and he beat me. He molested me, he tried to kill me…he *ruined* me."

Eden's eyebrows slowly furrowed into a look of horror listening to Travis talk, her mouth slowly opening in shock.

"I stayed to myself for years, and *never* got into any relationships because I had no blueprint on how to be a man. My father robbed me of my identity, my dignity, and my manhood. My girlfriend was my first chance at life, and I swear I thought I'd marry and grow old with her. When she died, I blamed myself for not being there to protect her. When I found you, it was my second chance at happiness," Travis sniffed, running his fingers down Eden's beautiful face. "I just wanted to protect you, and you weren't hearing me. It took me to another place— a *dark* place, and I blacked out. I'm so sorry. I'll get help if I need to, but baby, don't go. *Please*."

Tears fell from Eden's face as she stared. His words sparked a flare of sympathy inside her. "I didn't…I didn't know you went through all of that," she said, using her hands to dry Travis's crocodile tears.

"I've been through more than you could ever imagine. But it's no excuse to hurt the woman I love."

Eden's eyes slowly widened. "You love me?" She asked, making sure she heard correctly.

"I've loved you since the day I made you mine, baby." Travis gazed into her eyes.

Eden felt her heart growing sluggish at the sound of those beautiful words. She sometimes found herself thinking about what life would be like if she fell in love with Travis, but she refuted the idea every time the horrible experience with Jackson flashed through her mind. Travis meant a lot to her, and hearing those words flowing from his lips made her forget their horrible night.

Taking full advantage of the vulnerable moment he had just created, Travis picked Eden up, carried her into her bedroom and made the sweetest love to her, apologizing over and over again until he was sure she believed him. They scratched, tugged, and kissed all over one another until all of their energy had run out. Through her passion, the brutal beating she'd suffered at his hands briefly flickered through her mind, until the next wave of orgasms came and wiped it from her memory.

Twelve

Hello, Mrs. Hyde

Pop!

Loud noises sounded from outside, awaking Pandora out of her sleep. She snatched herself out of Jackson's arms and sat straight up in their king-sized bed, stiffening her posture with an incredulous stare.

"What was that?" She asked in a panic.

Jackson rubbed his eyes, sluggishly sitting up alongside her. "Probably just the wind knocking over the trashcans aga—"

The sound of glass shattering cut through his words. Seconds later, a car alarm sounded, and tires screeched, fading into the air.

"Okay, *that* was not wind," she huffed. They both jumped out of bed and rushed to the window. Pandora pulled the shade back, jogging her memory to remember where she had parked last night. Her mouth dropped open when her eyes came into contact with her car. "I'm losing my mind," Pandora graced her temples with her fingers, "I must be parked somewhere *else*."

Jackson's eyes bulged, angrily. He immediately grabbed his robe, and his gun from under the pillow, storming downstairs to see what was going on.

Pandora snatched her robe on and rushed down the steps to get outside. Her feet must not have been moving fast enough for her, because when she got to the last couple of steps, she jumped the rest of the way, and headed out the front door.

Pandora had video surveillance in, and outside every inch of her house, and everyone knew it. Who could have been that bold to destroy a lawyer's car? Certainly, she must have been dreaming. Much to her dismay, she slowly walked up to her brand new, *totaled* Aston Martin, realizing this was no dream.

Jackson walked around the car with a look of disdain. All four of Pandora's tires were slashed, a big heap of cement had gone straight through her windshield, and white spray paint vandalized her exterior with the words *Eden, I love your new hooptie. We match now!*

"Eden?" Jackson jerked his head back, "what is going on?"

"We're about to find out," Pandora hissed, storming back into her house.

"What was that noise?" Andre asked, turning on the living room lights with a look of concern. Quinn walked down the steps, adjusting Andre's oversized sweatshirt on her small frame. Pandora flew right past him in a rage, on a mission to get to her security system located in the closet.

"Someone just destroyed her car and drove off," Jackson responded, following Pandora through the living room.

Quinn gasped, peering outside at the horrific scene. Andre's mouth gaped open, looking at the big mess.

"Somebody's gonna *die* tonight," Pandora threatened, using her remote to turn on her forty-inch security screen that divided into eight different smaller screens throughout her home. She used her remote to rewind all of her cameras back, as Quinn and Andre joined them.

Quinn stood beside her friend, resting her arm across Pandora's shoulders. She could feel the venom seeping off of Pandora, and she knew without a shadow of a doubt, this night was about to get *ugly*.

Pandora's angry glare slowly melted into a look of horror when one of the cameras displayed Eden, performing oral sex on Joseph in her kitchen. Quinn's mouth dropped open, slumping her body closer to the television to make sure she wasn't seeing things.

"Is that Eden?" Andre asked with wide eyes.

Jackson confirmed with a disbelieving head nod. Pandora hit the fast-forward button on the remote, just as the camera halted to another segment of Joseph and Eden having sex across her kitchen table, their passionate moans vibrating through her surround sound. Out of respect, Andre quickly turned and walked out of the closet, shaking his head. Jackson followed, rubbing a hand down his neck at the embarrassing scene.

"You've gotta be kidding me. That was *her* under his bed?" Pandora couldn't believe it.

Quinn looked on, *speechless*. Her shocked expression was frozen solid across her face. All the color nearly drained from both of their faces when another camera showed Eden stealing money from Pandora's wallet. Pandora let out a painful gasp, as the emotions of betrayal sent her stomach lurching into her throat. Her nerves and senses heightened up, just before everything in her body shut down and grew numb. The remote fell from Pandora's hands, and she almost passed out. Quinn had to catch her before she hit the floor.

"Tell me I'm going crazy," Pandora's voice shook, clutching her chest, as a tear involuntarily slipped from her eye. She was completely devastated. Her childhood reality had taken her through enough experiences to want to shut down and not trust anyone, but with compassion and loyalty in the form of Eden and Quinn, Pandora was brave enough to be vulnerable. The three of them were like white on rice for the last *fifteen* years. They were the kind of friends that took everything you said to the grave. The type to put each other in their respective places when they were wrong but would protect one another and ride it out until the wheels fell off. They were that one person to each other, besides their mothers, that they counted on for anything. They were each other's sanity when all of their motor skills were nonexistent, and two plus two was no longer adding up to four. Within the realms of their friendship, they each placed their hopes, dreams, belief, and love.

Watching Eden disrespecting her home,

destroying her brother's life, and stealing from her, was torture. It felt like a knife ripping through her heart. The world around her froze like a statue, and she couldn't focus anymore. Another camera showed Eden driving away in Pandora's car and returning a short time later, getting into the passenger seat of her own car, and pulling off. Quinn quickly cut the television off, trying to protect Pandora's heart from seeing anything else that would hurt her. It was too late, however, because Pandora had seen enough. She was so angry that her skin began to tingle. Spinning around, she stormed up the stairs as Quinn followed in fear.

"Anna, why don't we sit down and breathe so you can calm down and gather your thoughts," Quinn proclaimed, watching Pandora put on her sweatpants and tie her sneakers.

Pandora threw a t-shirt on and grabbed her metal bat from her closet. She darted toward her bedroom door and Quinn closed it, blocking her path.

"Where are you going?"

"*Mannequin*, I will shoot you if you don't get the hell out of my way," Pandora darted, angrier than a trapped tiger.

"Joanna, please wait. You're gonna hurt her," Quinn shook her head.

"No, I'm gonna *kill* her," Pandora threatened, walking over to Quinn to push her out of the way. Quinn tussled with Pandora as best as she could to keep her from opening the door. Finally, Pandora took a step back and stared Quinn directly in her eyes.

"You know, I don't think you'd be this protective if you knew I lied to you earlier about picking Eden up from the market, because her car wouldn't start," Pandora hissed, putting a hand on her hip.

"What? Why would you lie to me about something silly like that?" Quinn winced.

"I *lied* because I didn't know how to explain to you that I was r*eally* going to pick her up from the police station. She got arrested for aggravated assault, spitting on a police officer, and being under the influence, all while Heaven was in the car," Pandora rubbed it in and pursed her lips.

Quinn tilted her head to make sure she heard correctly. "She did *what* with my baby in the car?" Veins she didn't even know existed started to strain through her neck.

"That was the same reaction I had. They were about to take Heaven to social services," Pandora admitted in a pitiless tone. "Honey, you and your hand-clapping, bible-believing husband, would have been plastered *all* over the news. I was able to get everything dropped, and I was going to tell you when we got in the house, but after listening to her sob story, I felt bad for her."

The most dangerous place in the world is between a mother and her children. At that moment, Quinn felt just as betrayed as Pandora. Quinn furrowed her eyebrows, spun around, and swung the door open.

Andre and Jackson were downstairs conversing about the entire situation when both of their wives came barreling down the stairs. Quinn grabbed the keys to Andre's truck, and they bolted through the front door.

"Where are you two going?" Andre asked, concerned.

"To hell, if we don't pray," Quinn responded. Opening the truck door, Pandora jumped into the driver's seat, and Quinn got in on the passenger side. Pandora rammed the key into the ignition, put the car in drive, and took off like a speeding bullet, making her way to Eden's with a bat and an intent to kick her behind.

Thirteen

Through exhaustion, Eden stared at her bruised left cheek and painful blacked eye, in the vanity mirror over her dresser. She was so tired, but the excruciating pain blazing through her face hurt so badly, she couldn't sleep. Travis felt terrible and had gotten up and gone to a twenty-four-hour Walgreens to get her some pain medication.

The bruises on her face looked pretty bad, but it also gave her a sense of comfort knowing that Travis wasn't the perfect Prince Charming she thought he was.

"This just proves he's human," Eden defended her dignity, "every couple fights here and there."

Travis's phone going off with a text message on her nightstand made Eden turn around. She didn't know he forgot his phone. He *never* left it when he went out. Eden walked over and picked it up.

It was almost 4 in the morning, she thought, *who could be texting him this late?*

Squinting at the phone, she began feeling guilty for attempting to invade his privacy. *Maybe it's an emergency.* She swiped her thumb across, unlocking the screen. The text was from an unsaved number. It was a picture of a dismantled, vandalized car, and a message that read, *"Keep your dog on a tight leash next time. Love always, Amber."*

If Eden could've jumped out of her skin, she would've, but her feet felt cemented to the floor. Her heart thrashed against the wall of her chest, and electricity surged through her body like she had just landed on a live wire.

"Oh no," Eden threw the phone on the bed and rushed into the living room. With her hands holding her head, she paced the floor in sheer panic.

"Shoot. Shoot. Shoot," she chastised herself. Her hands began shaking and her thoughts started to race out of control. "I'd rather burn in *hell* than have to explain this to Pandora. What am I gonna say? If she doesn't know it was because of me, should I not say anything? Yes! Bingo! Don't ask, don't tell."

Eden's mind grew so delirious; she swore she was going unconscious. The bullet flying through the padlock on her front door woke it up with the quickness. Eden quickly jumped out of the way as it hit the wall, just missing her torso. She glanced at the wall in shock and turned back around to see Pandora in the doorway. She glared at Eden with cold, chilling eyes, looking like she had checked out of reality a long time ago. Immediate fear paralyzed Eden from the neck down.

"You owe me one hundred and eighty-six thousand dollars and twenty-seven cents, and I want my money, *now*," Pandora gritted through her teeth, walking toward Eden with a vengeance.

"Okay, I'll replace the money for your car," Eden swallowed the lump in her throat, walking back from Pandora. She stretched her arm out arm in front of her to protect her, "but calm down, let me explain what happened. I had to—"

"Calm down?" Pandora's emotionless eyes turned to stone. "After you stole from me, you want me to calm down?" She roughly smacked Eden's hand out of the way as she moved in closer to her.

Eden's eyes widened, tripping over her bag while she continued backing away from Pandora. "*I didn't steal anything*," her voice shook.

Pandora's soul nearly jumped out of her body after she told that bold-faced lie. Eden's eyes widened in a bit of relief when she saw Quinn enter into the doorway.

"Quinn!" Eden, yelled, "Get—"

Before she could get the rest of her words out, Pandora's mind snapped, and she stormed at Eden like a hurricane in its perfect power. Pandora grabbed her by her hair and swung at her already blackened eye. She got a good grip on Eden's neck and choked her to the floor.

Quinn shrieked in terror, running over to them. She was angry at what Eden had done, but the drive calmed her down and she was able to think rationally about the situation.

Pandora, *not so much*. She let go of Eden's neck and hit her so hard, the whole house nearly shook. Quinn grabbed Pandora by her waist and tried to lift her off of Eden as best as she could, but it wasn't helping. Pandora was focused, precise, and ruthless, kicking Eden in her back, her stomach, and her mouth. Quinn's heart pounded the second she saw blood being smeared on the floor.

"Anna, that's enough!" Quinn was horrified, continuing her attempt to pry her off of Eden. She felt so relieved she was able to get the bat from Pandora before they got out of the car, otherwise Pandora would be on a boat to Alcatraz for murder one. She forgot about the gun she kept on her at all times. Ripping out of Quinn's grasp, Pandora dropped to her knees and began banging Eden's head into the hardwood. Eden tried to swing back, but Pandora was lightning quick. Eden didn't have a chance. With what felt like superhuman strength, Quinn grabbed Pandora by her waist again, and pulled her back from Eden, leaving Eden a battered, bloody mess as she cried uncontrollably on the floor.

"What the hell is this?" Travis hollered in the doorway, dropping the Walgreens bag as he raced over to Eden and knelt down to her, "are you serious?"

"You're gonna disrespect my house and screw my brother all over my kitchen table?" Pandora hollered, staring at Eden as her chest heaved up and down.

Eden wanted to respond, but she was too embarrassed and in too much pain. Travis stood up and balled his fists, his eyes furrowing into a rage.

"Both of you bitches need to get up out of here!" He yelled.

Quinn let Pandora go, and jerked her head back, her mouth flying open. No one had ever called her out before.

"Excuse me!" Quinn fussed back.

"Travis!" Eden hollered, finally able to sit up, silently begging every god on the planet not to let him hit one of them.

"Oh, *you're* Travis?" Pandora tilted her head to the side with a stony expression. With a hoodie on and scruffy facial hair, he looked completely different from the picture Eden showed them.

"That's right, and who—"

Pandora pulled her .32 caliber from her sweatpants pocket and fired two shots. One went into Travis's thigh, and the other went straight into his left foot. He yelped in pain, throwing his body onto the floor next to Eden. Eden screamed in terror, slumping her body over to see about him.

"I'm Anna, I believe we spoke over the phone. It's nice to meet you," she spat.

"Oh my *Gosh*, let's go!" Quinn screamed, grabbing Pandora by the arm, nearly dragging her toward the door.

"You're crazy!" Travis rolled side to side, writhing in pain.

"I'm not crazy," Pandora snarled, "admitting I was crazy would imply that I was mentally deranged, or insane, and that's farthest from the truth. There is nothing mental or deranged about me right now, and this is the sanest I've been in my *whole* life." Tears flooded her eyes as she turned to look at Eden's bloody face. "*Fifteen* years, Eden. This is what you do to fifteen years of friendship?"

Quinn rushed out of the apartment with Pandora in her grasp, praying that no one had called the police.

Fourteen

Eden sat in a hospital bed at the Bernard Thompson Emergency Room, covered in bruises, cuts, scrapes, and maybe some breaks. Her body felt like it had been in a car wreck. Her head and body hurt too much, and she kept her eyes closed, not because she didn't want to see where she was, but because it hurt too much to open them. As pain sheeted through her with terrible intensity, Eden rubbed her temples, desperately trying to massage it away.

"Miss Grant?" A doctor's voice radiated through her ears, making her headache worse.

"Yeah," Eden responded, squinting at the doctor.

"I'm Dr. Gooden. How are you feeling?"

"*Amazing*," she cut her eyes at him.

"I understand," he nodded. "Well, your x-rays came back. You have a fractured wrist, and some pretty bad contusions, but no broken bones. That's a good thing."

"Great," she muttered, "can I have some medicine for this splitting headache?"

"Not yet," the doctor shook his head. "After your blood work comes back, we're gonna send you for a CAT scan to get a good look at your head. I have to make sure we didn't miss anything. If that's negative, I can give you something."

"Okay, thank you."

"In the meantime, you sit back and try to relax.

You're lucky to have come out of that car wreck alive," he turned and exited the room.

Eden laid her head back against the bed and let out a deep sigh. She told the nurses she'd been in a car accident on the highway, and her car flipped over with her in it. She was too embarrassed to tell them another human being, about three sizes smaller than her, did this kind of damage with her own two hands. As Eden stared into space, her high cheekbones were sunken in, and her eyes were like dark circles. Her body was wrapped in pain, but the emotions running through her head felt much worse. Eden had no idea how Pandora knew she had taken her money, or that she'd been sleeping with Joseph. Joseph wouldn't put himself out there, and everyone was asleep when Eden left the house, so how could Pandora have known? Surely, Pandora had told Quinn what she had done with her baby, so Eden was certain that neither of them would want anything else to do with her.

Knowing that she'd just lost her best friends left Eden feeling withdrawn from reality, weightless and anonymous. The death of a friendship was worse than the death of a lover. Lovers are transient, but friends are supposed to be there for you, always. She never imagined life without them. They had a special kind of love that wasn't supposed to fade. The loneliness she felt knowing that *this* was the end, hit her like a wave of nausea.

"In life, it's given that you'll lose people," Eden could hear Ruby saying to her as a teenager after her father walked out on them, *"people will flow in and out like curtains through an open window, sometimes without any reason at all."*

But Quinn and Pandora were *always* meant to stay. As they got older and settled into their important careers and education, the three of them began to downsize and prioritize, trimming the corners of their lives. They kept what was important, and discarded what wasn't, but they're relationship always remained a priority. Now, just like that, their friendship went up in flames. Losing them felt like she had lost a part of her, and she would never be okay again. Not a person in the world deserved to feel that kind of pain. Eden cared about Travis a lot but catering to him cost her everything she loved. She wished she could take it all back. She wished she had told Travis to find some other way home and gone back to sleep. Eden's chin trembled and she burst into tears thinking about how badly she had messed up.

"Baby, relax, I'm alright," Travis grunted, limping into her room with crutches, "the bullets didn't hit any major arteries."

The sound of his voice made Eden feel even worse. She covered her face with her hands and sobbed violently, wishing he would just go away.

"Eden," Travis limped his way over to her bedside and wrapped an arm around her. "Baby, it's okay."

Eden snatched her body away from him. "Don't touch me. This is all *your* fault," she cried, shaking her head.

Travis looked at Eden like he could snatch her tongue out of her mouth. "I beg your pardon? *What's* my fault?"

"All of this! I told you when you called me that I would see you tomorrow," she cried, looking up at him, "but you refused to take no for an answer."

"Have you lost your mind, Eden? Shoot, maybe Pandora beat some screws loose in your head. *You're* the one that left the house against my wishes, *you* took her money, *and you* took her car. *I* came to your rescue and took two bullets from that crazy psycho," he glared, his eyes growing demented, "and this is my fault?"

"Travis, I just lost my friends because of you!"

"What friends? Friends don't run up in your house like that? She literally just beat you into a concussion, and then she *shot* me. What if that bullet had hit an artery, and I would have bled to death? Would they *still* be your friends?" Travis shook his head and limped his way over to the chair. "People like her don't deserve to be out amongst society. Jade's dad is the chief of police, and I'm calling him. By morning, she'll be arrested by the police while she's standing in the unemployment line!"

"Please, you'd be dead before you ended your phone call," Eden pursed her lips, wiping her face.

"*Whatever*, she's nothing but a barking dog, she's not about that life," Travis sneered.

"*She's* not, but she's got a rap sheet a mile long full of serial killers, assassins, and gang members at her disposal, who *are*," Eden shook her head, "she's one of the best defense attorneys in the freaking country! If she found out you threatened her career, she'd have these streets kidnap you, kill you, and send your body back to your family to *bury* you."

Travis looked up at Eden's straight face and jerked his head back. "I don't believe she's crazy like that. I feel like your gassing her up."

"Travis!" Eden raised her eyebrows. "She shot

you...*twice*. Thank Goodness you're alright, but if you had died, she would've shown up to your funeral with a gift and well wishes. Do you *really* wanna play Russian roulette with someone like that?"

Travis thought for a minute and then sucked his teeth. "I'll leave it alone because of *you*. However, it's very disheartening that after all I just went through for you, you're still trying to protect her."

"I'm not. I'm just saying—"

"YOU ARE!" He yelled, causing Eden to jump, and the nurses out in the hall to look toward the room. "I walked in here to see about you, and the first thing out of your mouth is that this is my fault. You didn't even ask if I was okay. What kind of support system are you? What kind of girlfriend are you?" Travis slumped his body in the chair.

The look on his face made Eden feel terrible. She did think it was Travis's fault, but he was right, if she had never left her house to begin with, none of this would've happened. Jade had gone back to Chicago, so now she had no friends. She didn't want Travis to end up leaving her too.

"Look, I'm sorry, okay? I just lost two very good people, and I'm *not* okay, but it's wrong to take it out on you."

Travis crossed his arms and rolled his eyes. "I see why you lost your friends. You don't know how to appreciate people who love you. Maybe I should make like them and leave you hanging."

Eden's eyes grew wide. "No, no, don't. I'm *sorry*."

"This is the second time you've apologized. I don't know if I believe you."

"Travis, I was wrong. I'm sorry. Please, don't leave me. You're all I have left," Tears flushed down Eden's face just as the doctor re-entered the room.

"Is everything okay?" One nurse asked, following the doctor in, "we heard yelling."

"Yes," Travis fixed his face and glanced at Eden. "We're just a little worked up about our situation, that's all."

Eden wiped her face and nodded in agreement.

"Well alright," the doctor nodded turning to face Eden. "Miss Grant, I was getting ready to send you over to CAT scan, however, your blood work came back. Did you know you were pregnant?"

"Pregnant?" Eden and Travis both replied.

"I'll take that as a no," the doctor chuckled. "Congratulations."

Eden's face was frozen in place, turning pale by the second.

"Are you *serious*?" Travis said with a building smile.

"There's a very unlikely chance of blood work being inaccurate, so yes, I'm serious," the doctor confirmed.

Travis's face filled with excitement as he jumped up from his chair, ignoring the pain that shot through his body. "Eden, baby!" He laughed hysterically with widened eyes.

"In the meantime, Miss Grant, we're just gonna give you some Tylenol for the pain, and let you go home. If you have any memory loss or blurred vision, come back and see us, okay?"

Eden nodded her head slowly, her mind still trying to process his announcement. The Dr. walked out of the room, and Travis limped over to Eden, nearly snatching her out of her hospital bed. He hugged her tightly, with tears of joy streaming down his face.

" Baby," he beamed.

Eden wasn't sure *how* to react. She wasn't emotionally ready to go through another pregnancy, not after the last experience. Was this really happening to her a second time?

"Wow," was all her flustered demeanor could muster up.

Travis let go of her, sensing her dull energy. "What's the matter?"

"Nothing, I'm just—" afraid to tell Travis how she felt, out of fear of it starting another argument, Eden just shook her head and forced a fake smile. "I'm just shocked. I wasn't expecting it, but I'm happy."

"Man, you have no idea how *badly* I've wanted to be a father, and now I have the chance!" Travis gripped Eden up again, hugging her tightly, "God answered my prayers," he confirmed with a head nod.

"What prayers?"

"About school, and just…everything. I came here with Jade to try something new and get out of Chicago, but after I met you my mindset completely shifted," Travis put Eden's hand in his and caressed it. "I saw so much pain in your eyes, and I wanted to be the one to make you happy. On my way to the store a while ago, I apologized to God so many times for my temper, and I begged him to forgive me. I told him I wanted you, forever."

Eden stared in Travis's sorrow-filled eyes, as tears filled her own.

"Eden, I love making you smile, and laugh, it's

music to my ears. I don't want to hurt you ever again. I want to take care of you. I want to get you away from all these bad memories and horrible people, and just start over. In less than twenty-four hours, God answered my prayer. It's time to put an end to school, and all this drama, and get for real. Let's move back to Chicago and start our life together."

Eden raised her eyebrows and backed her body away from him. "Chicago?"

"Let's do it," he smiled.

"Travis, I don't know," Eden stared at him uncomfortably, "I've lived here since I was twelve. I don't just want to pick up and leave."

"Why not? What do you have here worth sticking around over?"

"My mother's house. That's all I have left of her, and she worked hard to buy that."

"Just like she worked hard for the businesses you ruined," Travis shook his head, "you're too immature to handle responsibility like that. She left you all of that money, and you blew it because of your emotions. Let's start over, baby. Let me help you. Let's do it together as husband and wife."

"Wife?" Eden's eyes blinked rapidly, trying to make sure she heard correctly.

"Yes," Travis stated, standing up as he helped Eden out of the bed. "Marry me."

Eden's mouth fell open and her heart began to elevate. She never felt like she was worthy enough to be someone's wife, just like she thought she wasn't worthy of being a mother. Now, just like that, she was pregnant, and Travis was begging for her hand-in-marriage. Tears fell from Eden's eyes as she nodded her head. Maybe

Travis was right. Maybe God did answer prayers after all.

"Are you serious?" she cried, "yes, I'll marry you."

Travis scooped Eden in his arms. Both of them flinched from their pain, but they were too excited to let go. Eden couldn't believe what was happening to her.

"I don't need a fancy wedding with a bunch of people I don't like," Travis put Eden down and limped his way over to her chair to gather her belongings, "we can go to the justice of the peace tomorrow—just us. We can put the house up for sale, drop out of school, and use that money to take a weeklong honeymoon to an island somewhere. I don't care where, I just want you. I want us."

Eden stood there in awe with the biggest smile spread across her face. She was in so much pain, but her euphoria overshadowed it all. She felt a thawing in her ice-cold soul, the desperate relief of being loved. Finally, life was turning around in her favor. Eden rushed over to help gather the rest of their belongings, just as the nurse came in and gave her discharge papers.

Travis embraced Eden, planting a kiss on her that took her breath away, after which, they both limped out of the emergency room with smiles. To everything there is a season in life. For the last year, Eden felt like she was in a horrifying season that would never change. But in the blink of an eye, her shift happened. She felt like the worst was behind her, and the best was yet to come. *Or was it?*

Fifteen

Before the week had ended, Travis stayed true to his word, turning Eden Grant, into Mrs. Eden Rutherford, at the local justice of the peace. Eden never imagined getting married in a musty smelling courthouse. She was a hopeless romantic and often daydreamed of something much fancier. In the early stages of her pregnancy with Jackson's baby, she had visions of a rustic sort of farm-like wedding on a big piece of land they owned together. Andre would wed them, Quinn would be her Matron of Honor, Pandora would be her Maid of Honor, and Eden's daughter would be the flower girl. When the ceremony began, Ruby would make her way down the center aisle, smiling from ear to ear, dressed to the nines. The rest of her fancy wedding party would soon follow. When it was her turn to come down, everyone would stand up and stare at her with a face full of tears, gawking at her impeccable beauty. Eden was such a kid at heart. She loved bright colorful lights, teddy bears, and pinball machines, so her reception had to have carnival-style lawn games, a merry-go-round, and a Ferris wheel. She had a beautiful, twenty-thousand-dollar wedding dress clipped out from a magazine. It was a tailored, glamorous, forties inspired gown that accented her bust and fit snugly around her curves.

But just like Quinn said, there's no such thing as

a perfect world. There was no Jackson, no rustic farm, Andre, Quinn, or Pandora. She had no flower girl, and no mother smiling from ear to ear. There was no music, no fancy carnival reception, and the white, ankle-length Maxi dress she wore, only cost her fifty-five dollars from Etsy.

Although her dreams and fantasies were short-lived, it didn't stop her from falling completely in love with her new husband. By the time they said I do, Eden had forgotten all about their physical altercation and dove right into Travis's world. Over the next two months, Travis gave Eden heaven on earth. She had heard all of those ridiculous stories about love at first sight, but she never believed in them until it happened to her. Travis took her on a whirlwind of romance that left her more breathless than the first time she laid eyes on him. He stared into her eyes, rubbed her growing belly, and catered to her every beck and call. He was charismatic, caring, and captivating.

He surprised her with romantic dinners at restaurants, and a few trips out of the state. Travis was pleasant, fun, exciting, and he treated her like gold. He asked questions and listened to her answers. He *always* held her hand, opened her doors, and pulled out her chairs. He radiated such high-spirited energy, an exuberance— a magnetism. He was confident, intelligent, intense, and simplistic. However, even while she was having the time of her life, Eden found herself thinking of Quinn and Pandora often. She tried calling and texting them in an attempt to apologize and make things right, but they both ignored her. Eden cried a few times, and Travis held her in his arms, assuring her that a new state would change everything for the better. Eden really didn't want to move, but she felt as though she had nothing holding her back. Finally, she agreed to it. Within two weeks, Travis had sold Ruby's condo, and everything in it, for six hundred thousand dollars. Eden was so sad that he wouldn't consider taking some of her mother's antiques to Chicago with them. Travis said Ruby's taste was too feminine for his liking, and her things wouldn't fit in their new home. He dropped their graduate courses, sold Eden's car for eighty thousand dollars, and his car for one hundred and sixty thousand. They both arrived at the airport with a pocket full of money, and Travis's promise to give Eden the best life she could ever imagine.

"I still can't believe you donated *all* of my clothes to Goodwill," Eden fussed in disbelief, holding Travis' hand as they rushed through the airport, "that was almost a hundred thousand dollars' worth of clothes and shoes. What were you thinking?"

"I still can't believe you made us late."

"How did *I* make us late? You're the one that made me change my dress at the last minute. Not that I had a wardrobe to choose from *anyway*," she chuckled.

"We're rich, baby. I'll buy you a new wardrobe. Plus, I didn't like that green dress, you know I love the red one."

"But red isn't really my color. I don't understand why it was such a big deal."

"It's a big *deal* because we're going back to my home state with all my old friends and family. You're my wife, Eden. When people see you, I want them to say, *wow*, that's Travis' woman," he smiled with a head nod.

"Why can't I just be Eden?" she asked,

innocently.

"Babe, you're killing me with all the questions. We're late as it is. Here, stand here while I go check us in." Travis let go of her arm and walked up to the check-in counter.

"Well if I could have worn what I wanted, we would have b*een* here," she mumbled under her breath as she leaned against a wall and pulled out her phone.

"Eden," a familiar male voice sounded in her ear causing her to look up from her phone.

"Joseph?" Eden blinked her eyes, "how are you?"

"I'm good," he said excitedly, leaning in to hug her. Eden accepted his embrace and looked away quickly.

"Where have you been?"

"I've been...busy," she muttered.

Joseph scratched his head and glanced around. It was obvious that they were both uncomfortable.

"How's fatherhood? And Andrea?"

"Oh man, I love being a dad," he nodded with a grin, "it's a lot of work, but very fulfilling. Andrea is doing well, finally getting back to her old self."

"I'm so happy for you. That's awesome."

"She doesn't know about us by the way," he hesitated, stuffing his hands into his pockets.

Eden lowered her head and crossed her arms. "Is that a good thing?"

"I guess. I don't want to exploit you, nor do I wanna ruin my marriage. *We* had a moment, and I can't say I didn't enjoy it." He grinned, causing Eden to glance up at him and blush.

"Ditto. Thanks for sparing my dignity. I wish

Pandora never found out, though."

"Yeah, I heard you took a lot of heat from her, that was crazy. Then she told me you stole from her and got her car destroyed," he looked at her in confusion, "that's so beneath you. Even down to everything that happened with us. I don't understand."

Eden shook her head trying to fight back her growing tears. "I messed up *so* much, Joe, I don't even have an excuse. I've tried calling and texting, but Quinn or Anna won't answer my calls. So, I'm just trying to move on."

"Really?" Joseph winced, "last I heard, they had both tried reaching out to you, but said you ignored *their* calls."

"What?" Eden returned the wince just as a flustered Travis walked up to them. He wrapped an arm around his wife. He'd been eyeing them the minute Joseph walked up.

"Everything alright over here?"

"Oh," Eden quickly shook off her confusion. "Baby, this is Anna's brother, Joseph. Joe, this is Travis, my husband."

Joseph almost choked on his spit. "Husband?" His eyes widened.

"Nice to meet you," Travis said sternly, sticking his hand out for Joseph to shake.

"Yeah, we got married a couple months ago. I sold my mom's house and left school. We're relocating to Chicago right now actually, I'm—"

"Sweetheart," Travis laughed nervously, "just tell *everyone* our personal business."

"You sold your mother's house?" Joseph stared at Eden in awe. He couldn't believe it.

"It was a big pill to swallow, but there's nothing left for me here. My mother is gone, and my friends hate me. The only good thing in my life is Travis," she glanced over at Travis and smiled.

Joseph looked at her like she was crazy. "Where are you *getting* this from? Anna and Quinn love—"

"Listen, we really have to get going before we miss our flight," Travis interrupted, "we're late as it is." He nodded at Joseph before grabbing Eden's hand. "It was nice meeting you, Joseph."

"Take care, Joe," Eden waved with a smile, allowing herself to be pulled down the hallway, "maybe I'll be back to visit soon."

"Sure thing," Joseph said with a puzzled look, watching the two of them walk away. *Married? Left school? Sold Ruby's house?* He couldn't believe the drastic changes Eden had made in such a short period of time. Something about this situation *and* Travis made him very uncomfortable. After watching in complete shock as they disappeared around a corner, Joseph pulled out his phone to call his sister.

As Eden found herself being rushed down the corridor, she thought about Joseph's words concerning Pandora and Quinn trying to get in contact with her.

No way did they try to call me, she thought as she pulled out her iPhone to scroll down her recent call list. Their names were nowhere in sight. *But it's not like either of them to lie about calling me either.* Eden went into her contact list and searched for each of their names.

What? Her eyes widened when she realized why she'd never received their texts and phone calls. Pandora and Quinn's names were both set to *block*. Therefore, all incoming or outgoing activity between the three of them would never be received.

"What in the world?" She said out loud, shaking her head, "I didn't *block* them, and my phone doesn't do it automatically, either. How could—" Eden stopped dead in her tracks, causing Travis to jerk forward.

"*Travis*," she darted her eyes at the back of his head, as he turned to face her. "Did you go through my phone?"

"What? When?" He responded, quickly.

"Don't play dumb." She held her phone up for him to see. "How did my friends end up on my block list?"

"Baby, I don't know," Travis blew out a sigh. "We really don't have time for this right now. We have a flight to catch."

"Don't lie to me about something like this, *I mean it*," she spat.

"Don't lie to you about something so trivial, but it's okay for you to keep things from me?" Travis spat back, his forehead wrinkling in anger.

"No, don't avoid the question *or* change the subje—"

"That Joseph guy you were just talking to, is that the one you cheated on me with?"

Eden slumped her shoulders and slacked her mouth. She wasn't expecting *that* question. "What?"

"Don't *what* me?" He walked toward her, invading her personal space. "That night Pandora ransacked your house, she said something about you screwing her brother. I didn't mention it but trust and believe, I didn't forget it. Was that him?"

Her guilty stricken face was all the confirmation Travis needed. Eden couldn't think of a lie quick enough before she found herself being pulled into a nearby family restroom. Travis gripped Eden by her shoulders and slammed her against the bathroom wall, knocking the wind out of her. "Was-that-*him*!"

"Yes! That was him," she admitted in a shaky voice, "but I never cheated on you. We weren't together when it happened."

"So why didn't you tell me about it?"

"I didn't think I needed to!" She fussed back. "We're married, Travis. Why does anything that happened before you, matter?"

"It matters when you're hugged up on that faggot in public, disrespecting me like I wasn't less than ten feet away! Then, you're telling him our personal business, where we're going, where we'll be living! Were you telling him all of that so he can come see you?"

"What? No, I-"

"*Maybe I'll be back to visit,*" Travis mocked Eden's words, "*that's* what you said. Visit who, Eden? Visit *him*?" His face looked like it would explode at any minute.

"Travis."

"You still sleeping him? Is that *my* baby you're pregnant with, or is it his?"

Eden stared at her rage-filled husband. Tears rushed to her eyes as he squeezed the life out of her arms and showered her with questions, one behind the other.

"Travis, let go of my arms. You're hurting me," Eden choked out a cry.

The sound of her agony caused Travis to let go of her shoulders. He stepped back and watched her cry, his chest heaving up and down in anger. "So now you wanna play the victim role, and make me look like the bad guy?" He crossed his arms, "you flipped out when you saw Amber hugging me, and I never even touched her sexually, she was just a groupie. But I'm supposed to be okay with my *wife* hugging another man that she slept with?"

Eden cupped her face in her hands and sobbed louder.

"That's why your so-called friends don't like you. You're always doing something shady!"

"I'm sorry! It was a harmless hug. I didn't mean anything by it, but this isn't fair. You blocked my friends from my phone, and didn't tell—"

"You know what?" Travis walked up to her and snatched her phone from her jacket pocket. He slammed the iPhone into the floor and watched her screen shatter. The sudden noise caused Eden to jump as she looked up at him, terrified.

"This phone goes in the garbage with all of your other memories. When we get to Chicago, I'll buy you another one."

Eden watched in shock as he picked up her phone and flushed it down the toilet. "Travis, no!" She cried louder, running over to the toilet to try and retrieve her phone. "There were pictures and old text messages from my mother on there. I can't get those back!"

"You should have thought about that before you tried setting up an affair in front of my face," he said coldly.

Eden couldn't respond if she wanted too,

because her broken heart wouldn't let her. Her mother had purchased that phone for her three years ago. The pictures, videos, and messages from Ruby, and clips of her first ultrasounds were the last of her past that she had access to. Shaking her head in denial, Eden's mind grew delirious. She dropped to her knees and tried sticking her hand in the toilet. "Get my phone back, please?" She cried, hysterically.

"You want your phone back?" He yelled, "go get it then." Travis grabbed Eden's head and shoved it in the toilet bowl. He swished her head back and forth before pulling her out by her hair and then dumping it back in. "You want me to flush you down the freaking sewer so you can get it?"

Travis's shouting became incoherent as Eden's ears submerged in and out of the toilet water. Her heart pounded against her ribs, and her lungs struggled to intake sufficient air.

"You still want your phone now?" He snatched her entire body up from the floor and planted her on her feet.

Eden bent over and tried to catch her breath, frantically shaking her head no.

"I can't believe how immature, and selfish you are!" He bellowed, "I've shown you love in ways that you never even knew were possible! I *fixed* you. I made you happy, and I gave you everything! I'm trying to give you a better life, and you're gonna act like this because of some phone? If your old life is that important to you, then you stay here. I'm leaving."

Travis turned to walk away just as Eden jumped up and grabbed his arm. "No, wait." She begged, her eyes burning from the dirty toilet water.

"Get off me," he tore away from her and bolted for the bathroom door, "I'll find another woman that will appreciate a man like me. How dare you question me in an attempt to blame *me* for *your* friends not speaking to you? So what if I blocked them, I was trying to spare you the heartache. Even still, they knew where you lived. They could've come over if you were so important to them!"

Eden reached for his arm. "You're right, I'm sorry," she cried, "I'm overreacting, and I'm sorry."

"If we're gonna be together, I need you to let the past *go,*" he demanded.

Eden nodded her head, water dripping from her hair like a wet puppy. "I promise, I'll let it go. I can't just forget my entire life, but I'll work towards it. You've been nothing but good to me, and I don't want you to go, especially not without me."

The fire in Travis's eyes began to simmer down. He walked over to the bathroom sink and grabbed paper towels from the dispenser. "I forgive you, but don't let this happen again." He wiped the water from her face and attempted to put her hair back in place.

"It won't," she promised, "I'm sorry that I messed us up this morning. If I had just put on the dress you said, we would've been on time, and I wouldn't have run into Joe. I shouldn't have hugged him, I shouldn't have kept what we did in the past from you either," she tightened her eyes shut. "I'm sorry, Travis. I wanna fix it."

"Alright," he wrapped his arms around her and held her close while she cried in his arms. "Don't cry, baby, we'll fix it. The sooner we get out of here forever, the better."

Eden was so confused at this point. She was trapped between giving up the life she knew and embarking on the new one with Travis. She didn't know if she was right or wrong in the situation, but all of Travis's yelling and screaming had turned her into a bundle of nerves. For the last two months, she woke up on top of the world, but today, the world was seemingly on top of her. She latched on to Travis as tight as she could, finding it difficult to try to see her way off the emotional roller coaster she had just been forced on. Just before they exited the bathroom, Eden briefly thought about what her life would be like if she'd stayed. She then remembered that she had no house, no money, no school, no car, and couldn't even imagine explaining why to her friends.

Travis opened the bathroom door, being met with two security guards, and a few concerned onlookers who'd heard the commotion.

"Is everything okay, sir?" One of the guards asked, reverting his eyes between him and Eden.

"Absolutely, we had an emergency with some family issues, but we're okay now. Thank you."

"Ma'am, are you okay?" The guard asked. Eden saw a few women close by looking at her through fear-filled eyes.

"Yes, I'm fine. Thank you," she replied, lowering her head.

Travis grabbed Eden's hand and rushed down the corridor to catch their boarding flight. Both of her shoulders ached where Travis had grabbed them, and she was sure there would be a bruise by morning. *He didn't mean to hurt me though,* she thought. *He was just upset. Besides, love hurts sometimes, doesn't it?*

Sixteen

Rock-a-bye, Baby

3 months later...

Upon moving to the windy city, the plan was for Travis to enlist in the Chicago Metro Police Academy, and Eden would apply to the University of Illinois with Jade, to continue her graduate studies. Travis and Eden were supposed to purchase a home and furnish it together, along with brand new cars and wardrobes. Whatever money was left, was supposed to be split between the two of them, after which, they'd open separate bank accounts, and a joint account to share. Travis managed to make it into the police academy, but every other promise he made was null and void. He got Eden a cellphone in his name and secured it with parental controls to prevent Eden from having certain access to things. He set time limits for telephone calls and internet usage, telling Eden that spending so much time on her cellphone was unhealthy. Instead of the two-story house they'd originally picked out just minutes away from Travis's old neighborhood, he surprised Eden with a three-story home, forty-five minutes away from everyone he knew. He even had it furnished and decorated when they got there. Travis bought himself a new Benz but told Eden she didn't have any use for a car right now. He talked her out of going to college, telling her it would be too much stress on her five-month pregnant body. He requested that she take up more useful classes, like Lamaze or a prenatal exercise class to stay in shape. While he was away at the academy, he held on to all the money, paid the bills, and had all of the grocery shopping delivered to their home. Eden's only job was bathing herself, feeding herself, and reading the books Travis delivered, mostly about teaching her how to be a loving mother, and a respectable wife. He FaceTimed her every chance he got, in an attempt to see what she was doing, what part of the house she was in, and what clothes she had on. He limited the time she spent watching television and made sure she was in bed every night by 9 P.M.

Eden loved Travis to the moon and back, but she did think his behavior was a bit *much*. However, she also remembered being at the far end of happy during her lengthy relationship with Jackson. While Travis was extra caring, extra cautious, and extra attentive, Jackson was cold-hearted, ruthless, and insensitive. Even being away at the police academy, Travis always made his presence felt, but Jackson was almost *never* around, and it took him days to return phone calls and text messages.

Eden thought back to lonely nights, and vulnerable moments when she wanted Jackson to spend time with her, or make her feel special, but he never did.

She was in love by herself. The only thing that understood her, was her journal— a long, suffering friend that had taken everything she threw at it. Eden remembered the very last time she'd written in it.

As she ran her fingers through the thick pages filled with life, loaded with questions and tortured answers, she managed to find a fresh, empty page. Her pen stalled after one short sentence. *Jackson married Pandora.*

While it would definitely take some time to adjust to the added security, limited room to grow, or being able to come and go as she pleased, Eden would've rather have someone care *too* much, than not care at all.

As she and Jade sat on Jade's bed, eating sliced apples and joking one morning, the smell of hot buttermilk biscuits and sweet hickory bacon danced in the air. Eden gently closed her eyes, taking in the fulfilling aroma.

"What are you doing, weirdo?" Jade chuckled.

"Your mother's cooking," Eden sighed softly, "it reminds me so much of my mother's."

"Really? Maybe you should stay for breakfast then."

"No, it's okay," Eden said hesitantly, opening her eyes, "I have to get going soon. Travis is gonna FaceTime me when he's finished his morning physical training."

"*And*?" Jade raised an eyebrow, "does he not

want you over here?"

"No, it's not that," Eden giggled, "he just doesn't want me driving while I'm pregnant."

"Oh, I was getting ready to say," Jade toned down her annoyed facial expression just as her mother, Sandra, walked into the room.

"Breakfast is almost ready, honey. Eden, are you eating with us?" She asked with a smile.

"Good Morning, Mrs. Sandy. No——"

"No, she snuck out of the house and has to be back home before Travis calls," Jade cut her off.

"Well that sounds silly. I'm sure Travis wouldn't mind you staying for breakfast."

"I'm sure he wouldn't, but just like I was telling Jade, he doesn't like me driving pregnant, and I don't want to upset him. He doesn't like me leaving the house at all, really, but I got sick of being alone, so I wanted to get out."

"Mom, please tell her that's *stupid*. Like, it's Travis. Who cares if he gets mad over something so petty?"

"Jade…your slick mouth, sweetheart," Sandy darted her eyes at Jade, "you have to remember that while Travis may be like an annoying brother to you, he is a married man now…and that's his wife," She pointed to Eden. "I understand completely, Eden. I think it's very protective of him to take such good care of you. How about I make you a plate to go home?"

"That would be great, thank you."

"I mean, I guess it's kind of cute that he loves you and is extremely protective of you, but for the most part…it annoys me. You can't drive on your own, you can't come over, you can't shop…if that's the way marriage works, I'll *never* get married," Jade crossed her arms.

"You also have to remember the context in which he's doing this," Sandra walked over and sat on Jade's bed. "You remember what happened to Camilla and Denise…*and* that poor baby," she shook her head in remorse.

"Camilla and Miss Denise, yes, but what poor baby?" Jade tilted her head. Eden turned to stare at Sandra as well.

"His fiancé was pregnant," she confirmed. "I think she was about five months, you never knew that?"

Eden and Jade gave Sandra wide eyes glances. Travis told her he had a girlfriend, not a fiancé, and he certainly didn't mention anything about her being pregnant, but for the sake of sparing her embarrassment, Eden quickly fixed her facial expression and pretended she knew what Sandra was talking about.

"Pregnant!" Jade looked at her mother and then at Eden, "wow, he never told me that. I never knew."

"Yeah, that was a really rough time for him," Eden chimed in.

"Well, if that's the case, it makes sense that he's so overprotective."

Eden nodded her head. It made a whole lot of

sense, but why didn't he tell her?

"Travis is so special to this family," Sandra added, "he's always been a son to me, even when his mother was alive. There have always been women running after him, but he always stayed respectful of himself and his dignity."

"*Unlike me*, is what she's trying to imply," Jade laughed, looking at her mother.

"Well, if the shoe fits," Sandra playfully rolled her eyes. "This girl changed boyfriends like she changed underwear. And they were *all* bad influences. Every time we turned around, she was in trouble for truancy, shoplifting, stealing a transit bus, and the list goes on."

Eden's mouth flew open. "You stole a bus?"

"No. John, my ex stole the bus. I was just there while he did it, so I got in trouble too."

"…And her father is the chief of police. This girl gave us headache after headache. Thank God for a sweet, gentle boy like Travis," Sandra cut her eyes at her daughter.

"I hate to admit it, but I agree," Jade laughed, playfully nudging her mother, "Travis was a good kid, and what happened to him shouldn't have happened to anyone. He deserves the best, and he got it when he found you. I'm so happy for you two!" Jade squealed, beaming at Eden from ear to ear.

"Thanks," Eden returned the smile just as her cellphone went off. She pulled it out of her bag and saw it was her husband calling via FaceTime. Her heart nearly jumped through her chest. *Why was he calling so early?*

"Oh no," Eden stared at her phone. "It's him, and I'm not home yet."

"Uh oh, well…I'm going downstairs to eat," Jade laughed, rushing up from the bed, "I don't want him to see my face and think *I* talked you into coming over."

"Just tell him I came to get you for breakfast, that's all, I'm sure he won't be upset," Sandra smiled. "Maybe then you can come down and join us at the table."

"Hopefully that works," Eden stated, peering down at her phone. Jade and her mother exited the bedroom as Eden reached down and answered the phone. "Hey," she smiled into the camera.

"Hey baby, good morning."

"Good morning, how was training?"

"Ridiculous. Three more weeks of this crap, and I'll be home in your arms," he replied with a somber glow.

"I can't wait! I miss you so much."

"Same here, how's your morning?"

"My morning is going al—"

Travis peered into the camera, noticing that her surroundings looked different. "Where are you?" He cut her off, quickly.

"I'm…I'm over Jade's house," Eden muttered, hoping he would say okay and continue on with the conversation. Of course, her hopes were far too high.

"Jade's house?" He blurted out, frowning his face. "For what? What are you doing over there?"

"Well—" Eden stopped herself for a second in an attempt to gather her thoughts. She *really* didn't want to lie about why she was over there. The whole thing felt so silly to her. She should be able to talk to her own husband about how she felt. She also wanted to know why he kept an important part of his past from her.

"Listen," she looked into the camera, staring into Travis's confused face, "I asked Jade to come and get me, so I could use her car to go out."

"Go out? Where, Eden?"

"I wanted to go out— anywhere, Travis, anywhere but that house. Baby, that place feels like a prison to me. You don't want me to go to school, I can't get a job—heck, you don't want me to do anything but stay in the house, and I don't like it," her voice shook as she stood up for herself, "please don't be upset. I just needed to get out and get some air."

"Why didn't you talk to me about this before? You didn't seem to have a problem with it when we first moved here. Why is it a problem now?"

"There was *always* a problem, I just didn't want to get you upset."

"So you go behind my back and leave instead of just talking to me like you're doing now?" He glared, angrily.

"I—I guess I should have said something," she

stuttered, "but you're not the most innocent spouse either," she defended.

"What are you talking about?"

"You never told me you were engaged to your ex, *or* that she was pregnant. Apparently, Jade never knew either. I had to find out an important piece of my husband's past from someone else. It was extremely embarrassing."

Travis looked like a deer in headlights mixed with an angry bear. "Are you over there running your mouth about what's going on in our marriage?" He yelled.

"What? Travis, no. I—"

"So how did the subject of my ex even come up?" he yelled.

"Can you stop yelling please?" Eden winced, turning down the volume on her cellphone.

"I don't want those hoes in my business. I told you from the very first time we started dating, not to run your mouth to them, or anyone else about what goes on."

"Are you seriously gonna refer to them like that?" Eden spat, annoyed, "after that woman took care of you? You and Jade have been like brother and sister."

"Yes!" He exploded into a rage, "I had a long morning, and I was expecting to call you and unwind. Instead, I'm being met with drama and questions. See what I mean? I don't have time for this. It's nobody's business what goes on in our home!"

"They weren't starting any drama."

"I think it's time for you to go home! Now!"

"Travis, you're being extra sensitive over nothing," Eden fussed, feeling her eyes tingle with tears. She was frustrated and confused as to why he would make such a big deal about her being there.

"Eden," he said in a calm, but threatening voice.

"You know what? Fine!" Eden popped up from the bed and grabbed her purse, "I'll go home, and I'll never come out of the house again. I won't even ask Jade to take me back home. I'll take the bus!"

"I don't want you on the bus. I want you to—"

"It's always about what *you* want!" Tears ran down her face, as she stormed out of the bedroom. She knew it was daring to spill her feelings in such a heated way, but she didn't care. "I don't get you, just because you lost your baby and your fiancé, doesn't give you the right to keep me in a bubble!"

"Keep your mouth off of things you don't understand," he warned.

"Well, maybe I would understand if you informed me. I'm your wife. I am not your daughter…or slave… or your freaking arm charm!" Eden swung her purse over her shoulder and bolted to the staircase. She had enough of Travis's controlling ways, and it was time for him to see how over it she was.

"I'm not gonna talk about this anymore. Call me when you get—" before Travis could get the rest of his sentence out, Eden put one foot on the staircase and tripped over the rug. Her phone flew out of her hand as she plummeted toward the landing of the long staircase. Her limbs tumbled over one another, twisting and hitting against the rise and runs of the stairs.

Eden was paralyzed in shock. Her elbow slammed into a sharp corner, and her head tossed around like a single grape in a blender. The minute she felt her body hit the floor, everything began to spin. She struggled to catch her breath.

Sandra and Jade stormed into the hallway, screaming in sheer panic.

Seventeen

Eden lay in her dark, depressing bedroom staring at the floor for two days, with Jade next to her bedside. Relentless pain echoed through her entire body, needling in specific spots in her now barren womb.

Another baby, dead. She was emotionally fragile from all of the agony swirling around inside of her, but a large portion of it was anger. She was *angry* that her body was taking too long to recover, *angry* that life carried on as usual and a*ngry* at God for putting her through this a second time.

She felt cursed—like she was being punished for something.

Why does this keep happening? She thought.

Throughout her five-month pregnancy, Eden stayed strong and hopeful because of Travis, but deep down, she was an emotional wreck. During each ultrasound appointment, the threat of another stillbirth or miscarriage sat right in the exam room with her. Because of liability issues, technicians aren't supposed to say much, but their body language and demeanor said enough. When the technician cheerily pointed out the baby's head, its chin, and its heartbeat, her fears quickly alleviated, being replaced with the joy of becoming a mother. But her joy was short-lived, as death and disaster had returned for an encore.

What had I done wrong *this time?* Her thoughts chastised her for the last forty-eight hours. Eden took her prenatal vitamins, sang to her baby, rubbed her belly, and made sure to eat healthily. None of that mattered... Much like the first child she lost, it was very abstract and intangible. There was no grave, no funeral, and no grand goodbye. Just the emotional aftermath and psychological distress that had the magnitude to finish off what was left of her sanity.

Travis opted out of his training to be by her side. In doing so, his dreams of becoming a police officer disappeared right along with their dead baby. Both of them had to reconstruct their futures and neither one of them was up for it. Eden was mentally detached, and Travis kept to himself. When he walked into the hospital room, he refused to even look at Eden. He never said hello or asked her how she was feeling. The doctors informed him of what had happened, and he just nodded, giving them an empty stare. He drove Eden home, left and went back out, and didn't return until the following day. If it weren't for Jade coming over to be with her, Eden would've gone through the last two days alone.

"Listen, I know it's been a couple of days, and I know you're still suffering, but it may do you some good to get out of the house for a while," Jade smiled rubbing Eden's hand, "maybe we can go see a movie and grab a bite to eat."

Eden snatched her hand away. "You can go. I'm not interested."

"Eden, you can't stay in this room and just sulk, it's not healthy. Here, at least let some light in and turn on the TV." Jade flicked the switch on the television and opened the curtains, allowing an array of sunshine to beam through the window.

Eden shook her head and sighed. When she lost her mother and her daughter, Quinn stayed with her for an entire month and took the best care of her. She missed her friend *so* much and could really feel the lack of her presence. Not everyone could be as comforting, wise, and all-knowing as Quinn, but Jade did the best she could, which wasn't much considering she'd never been pregnant or lost anyone close to her. Jade was a good companion for smoking and partying, but other than that she was a pain in the behind.

A few times, Eden almost lashed out at Jade and sent her home, but she caught herself and tried to remain appreciative.

She couldn't stand to lose any more friends at this point. Averting her gaze as Jade flipped through the channels, Eden was met with a myriad of tremors. From diaper commercials to the teen moms on Maury Povich. These things went on every day on daytime television, but after losing a baby a second time, Eden took it personally. "Turn it off…please," she begged, as tears welled up in her exhausted eyes, "just turn it off."

Jade quickly obeyed. "I'm sorry, Eden. I feel like I'm adding to your pain instead of helping you."

"It's okay, really. You're trying, and I'm grateful. *Much* better than my husband is doing," she sniffed, frowning her face.

"Oh no," Jade sighed, feeling terrible, "he still hasn't come in to see about you?"

"That bastard won't even *look* at me. He's been home for two days, in and out of the house. He hasn't said one word about it at all. He woke up this morning, came in the room to see if I was still alive, and then he left."

"My mom tried reaching out to him, and my dad, but he won't return any of their phone calls. My dad said he was really upset about having to leave the academy."

"I can imagine, and I feel so terrible about it," tears fell from Eden's face. "I feel like this is all my fault. He told me he didn't want me leaving the house, and I did. Now I've ruined *both* our lives. I shattered his future and his baby. He doesn't love me anymore."

"Honey don't say that," Jade walked over and rubbed her back.

"Jade, he *hates* me, I know he does. Part of me is angry because he's mad at me and won't come to see about me, and the other part is mad at myself. I feel so stupid. Every time I make my own choices, they backfire. I should've just listened to him and accepted the fact that I'm immature and cannot survive on my own," Eden sobbed.

Jade looked at Eden like she'd been sucking on lemons. "He *said* that to you?"

"I should have listened, I should have—" Her words became inaudible as she cried uncontrollably.

"No..." Jade wrapped her arms around Eden as tight as she could. "First of all, I'm sure he didn't mean any of those horrible things," her voice was hesitant. She *hoped* he didn't mean any of it. "Secondly, he's under a lot of pressure. Travis loves you. I've never seen him look at a woman the way he looks at you. Granted, his methods are a bit extreme in my eyes, but what do I know? I've never been married. He's probably just trying to process everything and get his words together so that he doesn't say the wrong thing."

"I can't face another day of him in this house not speaking to me."

"Well when he comes in, *say* that to him," Jade wiped away Eden's tears, "tell him that you can't take all of the disconnect and that you need him. When he lost his mother and Camilla, he shut down the same exact way. He wouldn't talk to anyone or accept help. He wouldn't even go to their funerals."

Eden looked up at Jade, partly shocked.

"Exactly," Jade nodded, "I don't wanna tell you not to take it personally, but I don't think it's you. I think the situation has caused him to shut down."

The sound of the front door slamming startled both of them. Jade could hear Eden's heart beating through her chest wall. Eden got up from the bed and walked over to the mirror to fix her hair and wipe her eyes.

"I'm gonna take your advice," Eden cleared her throat.

"I wish you two the best, and I love you both. You'll get through it. I'm gonna get going. I don't want my presence to make anything awkward," Jade got up from the chair and grabbed her belongings just as Travis stepped into the room.

"Hey Jade, good to see you."

Jade looked up, partly shocked that he spoke to her, as Eden turned around. "Hey, what's up? How are you?"

"I'm doing alright. I just took a jog on Front Street with your dad. He said he was looking for you."

"I was here with Eden, I'm headed home now."

Travis moved out of the doorway so she could get by.

"Listen, I'm really sorry you guys are going through this. I'm praying for you both," Jade smiled.

"Thanks a million," Travis nodded, "tell your mother I said hello."

"I will do that. Eden, call me, okay?"

"I will," Eden forced a smile as Jade walked out.

Eden and Travis gazed at one another through pained expressions. Just as Eden opened up her mouth to talk, Travis turned and walked out of the room.

So much for him not being mad. Eden gasped in shock, crossing her arms. Travis had a lot to say to Jade, but nothing in his heart to at least *try* and comfort his wife.

How dare he walk out of the room without even acknowledging me? Eden was tired of him ignoring her. In some instances, silence was golden but this was driving her crazy. She stormed out of the room and down the steps after Travis. He had just entered into the living room and was sitting down on the couch.

"So, you can speak to Jade and ask about her family, but you can't even say hi to your wife?"

Travis rolled his eyes and stared at her. "Hi," he replied emotionless, reaching for the remote.

Eden walked over, snatched it off the couch, and threw it across the living room. "Stop it! We're not about to do this for another two days. We need to talk to one another, Travis."

"Don't tell me what we're about to do. I'll talk when I'm ready, not when you demand I do."

"Oh really?" Eden jerked her head back, "but it's okay for you to dish out demands twenty-four seven and tell me what to do?"

"Whatever Eden," he looked at her in disgust. "I don't wanna deal with you right now, go somewhere else."

"I *can't* go anywhere else, baby, *I need you.* Don't shut down on me. Not here, not right now," her voice shook. "You've handicapped my mind and my heart. It's like I'm mentally and physically dependent on you—"

"Eden, not *now*!" He snapped, "I don't feel like listening to this."

"Travis, please?" She pleaded, "I feel so damaged— like I can't face life on my own anymore. I'm sorry about all of the—"

"Will you *shut up*?" He sprung up from the chair with a demented stare, "I'm sick of hearing your voice. I'm sick of looking at you, *period*. I wish it was you that died instead of the baby!"

Eden clutched her chest. If words could kill, she would be on her way to reunite with her mother. A knot quickly formed in her throat, too painful to swallow.

"I need an all-weather *wife*, not a seasonal *woman*," Travis gritted. "You don't respect me as your husband, nor do you value and appreciate anything I do for you! You refused to listen to me! *You* killed our baby, and *you* destroyed my future! You have become a liability instead of an asset!"

At that moment, Eden was too hurt to even cry. Her tear ducts felt as dry as a desert. She was completely devastated. She was brave enough to be vulnerable with him, and he just squashed her feelings like a roach.

"*Oh my God*, now you're gonna stand in my face like a mute? What are you, retarded now?" He flung his arms into the air.

Eden swallowed hard, clearing a pathway to speak. "Do you hear yourself? How *dare* you blame me for everything? Maybe if you weren't so controlling, I wouldn't have felt the need to sneak out! Where is the man I fell in love with? Ever since we've gotten here you've kept me in a box!"

"And ever since we got here, *you've* made it hard for me to take care of you!" He violently waved his finger in her face.

"This doesn't feel like a marriage. This is some type of ownership. Quinn and Pandora built empires with their husbands. We don't do anything togeth—"

"Quinn and Pandora also have law degrees and Ph.D.'s. Their husbands must be proud of them!" He sneered, "meanwhile, *my* dumb as a doorknob immature wife can't even do what God designed her body to do…carry a *baby*!"

Eden took a few steps back. Without warning, she drew back her neck and spit in his face. "Go to hell!" She screamed.

Travis grabbed her by her neck and tried to choke the life out of her. She could see the flames etched in his eyes.

"Are you crazy?" He grabbed her hair with his other hand, nearly ripping her edges out at the root. "It's about time you learned some respect!" Travis released his grip and backhanded her across the face. Eden fell onto the arm of the recliner nearby.

Before she could feel the sting of the first hit, Travis hovered over her body and slapped her once more. Blood flew out of her mouth as she fell to the floor.

Eden kicked and screamed, as Travis dragged her across the carpet by her hair. She held tightly to his wrist, digging her nails into his skin. Travis raised his foot and drove it into her chest as hard as he could, forcing her to release her hands. His face was distorted into a dangerous rage. He was transforming into the devil, right before her very eyes.

Eden screamed in agony, begging him to stop. He stomped her again, just before grabbing her by the shirt and tossing her across the room like a rag doll.

When Eden spotted the front door within arm's reach. She opened it as fast as she could and crawled out of the house. Travis sprinted behind her and grabbed her by the hair just as she reached the front lawn. It didn't matter if they were outside, he continued his brutal beating.

Ruby cringed at the horrible sight, turning to face her daughter. "Remember all that good loving he gave you in my bed, that had you singing Drunk in Love by Beyonce? Ruby belted out a laugh, "sing it now."

"I'm glad you think this is funny?" Eden lowered her head. Watching the man she loved beat her down was worse than the beating itself.

"What else can you do in a situation like this? Especially after making so many enemies. I can't tell who smacked you around worse, Anna or Travis," Ruby sighed.

"This wouldn't have happened if I didn't spit at him.

"Honey, before you even said *I do*, it had already happened. Many times, however, the woman in the abusive relationship is too far in to get out. By the time she realizes she's in trouble, he's isolated her from her family and taken financial control of everything, leaving her completely dependent on him."

"None of these signs warned me of an abusive relationship, mom. Call me crazy, but I still felt like I had control. Yes, he had a bit of a temper, but so did I."

"You sure did…and look at him beating it out of you," Ruby pointed to the vision in front of them. "When are you going to stop with the excuses and understand what I'm trying to show you?"

"I don't need you to show me *now*," Eden hissed, "I needed you to show me *then*. I needed you to come down from whatever high horse you were on and show me how messed up I was. I loved Travis, and for about two seconds, I got to know what being a happily married woman felt like," tears flushed from Eden's face. "Quinn, Pandora and I, we had plans. While theirs played out like the fairy tale they imagined, I ended up in a horror film. I get it, I understand. I shouldn't have been so naïve, but I wanted my fairy tale too."

Eden's voice lost power as she spoke. Her pride finally crumbled to pieces in front of her mother.

"Well, your two minutes of fame are up and the clock is striking twelve, Cinderella. It's time to run away from the castle."

Eighteen

Eden felt herself being lifted off the ground and tossed over Travis's shoulder. Pain ripped through her body from places she never knew existed. Travis walked into the house and up the stairs, gently placing Eden face up on the bed.

Gripping her head, Eden screamed. Her head pounded like a bass drum and her ears wouldn't stop ringing. She tried to pry open her eyes but only managed to get a squinted view through her swollen lids.

"Baby, why do you make me act this way?" Travis paced the floor.

Eden could see him pacing back and forth with his hand planted on his waist. She wanted to spit at him again, but she knew she'd lose her life if he threw another blow.

"Why do you have to disrespect me so much? Why can't you just let me love you?" Travis got up and rushed into the master bathroom. He ran warm water in their Jacuzzi tub before searching around for Eden's favorite scented candles.

Eden sat up in the bed just as a wave of dizziness sent her falling forward onto her knees. The room spun, as nausea swirled around the pit of her stomach. Before she knew it, she was vomiting all over herself and their beautiful, white carpet. The more she gagged, the more vomit flew from her mouth like hot lava.

When Travis heard Eden choking, he dropped the glass candles. They crashed to the tiled floor, glass shattering to tiny pieces. He grabbed a towel from the hook and ran to help her.

"Eden!" He shrieked, his voice filled with terror. "Baby, let me help you."

Eden could hear his footsteps getting closer. She tried getting up quickly to get away from him, but her legs wouldn't work.

Travis dropped to his knees beside her, patting her back in an attempt to help her stop throwing up and catch her breath. As Eden finished heaving out the remaining remnants, she yanked away from his touch and crawled to the other side of the bedroom like her life depended on it. She found the nearest corner and curled her body up in it.

Travis stood up and followed her. "Eden let's talk. I'm sorry," he sat down on the floor in front of her. When he reached out to touch her, Eden flinched, extending her arms out to shield herself from him.

"Leave me alone, *please*," she managed to speak through her sore, swollen lips.

"I'm not gonna hurt you, I promise." As he wrapped his arm around her, against her will, Eden's entire body trembled under his touch. There were no words to describe her fear of her husband. Blood trickled down her nose from the impact of having her face slammed into the concrete.

"I'm sorry, Eden," he repeated. "I love you...I swear I love you with all my heart," Travis held on to her fragile body, using his hand to caress her bruised cheek. He rocked her in his arms like a baby as he began to cry.

Eden was all too familiar with the song he was singing. So much, she even knew the lyrics. She didn't know if she believed him anymore, but she was scared for her life to go against him. In that moment, she made up her mind that life would be much easier, and situations like these could be avoided if she stopped fighting and just followed his directions.

As her hearing faded in and out, Travis lifted her up from the floor and carried her into the bathroom, asking her questions about loving him and making their marriage work. She couldn't make out what he was saying, but she obliged and nodded anyway as he gently removed her clothing and placed her in the bathtub...

A few weeks had gone by. Travis somehow managed to make up for the damage he'd done. He opened Eden her own bank account and placed half of their money in it. He purchased her a Mercedes to match his own, along with the freedom to come and go as she pleased. He still didn't want her going to school or work, but he did promise her that she could go back or find a job after the New Year.

Travis took all the parental settings off Eden's phone and gave her breathing room to make her own choices. Since her bruises were still very noticeable, he couldn't take her out on dates or to mingle with any of Jade's family or his friends. However, he cooked her five-star meals, spent time holding her in his arms, bathing her, and taking on all of the chores while her body and soul recovered. He found a local nine to five job at a welding company with a good salary and benefits. Each day when Travis got in from work, they would eat dinner, he would wash the dishes, and at night, they'd fall asleep talking about their future and when the time would be right for them to try for another baby.

Once Eden's face healed up properly, she spent most of her days with Jade and her mother or riding around getting familiar with her new town. Even though all was well physically, Eden had a hard time forgetting the horrible beating she took at the hands of her husband. The dreadful memory replayed in her mind every single night to the point where it gave her nightmares. She'd wake up in his arms screaming. Her anxiety attacks were at an all-time high. Eden ended up needing her medication again…double doses of it.

Travis didn't feel comfortable scheduling any type of doctor's appointments until the bruises on her back and stomach cleared up, so he bought Xanax from local drug dealers. Other than her nightmares and random attacks, everything had gotten back to normal between them…well, *their* normal anyway.

Eden was sitting so high on cloud nine, she almost forgot about Travis' birthday. After running to the supermarket and craft store, she rushed home to make him a three-course meal. She prepared an appetizer of homemade spinach dip with nachos, a delicious entree of rib-eye steak, lobster, rice pilaf, steamed broccoli, and cheddar biscuits from scratch. For dessert, she baked him a red velvet cake complete with her mother's homemade icing. Eden hand-folded blue and silver napkins she purchased from the craft store, into hearts. She spent almost two hours setting the table with China dipped in his favorite color; silver. Once the food was done, she placed it into matching silver bowls in the center of the table. She looked at her watch and after realizing it was past five o clock, she went upstairs to change her clothes. Travis usually got in from work around five forty-five, so she had plenty of time to adorn herself for him.

Eden took a quick shower and spiced herself up with all the fragrances he loved to smell on her. She put on a form-fitting, black cocktail dress that exposed her cleavage just the way he loved to see her in private. She put her hair in a simple bun, and diamond studs in her ears before she walked back downstairs. Eden dimmed all the lights in the house, setting the mood with candles while Luther Vandross played softly in the background.

By the time she sat down at the table, it was six-fifteen and there was no sign of her husband. He hadn't called or texted saying he would be late.

"That's weird. Maybe traffic is backed up," she said aloud, playing around on her phone. After twenty more minutes of sitting at the dinner table alone, she got up and placed covers over the food, and stuck the lobster into the fridge so it wouldn't spoil. Part of her wanted to call him, but Travis hated to feel like he was being tracked. She wanted this night to be special, so she decided against it. Walking into the living room, she grabbed her kindle from the coffee table and sat down on the sofa to finish up another chapter of *Life and Favor* by one of her favorite authors, V.M. Jackson. After a few pages, fatigue kicked in, and Eden drifted off to sleep.

The sound of the door opening and closing startled her out of her sleep. She removed the kindle that had fallen to her chest and placed it on the seat beside her. Checking her watch, her eyes bulged when she saw that it was after eleven o'clock.

She walked into the kitchen as Travis walked in through the kitchen door, turning on all the kitchen lights.

"Why are all the lights so dim?" He asked with an attitude.

"Hey," Eden walked into the kitchen entrance looking confused.

"Where are you going dressed like *that*?" He asked, opening the refrigerator door and pulling out a bottle of water.

"H…happy birthday," she replied, hesitantly, "I cooked for you and got all dressed up. I wanted to surprise you."

Travis glanced at the fully decorated dining table and then back at Eden. "Oh, thanks," he replied, dryly. "I was actually gonna go out with the boys tonight, but I'll eat real quick." He took his work jacket off and sat down at the table.

"It's after eleven o'clock, why are you so late getting in?" She took a seat across from him.

"Why are you questioning me about why I'm late? Do you not trust me or something?"

"Of course I trust you," she nodded, staring into his eyes, "you're usually never *this* late, though. I wanted to know what took so long, that's all."

"I had a late job, sorry. I didn't know you were clocking me," Travis picked up the bowl of rice, slamming his spoon into it.

"Travis, I wasn't clocking you, I'm sorry. I just wanted to do something special for you to show my appreciation," she smiled, reaching for the bowl of broccoli before standing up to put it in the microwave.

"Here, let me microwave the rice for you."

"So now you're telling me how to eat my food too?" He hissed, tossing the bowl down on the table.

"No," she scrunched up her face, "it's just been sitting for hours so I thought you'd want it warm. Look, let's just have a good evening, okay? I have a whole night planned out, maybe you can meet up with your friends tomorrow. I really wanna do—"

Travis angrily slid his chair out from under the table and sprung to his feet.

"Where are you going?"

Travis picked up a plate and threw it in her direction.

Eden moved out of the way, just as it shattered against the microwave door.

"I'm sick of you trying to control me!" He shouted, "you're not my mother!"

"Baby, what are you talking about?" She looked confused. "I'm not trying to control you."

He picked up another plate and threw it across the room, watching it break against the fridge. He then grabbed every bowl of food from the table and tossed it at Eden like he was a pitcher in the World Series.

Eden dropped the bowl of broccoli, dodging the bowls like they were bullets. She watched as Travis reached for the wine glasses. Dropping to her knees, Eden hid behind their oversized kitchen island.

Travis threw knives, forks—hell, he would've thrown the entire table if he had the strength to do it.

When the coast was clear, Eden ran into the living room to get away from him.

Storming behind her, Travis looked like Satan in all of his splendor. "You are not the boss of me, I'm the boss of you!" He yelled at the top of his lungs.

Eden turned to him. She wanted to look him in his eyes so he could see that she was sincere and didn't mean any harm, but she couldn't take her eyes off his balled-up fist. The closer he walked to her, the tighter his fist seemed to get.

"Please don't get mad. You hung out with your friends last night, I thought this night would be reserved for me, that's all," she pleaded with him.

"You know what?" Travis adjusted his posture, "I'm not gonna get mad. I'm not gonna let you get me riled up. I'm just gonna leave. I'm gonna go hang out with my boys," he confirmed, calmly walking back into the kitchen as if nothing happened.

"Listen, just forget what I said, ok? Don't leave," She cried, walking behind him as he grabbed his jacket off the kitchen chair and put it on. Just as he opened the door to storm out, he grabbed an envelope off of the counter with his name on it. It was full of slips of paper Eden had made for him for his birthday. Each slip contained a reason why she loved him, and she spent an hour making it. She cut out each slip carefully, typing up the reasons. She even colored an elephant made of heart-shaped cutouts taped to the front.

"Baby, *please* don't leave, I don't wanna be alone," she followed him out the door and into the driveway.

"You're such an *idiot*. I can never have a good time with you," Travis pressed the unlock button on his keypad.

"I'm sorry, Travis," she pleaded. She tried to embrace him, but he kept pushing her away like she was some kind of beggar pleading for his riches.

"That's *exactly* why Jackson married Pandora, you're so clingy and annoying." Before he got into his car, he ripped open the envelope Eden had made him. Grabbing a handful of slips, he took one glance before ripping them into pieces.

She numbly watched her feelings for him flutter to the ground. Travis got into his car, backed out of the driveway, and pulled off, blasting his music. Eden watched him disappear around the corner. She stood there in a state of shock and heartbreak.

What did she do so wrong that would cause him to change up like that? Did he not like her dress? Did someone at work upset him? She didn't understand his sudden erratic behavior shift. While Eden always believed that there was good in everyone, she didn't realize that some people were just plain *evil*.

Nineteen

Love is blind

Tears silently fell from Eden's face as she walked at a snail's pace back into her home. She tried her best to mentally process what had just unfolded, but she couldn't. After closing her back door, she turned to face the catastrophe all over their once beautiful kitchen. Broken dishes littered the floor, there was silverware scattered about, and food splattered all over the cabinets and appliances. Eden looked around her kitchen shaking her head, trying to understand what she did wrong. She tried so hard to make things right for Travis. She did everything he required of her in an attempt to keep him happy, but his behavior was beginning to become unpredictable. One minute he loved her, the next, she disgusted him. She had no idea how to fix it and was starting to feel it really wasn't worth trying.

Eden felt like over the years Travis had lost so much and developed major trust issues. She so desperately wanted to be the one to save him like he did with her, but her efforts at trying seemed to all be in vain.

Too drained to clean up the mess in the kitchen, Eden walked into the living room and sat down on the couch. She wanted to finish some more of her book, but her thoughts wouldn't stop spinning long enough for her to concentrate. Flopping down on the sofa, she turned on the television instead. The second the screen loaded, Eden saw a scene from the nightly news that displayed Pandora, destroying her competition to win yet another case. Eden smiled, watching the friend she once knew strutting around the courtroom like she owned it.

Pandora was competent and ruthless, showing no pity or compassion for *anyone* standing in the way of her victory. A slow trickle of tears fell from Eden's face, remembering all of the good times they shared as friends. The world only saw the merciless side of Pandora, but Eden knew *her*. Without a thought, she picked up her cellphone to dial Pandora's number. She didn't have it saved in her new phone, but that was alright, she knew her number by heart. Just as she got ready to press the call button, grief stopped her. Eden remembered the heartbroken expression on Pandora's face the night she bailed her out of jail. She remembered the hurt in her eyes after she found out Eden had stolen from her, seduced her brother into adultery, and was the culprit behind her car getting destroyed.

"What could I possibly say to Pandora after that? *I'm sorry*?" Eden shrugged. Even after all the months that passed, surely it wouldn't mean anything. Eden tossed her phone on the other side of the couch and continued watching her on the news. After everything Pandora had gone through in her life, she was still bold, beautiful and had risen to the top.

If God could bless such a menace like Anna, why didn't he do the same thing for me? Eden thought back on all the wrong she had done, and she felt *terrible*. Getting up from the sofa, she went upstairs into her bedroom and stood in front of the mirror. Strangely enough, she couldn't even recognize her own reflection. What had become of her identity? Her entire world unraveled, and it was the darkest, loneliest feeling she'd *ever* encountered.

"Come back, Eden," she said to herself, "I know you still exist. Come back, please." Sighing deeply, she walked into her bathroom and popped two Xanax from her medicine cabinet, washed her face and changed into her oversized nightgown. At least she'd get a peaceful night to sleep it away for a few hours.

Just when she dozed off, the front door swung open. Travis's slurred profanity bounced through the hallway. Eden sighed, rolling her eyes as hard as she could. The peaceful night she'd prepared for was over...especially since Travis had been drinking. She listened to him stagger toward the stairs, knocking things over along the way. She didn't even bother to get up and turn the hall light on to help him. Just before he stumbled into the bedroom, Eden rolled on her stomach and turned her head in the opposite direction so he would think she was asleep.

"Baby," Travis whispered loudly, neglecting to take off his clothes as he fell into the bed beside her.

"Eden, wake up sweetheart, I wanna talk to you," he slurred, filling the bedroom with the stench of vodka and bad breath. Eden didn't move a muscle. She hated dealing with the drunk and disorderly and had nothing to say to his trifling behind after the stunt he pulled at dinner. She kept her head turned away, in hopes that he would just pass out. Moments later, she felt her hair being pushed from her face, and his sloppy tongue raking down the side of her neck.

"Wake up baby," he kissed her, easing his hands up the back of her thigh, "let me talk to you."

"*Travis*," Eden pushed his hand away. "It's four in the morning. I'm sleepy."

"Baby, I'm *so* sorry for the way I acted earlier. I couldn't stop thinking about you while I was out. I had to come home and touch you," he rubbed one hand down her backside, and the other through her hair.

"Not right now. Later, I promise."

Ignoring her request, Travis turned Eden over and straddled her body. He put his hands around her neck and lowered himself to kiss her. Eden could feel the rough stubble on his chin from not shaving, cutting at her skin.

"Travis, *come on*, stop it," Eden used her hands to pry his fingers from around her neck, wiggling him off of her.

"You listen to *me*," he slapped her hands away, "I'll kill you if you ever deny me my rights as your husband," he tightened his grip even more, roughly shaking Eden by her neck. You hear me?"

She quickly nodded.

Travis stood up, snatched her out of the bed with one hand, and punched her in the stomach with the other. The immediate pain sent her plummeting to her knees. She could hardly breathe. Travis pulled down his pants and exposed himself.

"If I don't come in thirty seconds, I will shove my dick so far down your throat, it'll come out through your behind," he glared at her, angry and disoriented.

Eden was *mortified*, but she quickly obeyed with no questions asked. Wrapping her hands around his manhood, she leaned in. When she got close enough, Eden noticed smudges of red lipstick ringing around the head of it.

*You've gotta be kidding me…*were the only words that came to her mind. In that moment, what was left of Eden's heart had dropped into the pit of her already sore stomach. *The nerve of him,* she sneered. After everything she'd sacrificed and taken from him, he had the audacity to be *unfaithful*? A delirious rage spread through her mind like a wildfire. She had given up everything she owned and suffered for her marriage, yet *this* is how he repaid her?

Eden glared at his penis, contemplating whether or not she should bite it off and shove it down *his* throat until it fell out of *his* behind. The longer she neglected his shaft, the limper it became until it shriveled up in her grasp.

Wham! A rock-hard fist connected with her left eye, causing stars to appear in her vision. Eden immediately fell to the floor.

"You can't even keep me turned on! My dick doesn't even want you anymore!"

Crack! A size fourteen Ugg boot came soaring down on her rib cage. The pain nearly knocked her out cold. Travis jumped on Eden, raining down blows like a thunderstorm.

The rage in his eyes was so chilling, Eden thought Travis was getting ready to kill her. *God, if this is it, please don't let me suffer,* she thought.

After dragging her across the room, he picked her up and threw her against the wall. Eden screamed in pain as she felt her spine connect with the doorpost. The minute she hit the carpet, she heard a bone-chilling crack, just before a surge of pain filled her wrist.

Two hours later...

Eden sat upright on top of the hospital bed of the Illinois Emergency Room feeling like she was in a heavy, black cloud. She couldn't see or hear; there was just a heaviness throughout her entire body. As she slowly came to, she felt a gentle hand caressing her swollen jaw.

"It's okay Eden, I've got you," Travis's soft voice echoed through her ear canal, bringing her hearing back into fruition.

"They put a cast on your broken wrist," he gently

touched the hard shell on her left arm, "they were getting ready to give you a red one, but I made them give you pink, because I know that's your favorite color."

Suddenly, all types of noises filled the room. Machines sounded, hard soles clacked against the floor, and random voices flooded her hearing like a traffic pile up. Her mind began to register where she was, and her memory traced back to how she got there. She flinched a little as Travis tried to wipe her tears away.

Unlike earlier, his touch was soft and subtle. She guessed maybe the hulk had turned back into Bruce Banner.

No. She thought. *Hit me like you did in our bedroom. Beat me down in this hospital so everyone can see the monster you really are!* Her thoughts ran wildly with the courage her mouth dared not let slip out.

Eden struggled to prop her body upright. Travis offered his assistance, handling her like a fragile package.

"Baby, you know I love you right?" Travis kissed her cheek, using a wet cloth to dry the clotted blood off of her eyebrow. The same routine began yet again as he tried to clean up the mess he'd made of her body. He smiled at her like the world's greatest husband. Eden was so disgusted she wanted to spit.

I can't keep doing this with him.

Leaning into her, Travis flooded her ear with constant reminders of how intensely good things were when they first met, but for each good encounter, Eden noted a bad one. By the time he was done his list, hers still had a long way to go. The bad certainly outweighed the good.

"Hi, Mrs. Rutherford," a female doctor entered the room. "How's that wrist doing?"

"It still hurts a lot," Eden forced the words out.

"Well, I did give you some Percocet. It should kick in soon. Now, what did you say happened again?"

"She fell off the porch," Travis answered before Eden could even formulate any lies in her head.

"Wow," the doctor nodded her head, "I'm so sorry to hear that. Eden, do you mind removing your gown so I can take a look at your other extremities? I want to make sure nothing else is broken."

"Um...O-okay," Eden replied, lowering her gaze to the floor.

Travis helped her undress and covered her up with the white paper sheet the doctor had given her. The doctor examined Eden's body from head to toe, leaving no stone unturned. She kept quiet the entire time, but Eden knew she saw the obvious bruises all over her body. Hell, even Stevie Wonder could see them.

"All of this happened from falling from a porch?" The doctor winced.

"We have some very high steps. If someone falls from it, it can do some pretty bad damage," Travis confirmed.

"I see. What about all of these old, yellow

bruises right here?" The doctor softly touched the discolored areas, "did you fall off the porch last week, and the week before that too, Mrs. Rutherford?"

Travis cut his eyes at Eden. All she could do was hold her head down in shame, and nod her head, yes.

"Well, other than that wrist, nothing else appears to be broken," the doctor helped her up. She looked Eden directly in her eyes for a few seconds, before slightly shaking her head. "Here are your discharge papers. You can sign right here at the bottom."

Grabbing her clipboard, the doctor gave Eden a pen and watched her sign the form. "You two have a *safe* night," she glanced at Travis, then back at Eden, "if you feel faint or dizzy, of course, come back and see me, alright?"

Eden forced a smile as Travis helped her off the bed. "Thank you."

As they exited the ER, Eden walked two steps behind Travis, leaving him enough room to lead. She didn't want him to think for a second that she was trying to control things.

"Eden, you know I care about you, right?"

"Yup."

"And I only want the best for you."

"Uh-huh…," she said without making eye contact.

"I see now that I have a problem, and I'm gonna get help. I don't want to keep hurting you." Reaching for her hand, he gently pulled her up to his chest and planted a kiss on her swollen cheek. "I promise."

"Great…" she said in a low tone.

As they reached their car, Eden walked over to the passenger side and stepped to the right, allowing him to open her door.

Anything to feel like a man…I guess, she watched him reach for the door handle. Once she was securely inside, Travis hurried around to the driver's side and hopped in.

"1…2…3…4….5," Eden counted the seconds in her head before reaching over to adjust her seatbelt, careful not to move too quickly and let Travis think she was trying to rush him.

Travis started the car and pulled off, turning on a gospel station.

Gospel? Really? Eden discreetly shook her head, listening to him thank God for life, health, strength and his beautiful wife. Meanwhile, she sat back in the seat wrapped in pain trying to rid herself of the self-pity, loathing, held back tears, and urges of suicide. She'd never felt so low in her life, and this gospel music was only boosting her pain. No way could there be a God, at least not the one she learned about. The God she knew wouldn't let her suffer like this. The God she knew promised to never leave her nor forsake her. She needed him, and he was nowhere to be found.

Twenty minutes later, Travis pulled up in their driveway. Eden sat with her hands folded, waiting patiently for him to finish checking his phone before getting out to open her door. Staying in her lane, she allowed her *husband*, her *king*, her *protector*, to escort her out of her chariot and walk her into the sunset…or over a cliff. Whichever would release her from her misery the fastest.

Travis unlocked the front door and ushered Eden to go inside. She quickly walked into the living room and pulled the contents from the bag out that the nurse had given her. Stuffed between her discharge papers and her pain medicine prescription, was a pamphlet for Domestic Abuse.

Are you afraid of your partner? Has your partner ever hurt you? Do you constantly worry about your partner's mood? Call the National Domestic Abuse Hotline.

Eden stared at the pamphlet in her hands. Sadly, she could answer yes to all the questions listed. A tear fell from her cheek, allowing her conscious to answer her. In the past, Eden would often wonder how her own mother stayed in an abusive marriage for fifteen years. From the very first day she met Travis, all the precise, psychological games he played had brainwashed her. He made it so easy to fall in love with him, carelessly ignoring the red flags.

Before she could wipe the tears from her face, Travis snatched the pamphlet from her hands and shoved her body into the flat-screen television, mounted on the wall.

"So, you're in an abusive relationship? Is that

what this is?" Travis hovered over her with deadly eyes.

"No, baby. It's not. I just— this was in my bag. I—"

"Whatever. I saw the faces you were giving that doctor. You're trying to bring drama into my already complicated life."

"No, Travis, I swear."

"You're gonna leave me now, huh?"

Eden didn't respond.

Travis grabbed her by her hair and threw her onto the ground. With all of his might, he dragged her through the living room, into the kitchen, and out the side door, into the backyard. Eden thought every strand of hair on her head would be ripped out of her scalp. He dragged her down the cement steps, skinning her back raw along the way.

"Since you're in an abusive relationship, stay away from me. You sleep outside in the cold with the animals." Travis threw the pamphlet in her face and turned to walk back into the house.

Eden heard the backdoor lock and watched the kitchen lights go out. She wanted to get up and move, but her back was on fire. She literally had no fight left in her. Covering her face with her hands, she laid on the backyard grass in a fetal position, cupped her face into her hands, and cried herself to sleep.

Twenty

"On time God"

Tiny droplets of rain burst against Eden's face, awakening her from her uncomfortable slumber atop the dewy grass. As more droplets fell, she squinted her eyes, trying to ward them off. The more conscious she became, the higher her pain scale rose. Her broken wrist ached badly, and she had a splitting headache. Eden opened her eyes to the gloomy, mid-morning sky as the grey clouds hovered over her. Trees moved gently in the breeze, and the wind rustled the crunching leaves around her. She had no idea what time it was, but judging from the sun hiding in the clouds, it had to be approaching noon.

Eden struggled to stand up, wiping the wet grass from her jeans as best as she could. The agony traumatizing her body felt endless…it even hurt to breathe. Suddenly, it was as if the sky cracked in two because the rain began to fall relentlessly. Thunder rumbled over her head and bolts of lightning periodically flashed. With her hands shielding her face, Eden staggered to the back door looking like a wide-eyed psychopath. She felt like death, and truth be told, dying seemed like a much better option than her reality. Approaching the back door, she was almost afraid to knock, but as the lightning and thunder magnified, she took her chances and knocked on the door anyway. Eden crossed her arms, shivering from the cold air hitting her wet body.

"*Come on*, Travis. Open the door," she pleaded in a low tone. She wished so badly she could be like Dorothy in The Wizard of Oz. She would've given away one of her limbs to be back in Virginia right now. If Travis would've thrown her wallet out with her last night, maybe she would have. She put her fist up to the door to knock again, but the sound of the front lock unlocking stopped her. The back floodlights turned on, and Eden watched in terror as the door opened. Her heart rate and pulse elevated, trying to figure out what kind of mood Dr. Jekyl and Mr. Hyde would be in today.

Travis peered out through red, puffy, sad eyes. He almost looked like he had been crying all night. "Hey," he spoke softly, staring at Eden as if he felt sorry for her.

"Can...I come in?" She hesitated, "It's- it's raining pretty hard, and—"

Travis pulled Eden into the house, her body flinching from the sudden jolt of pain. Tears fell from his face as he wrapped his wife in his arms and started to cry. "Eden, don't leave me, *please,*" he begged, "I'm sorry for all of this, but don't leave."

Eden sighed. She wasn't in the mood to listen to his pathetic pleas again. She'd already made up her mind that the second she got her wallet, and a clear getaway, she was leaving.

"I just want to take a bath, grab some pain medicine, and lie down on something *comfortable*," she told him.

"Baby listen to me, okay? I've been praying to God all night, and I feel extremely convicted." Travis held her hands and looked at her. "I've said this to you a million times, but I'm *sorry*. Please believe me."

Hell no she didn't believe his *sorry* behind. In that moment, she wished the lightning outside would've torn the roof off her kitchen and struck him to death for his repetitive lies. *Enough was enough.*

"I accept your apology," she lied, "but I don't feel good. I just want to go to bed. Is that okay?"

"Eden, I'm sick," Travis got down on his knees in front of her, looking like a lost puppy. "The way I treat you isn't healthy, and it took me until *now* to realize it. The minute I saw that pamphlet in your hands last night, my mind snapped, but it was also a revelation. This whole time I'm blaming you—"

"Travis...please," she looked down at him. "Right now, I just want to clean myself up and lie down...*Please.*"

A tear fell from Eden's black eye and rolled down her bruised cheek. Travis wiped it away before standing up in front of her.

"Eden, I have a problem. I'm accepting it. *I need help*," his voice shook, "and I'm gonna get help. As a man with so much pride, it's embarrassing to be in such a vulnerable state in front of you, but I'll do anything not to lose you."

His pleading soul bore into her eyes to the point where Eden could feel his sincerity and partly believed him. She didn't know how to react, or what to say in return. Her intuition told her to head for the nearest exit, and she had every intention of doing so. But no matter what, Travis *did* need professional help. As his wife, she considered it her duty to be sure that he got it.

"Okay," she whispered softly.

Later that afternoon, Eden agreed to a night out with her husband. He told her he wanted to apologize the correct way for his actions. Lunch at *The Fortune Cookie,* an upscale restaurant, was a start. Although her body disagreed, she did what she could to keep the peace. *It's only dinner*, she coached herself.

Travis pulled up to the restaurant's parking lot. Originally, he planned to let the valet park his car like everyone else, but he wanted to make sure Eden's makeup properly covered her bruises.

"How do you feel, baby?" Travis looked over at her, "because if you don't feel up to it, we can just go back home and order in."

"No, it's fine," Eden pulled down the overhead mirror to check her makeup, "we're here now."

"Okay, but if your wrist or anything starts bothering you, you'll let me know so I can get you home?"

"Yes," she nodded, "I can do that."

Travis got out of the car and walked around to the passenger side to help Eden out. The Percocet she took did nothing for her back or wrist, but she played off the pain and slid her arm into Travis's as they made their way into the restaurant.

Travis wore black slacks, a collared dress shirt, and a long black pea coat. Eden complimented him with a calf-length black dress, black pumps, and a matching trench coat. They walked into the place arm in arm, fitting in perfectly with the rest of the crowd.

"Reservations for Rutherford," Travis smiled, approaching the front desk.

"Oh yes, absolutely, Mr. Rutherford," the receptionist marked his name from her clipboard, "someone will be right in to seat you in just a second."

"Awesome, thanks," he nodded.

"This place is amazing," Eden stared in awe at the grand fountain, stretching from the ceiling to the floor. It sparkled like a frozen waterfall in the center of the pathway. Glass chandeliers, rose bouquets, and a floor covered with velvet were just a few parts of the eye-catching decor.

"I know, isn't it?" Travis smiled, wrapping his arms around Eden's waist from behind.

Even though she didn't welcome his touch, she wasn't going to act out in such a fancy place. Clearing her throat, she continued with their minor conversation. "You been here before?"

Travis shook his head. "No, I saw it online and immediately called to reserve. It actually looks better in person. I thought this would impress you."

"Well you *definitely* impressed me," she replied.

Travis kissed her softly on the cheek.

"Mr. Rutherford?" A waitress walked up to them, dressed in a white pantsuit.

"That's us," Travis looked at her.

"Right this way, sir," she smiled.

Travis held Eden's hand and they followed the woman into the extra-large dining area. It was starkly modern with fancy wall art, and cozy tables dressed in pristine table linen dotted the room with white leather chairs accompanying them. Soft music danced in their ears and dimly lit lighting accented the beautiful atmosphere. The waitress escorted them to a table, pulling out both of their chairs.

"Here you are. Your host will be with you shortly."

"Thank you," Travis said as the woman walked away. He took his coat off and helped Eden remove hers. He helped her into the chair, pulling it up to the table, before taking his seat. "I checked out the menu before we got here. I know you don't eat pork or beef, so I made sure they had a good selection of chicken and fish."

Eden looked up at him and smiled, masking the truth. She *did* eat pork, and she *loved* beef. It was him who made her stay away from it because he said it would clog her arteries. Maybe he forgot.

"Welcome!" Their server announced as she approached the table. "My name is Amy. Can I start you both off with a glass of wine?"

Eden reached for her menu. Before she could grab it, Travis spoke up.

"Amy, my wife and I are ready to order."

"Oh, that was fast," Amy smiled, pulling out a white piece of paper and pen from her pocket. "What can I get for you two?"

Eden's smile slowly faded listening to him order tonic waters, the nasty soup of the day, and an entrée full of food she didn't like.

"I think it's so sweet that you know your wife like the back of your hand," Amy smiled at Eden, "I wish my husband was like that."

Eden forced a smile. He sure did know her like the *back of his hand.* As the server walked away, Travis reached for his pocket to grab his ringing cellphone.

"Oh, baby, this is my job calling about the overtime I inquired about last month," Travis said, just before looking at his screen and answering.

Eden scanned the restaurant at all of the well-dressed couples, laughing amongst one another. Suddenly, she felt out-of-place. Everyone looked so happy and connected. As her eyes traveled from table to table, all of the women seemed to be head over heels in love with their significant others. They gawked at them through glossy eyes, held hands across the table, and ordered their *own* food. Their makeup was lightly spread throughout their faces, accenting their different types of beauty. Underneath hers were bruises and scars. She kept her left wrist under the table so she wouldn't draw attention to the big cast wrapped around it.

The more Eden's eyes danced around the different tables, her mind warred endlessly trying to figure out where she went wrong. She remembered moments where Travis *did* make her feel alive and limitless, before the first black eye he gave her and the first lie she had to tell about how she got it. It took everything in Eden not to burst out into tears at the table.

"I'm gonna use the ladies' room," she said quickly, trying not to blink.

Travis gave her a smile and a thumbs-up as he continued his phone call. Eden sprouted up from her chair and spun around to rush to the ladies' room. She halted in her tracks when a large-frame security guard blocked her.

It took her a second to realize what was going on. A few couples sitting at tables smiled in awe, grabbing their cameras in an attempt to get a picture of the couple shielded behind the guard.

"Pastor Bentley, can we have a picture?" One onlooker asked, getting up from his chair. He pulled out his phone, but the bodyguard stood in his way to block him.

"No personal pictures today. Please keep your distance," the guard replied.

Every muscle in Eden's body tensed up, as her widened eyes locked on Quinn and Andre. It was like looking into a mirror of her past, staring at a reflection of who she *used* to be. Chills traveled up and down Eden's spine watching Quinn beaming and waving at some of the onlookers. Oh, how she missed that smile in her life. Eden missed the old Eden, period. Her throat felt like it was closing in on her, as the realization of who she had become over the last six months was a hard pill to swallow. She was numb and empty. Her world had become a sad place. She wanted to turn around and run the other way but her legs felt cemented to the velvet carpet.

She watched the way Andre smiled at Quinn like he was the luckiest man alive. They held hands and proceed to turn in Eden's direction. Both of them accented each other, *beautifully*. There was something about the way they touched each other and stood together that intuitively made sense. They were like a walking work of art…a match made in heaven.

Eden tried her best to hold in her tears, but she couldn't help it as one escaped her eyes and rolled down her cheek. Just as Andre and Quinn turned to walk in Eden's direction, she quickly spun around to walk the other way. Andre's deep, baritone voice stopped her dead in her tracks.

"Eden?"

Twenty-One

Eden swallowed hard, wiping a tear from her cheek. She hesitated before turning around to face Andre. Travis looked up from his phone call and almost had a heart attack when he noticed Andre and Quinn.

"Hey...Andre," Eden said softly, trying to mask the emotion in her voice.

Quinn gasped, her eyes widening in disbelief. "Eden!"

Before Eden could open her mouth to answer, Quinn rushed over and nearly melted into her, gripping Eden into the warmest embrace she'd ever felt. Eden wanted to keep herself composed, but she couldn't. She wrapped her arms around Quinn and held on to her for dear life. Eden closed her eyes as another tear fell from her face onto Quinn's coat. It felt as if all the noise in the room mellowed out, and everyone else around them ceased to exist. The pain in her back seemed to fade away, and she suddenly felt safe and comfortable.

"Baby *girl*," Quinn could barely get the words out, loosening her grip. She stared at Eden through her own tear-filled eyes. "Where have you been? We've been looking all *over* for you. You changed your number, you moved...Joseph told us you got mar—"

"We did," Travis interrupted, cutting through their moment as he walked up and grabbed Eden's hand. "It's good to see you, Quinn," Travis smiled.

Quinn's eyes immediately locked onto Travis. If

looks could kill, that would have been the end of him.

"It's a pleasure," Quinn forced a brief, fake smile. "Pastor?" She called for her husband, "*this* is Travis, the one I told you about," Quinn never took her eyes off of Travis.

"Oh, hello Travis," Andre walked up to him with a straight face, extending out his large hand.

"How are you, Pastor Bentley?" Travis smiled, shaking Andre's hand, "I've heard a lot about you."

Andre's hand came crashing down on Travis's shoulder while his other hand shook Travis's, squeezing the life out of it.

"*Ditto*. I heard you mispronounced my wife's name," Andre glared at Travis, moving into him to keep people from seeing what he was doing. Biting his bottom lip, Andre tightened his grip, forcing Travis to close his eyes and cringe in pain. At any moment Travis swore the bones in his hand would crumble like dust.

"That was an accident," Travis grunted softly, "I'll be sure to get it right from now on." Beads of sweat protruded from his brow.

"If it happens again, I'll snap every bone in your body," Andre threatened in Travis's ear.

"It won't…" Travis writhed.

Andre smiled gracefully, letting Travis's hand go. "Praise the Lord," he winked.

Travis lowered his head, embarrassed. He wanted to kill Andre, but his six-foot basketball build was no match for Andre's six foot four, wrestler's physique. Putting his hands into his pockets, Travis moistened his lips and held in his anger.

"Are you guys just getting here? Let's catch up," Quinn broke through the tension, slightly smirking at

Travis's frustration.

Travis set off all kinds of alarms in her psyche. She didn't like him one bit and she was happy her husband made him sweat.

"Yeah," Eden's eyes lit up, "we—"

"We were just finishing up, actually," Travis chimed in. Eden cut her eyes at Travis, sensing his irritation. She quickly averted her gaze to the floor. "It was very nice running into you two, but we're gonna head out. We have some important business to attend to."

"Is there any way you can reschedule?" Quinn asked sweetly, "I'd really like to spend some time with Eden."

"I'm afraid not, we're running late," Travis answered coldly, turning to grab Eden's coat.

Quinn quickly noticed Eden's eyes cast downward and could sense her fearful energy. Travis put his coat on and stood behind Eden, opening her coat for her. Refusing to look up, Eden raised her arms to slide them in her sleeves.

"Honey, what happened to your arm?" Quinn gasped, looking at Eden's cast.

"I-I fell off a ladder a few weeks ago," Eden hesitated with a forced laugh, "you know how clumsy I can be."

"Super clumsy," Travis laughed boisterously, "she was on the ladder helping me paint the asphalt shingles on the roof She had the paintbrush in her left hand and the phone in the other. Next thing you know…BAM!"

"My goodness," Andre winced, "Glad all you broke was an arm."

Quinn furrowed and crossed her arms. She wasn't buying it. Eden was *far* from clumsy. Since she was a kid, she was often teased for being too *careful*. She was also afraid of heights, so it was extremely unlikely that Eden would be on somebody's roof. Quinn also knew that her friend was right-handed, so it made no sense that Eden would be using her left hand to paint.

"I'm so sorry you guys have to go. Eden, will you walk me to the ladies' room?" Quinn looked at Travis, "it'll just be a few minutes."

"We don't have a few—"

Andre put his arm around Travis and moved in closer. "Surely, you have thirty seconds," Andre laughed, "let the women get some time in or I'll never hear the end of it."

Travis laughed nervously, cutting his eyes at Eden. Quinn slid her arms into Eden's and walked toward the ladies' room.

"Hurry back, sweetheart," Travis muttered in a sweet, but subliminally threatening tone that sent immediate fear to Eden's heart.

The minute they got into the family bathroom, Quinn locked the door and spun around to see Eden's wide, fearful eyes.

"How about I just give you my number? He's ready to go, and—"

"Eden?" Quinn cut her off, "what's going on?" Quinn folded her arms and leaned against the door. Eden looked at Quinn with pleading, scared eyes that almost made Quinn's heart stop.

Eden blew out a sigh.

"You just fell off the face of the earth. That's not

like you," Quinn shook her head, "Anna and I searched *everywhere* in the system for you, and your number isn't listed. What's- going -*on*?"

Eden looked down at the floor to keep herself together. She wanted to open up and tell Quinn everything, but she couldn't find it in her heart to." Travis had such a hold on her. There she was…Quinn. Her way out. Yet, Eden couldn't speak.

Uncontrollable tears began running down Eden's face, as she wiped them away as fast as she could. Being face to face with Quinn did something to her. Her soul was crying out for help without her permission.

"Nothing's going on," Eden tried moving toward the door.

Quinn walked into her and stood in her face. "Eden…"

"Mannequin, I'm fine, I have to go," Eden replied through a shaky voice, as more tears plummeted down her face.

Quinn blocked her path a second time and Eden dodged it again. The more they tussled for the door, the weaker Eden became until finally, she couldn't contain herself. Eden burst into tears, nearly falling into Quinn's arms.

Quinn caught her, holding on to Eden as tight as she could. "Is he hurting you?" Quinn asked, shaking her head. She already knew the answer, but she knew Eden needed to admit it herself.

Without any more hesitation, Eden nodded her

head yes before she pressed her face into Quinn's chest and cried harder. Quinn could literally feel Eden's broken heart as she clung to her like a lifeline. She wanted to cry with her, but she was too angry and scorned. Quinn never had a hatred in her heart for anyone, but Travis had just made the list. In that pivotal moment, Quinn searched for the exact words to say, but all she really wanted to do is tell her, in no uncertain terms, *to get out.* Quinn had been in situations like these dozens of times with clients, but *neve*r with someone who meant so much to her. Holding Eden close to her, all she could say was, "I'm so sorry this is happening."

"Mannequin, help me," Eden let her go and looked into Quinn's eyes, "I feel so paralyzed. I'm afraid. I don't know how I got into this." As Eden wiped her eyes, her mascara smeared as well.

Quinn clutched her chest when she saw traces of a blackened eye and faded bruises on Eden's face. A tear rolled down Quinn's face. She was beyond crushed.

"I just wanted to fall in love. I didn't see any of this coming," Eden shook her head, "am I stupid?"

"No, of course you're not *stupid*," Quinn wiped away her tears and helped to dry Eden's as well. "At the start of any relationship, we all tend to blind ourselves to the faults and inconsistencies of our new partner. It's natural. We see them through rose-tinted spectacles, and all the attention- even jealousy, is flattering."

"Travis showered me with love…I *needed* that in my life and he gave it to me. Then, somehow, he took it back, along with my money, my sanity, and my self-respect. He took away my phone and cut off my communication with you guys. What's insane is that in all of this, I *still* love him. A big piece of me wants to leave, but a small piece of me remembers all of the good times and I want to stay, thinking he'll change."

"*Don't* fall for the trap of feeling that the good times are worth the bad, because as sure as night follows day, the bad times will, bit by bit become all there is."

Quinn's chilling response caused Eden to look directly into her eyes.

"I'm sure he has *plenty* of attractive elements to him, but all traps do," Quinn said, "you have to get away from him."

"How? I don't have anything left, Quinn. My phone, our house, my car, *everything* is in his name."

A hard knock at the door startled both of them.

"Eden, baby I need you to come on, we're twenty minutes late," Travis fussed. Eden and Quinn traded glances.

Quinn reached into her purse for her spare cellphone. "Listen, this is the phone I use for work. Take it, hide it, and keep it with you wherever you are. There's a locator inside of it that will tell me where you are. I'm *gonna* get you out of this before the day is over and you're coming back home," Quinn promised.

"I'm afraid he's gonna hit me again," Eden looked terrified, "he's already gonna be upset that I came in here to talk to you."

"Listen, I can walk out of this bathroom, cause a ruckus, and expose him. I can have the police called and I can get you away from him…but at this point, it would be your word against his. He hasn't attacked you in front of anyone, and I'm assuming you haven't reported him at all, so there's no record of it. He won't pay for *anything* he's done, and the police won't even lock him up. They'll grant you a restraining order and send him on his way," Quinn shook her head. She'd dealt with so many cases like these in her career, she knew the process like the back of her hand. "Take my phone and go. I'm gonna figure this out so that when we get you out of this, it's for good."

Eden took a deep breath and nodded. "Okay," she coached herself, "okay." She tucked the phone Quinn gave her safely into her bra, and turned the doorknob, being met with Travis's impatient face, and Andre standing beside him.

"I'm sorry," Eden looked terrified, "I'm ready now. I was—"

"It's fine," Travis tried his best to maintain his composure. He grabbed Eden by the hand, squeezing it. "Let's just go," he cut his eyes at Andre before rushing out of their view.

Quinn looked on, silently praying to God she'd made the right decision by letting Eden out of her sight. The entire time Eden went missing, deep down, she *knew* this was why. Quinn tried everything in her power to find Eden, but she felt guilty for not trying harder.

She'd seen so many battered women throughout her career, and now her best friend was one of them. Quinn walked out of the bathroom and stood in the corner by the phone booth, trying to take it all in.

Sensing her disheveled demeanor, Andre walked over to her. "Sweetheart, what's wrong?" he asked, "you know, you were right about that Travis guy. I don't like his energy at all—"

Quinn lost her composure, sliding to the ground with her hands covering her mouth. Andre's eyes widened in concern.

"Mannequin," he squatted in front of her, taking her into his arms to see what the problem was.

Twenty-Two

"Grenade" -Bruno Mars

During the drive home, Travis glared at the road the entire time. Gripping the steering wheel, he seethed in anger. He didn't say a word to Eden, but he didn't have to, she already knew she was in for it. As her thoughts swirled through her mind, the butterflies in her swirled in her stomach, making her nauseous. Would Quinn come to her rescue in time, or would this man officially succeed in beating her to death? Travis sped into the driveway, put the gear in park, turned the car off, and snatched his keys out of the ignition.

"Travis," she spoke gently, "can you—"

Ignoring her, Travis exited the car without the bother of opening her door. Instead, he walked up to the back door and searched for his keys. Eden softly shut her eyes, taking in a shallow breath. Reaching for the cellphone Quinn had given her, she typed in her home address, followed by a text message that read:

Quinn, he's angry and I'm scared. Please hurry.

Making sure the volume was on silent, she placed it back into her bra. Eden got out of the car and took her time walking up to the door. Travis unlocked the side door and opened it, stepping aside for Eden to walk in. Her foot barely made it through the entrance before her head went flying into the glass window connected to the door.

"I swear, you take me there every single time!

What the hell was that about?" Travis screamed at the top of his lungs, slamming the door behind him.

Eden didn't speak. Her voice was never any use anyway.

"Did you set me up?" A hard shove sent her crashing into the refrigerator, knocking the wind out of her.

"No!" Eden's eyes widened in fear.

"Shut up!" His rage-filled voice scared the life out of her. She winced, biting her lip, begging God to get her out of this mess as quickly as possible.

"That big giant ape looking pastor had the nerve to *embarrass* me in public like that?!" He circled the floor with his eyes closed, periodically punching the air, yelling out obscenities.

Eden had never seen him so angry.

"And you let him! You took pride in watching him trying to break my arm, didn't you?"

"Just stop it!" Eden yelled, "you talked all that crap about trying to change and it was *all* lies…just like I knew it was! You can knock the wind out of *me*, but you didn't have the balls to stand up to another man. How *dare* you treat me like this. All I've ever done was love you, this isn't fair," she hissed, finally letting out everything she'd held in for the last seven months. Eden had no idea where she mustered up the faith to stand up for herself, but she couldn't stop.

Travis pierced his eyes at her, glaring like he could burn a hole right through her soul. "What did you just say to me?"

Eden could see the rage building up inside of him, but she didn't care anymore. "Look at you. What *happened*? You told me you would never hurt me and you've done more damage to me than *anyone* in my life.

At this point, Travis's eyes were as black as a night sky. Eden could hear his heart thudding loudly. His fists were clutched so tightly that his fingernails had begun to cut into the palms of his hands. As he moved into her, Eden grabbed his hands without thinking about what she was doing.

"Let go of my hands, Eden," he threatened.

Staring at him, Eden held on to his hands for dear life, knowing there was no telling what he would do if she let him go.

"Get help, *please*," she pleaded with him, refusing to let go of his hands. They both struggled around the kitchen.

"Eden, let go of my hands!" He barked.

Eden was scared for her life, begging God to give her the strength to hold on. God must've missed the memo because before she knew it, Travis tore away from her grip and punched her in the face.

Eden fell into the wall just as another fist came crashing into her. Grabbing Eden by the throat, he threw her onto the kitchen floor and dragged her around like a mop as she kicked and screamed.

"You must've lost your mind. Maybe you need it beat back into you!" His foot came down onto her chest, silencing her screams.

*****

Pandora sat in her office with her feet propped on top of her desk, reading notes from a case she'd been working on. She'd been going over her notes all week and couldn't find any loopholes in the situation to get her client found not guilty, or at least a lesser charge. She was the queen of defending the indefensible, but this one seemed impossible.

The sound of her phone ringing on her desk broke through her concentration. Lowering her feet to the ground, she answered it. *"Joanna,"* she said politely.

"Anna, Detective Steed is here to see you. He says it's important," her secretary answered.

Pandora jerked her head back, looking at the phone to make sure she heard correctly.

Just as she went to respond, her office door opened, revealing a six-foot-four, almond mocha of a man. He had jet black waves, beautiful full lips, and a fire blazing stare. He stood in the doorway in all his glory, boldly staring at her.

"Sorry, Anna," the secretary rushed in behind him, "he brushed past security and ran up the stairs

"It's fine, thank you," Pandora hung the phone up, lifting her eyes to meet him.

"Miss me?" He leaned against the door with his hands in his pockets. Pandora stood up and leaned over her desk.

"You *do* know you're trespassing. I can have you arrested."

"Nonsense," he smiled, making his way to her. "I have a right to access any property that's open to the general public."

"Not all property owned by the government is accessible by the public. *My* office is one of them," she glared.

"It would make sense they'd give *you* more security," he laughed, "especially considering all the things I've heard about you this year."

"And what horse's mouth did you hear it from?" Pandora glowered, "the men that can't have me or the women that can't compete with me?"

"Ouch. You're still feisty, just like I like you," he walked around her desk, catching Pandora off guard with his blatant boldness.

Pandora stepped away from her chair. "Bruce, what do you want?" She asked, impatiently.

Moving into her personal space, Bruce backed her into the nearest corner, the things he wished he could do to her again lay in the pupils of his eyes.

"I was in the neighborhood, so I thought I'd drop by," he grinned, devilishly.

Bruce Steed was a detective in California. He and Pandora had known each other since elementary school. Years later, they reconnected after working on a case together. It wasn't long before the sexual tension built up between them, made its way out. One time was all it took, and Bruce was hooked like white on rice.

For over eight years, he dipped out on his wife to open Pandora's box. He'd fallen so in love with her he filed for divorce and tried leaving his wife so they could be together. By that time, Pandora was already caught up with Jackson.

When Bruce found out Pandora had gotten married, he lost it. He tracked her every move, hacking into her computers and cellphones to figure out her whereabouts. He had questions, and Pandora owed him answers that she refused to give. She had to heighten her security just to keep him away. Eventually, he got over it and went about his business. *Or so she thought.*

"Virginia isn't in your jurisdiction *or* your

neighborhood," she crossed her arms. "*What* do you want?"

"You know what I want," he gazed at her beauty. "Why did you do that to us?"

Pandora sighed, nudging him out of the way as she walked to a safer distance.

"Anna, seriously?" His head followed her, "I gave up everything for you. I disappointed my daughter and went through a nasty divorce...for you."

"And if good kitty cat can make you destroy your family, what would you have done to me when *another* woman threw hers in your face?" She pursed, "would you have done to me what you did to your wife?"

"Don't be stupid," he furrowed, "you and I both know that would've never happened. I can't believe you'd go out and get married on me."

Pandora stared back at Bruce with a straight face, keeping herself composed. She made a bold move to marry Jackson, b*ut she still missed Bruce.*

Her phone rang, shaking her out of her moment. *Saved by the bell.*

Walking over to it, she saw Quinn's name flashing on her screen. "Hi honey," she answered.

"Anna, there's a h*uge* problem," Quinn blurted into the phone.

"What's the matter?" Pandora furrowed.

"Andre and I are in Chicago at a retreat, and we saw Eden in the restaurant with her poor excuse of a husband."

"Wait, you *found* her?" Pandora clutched her chest.

"Anna,, she looks awful. He's abusing her to the

point of no return."

Pandora gawked as Quinn ran down the entire encounter. Her body shut down completely.

"I want to call the police, but I don't—"

"Don't!" Pandora warned, bellowing into the phone, "police aren't helpful in situations like this. I'm coming to where you are, I'll be on the next flight out. Don't do anything until I get there."

"The text she sent really scared me. We need to figure something out, *now*."

"Do you have an address?" Pandora rushed over to her closet for her coat and purse.

"55 Greenhouse Lane, Chicago Illinois."

"Got it. Text me the information to where you are. I'll be there as soon as I can," she hung up the phone and turned to Bruce. "I need a favor."

"Sure. I'd love to help the *trifling* woman that ruined my life," he rolled his eyes sarcastically. His reaction quickly faded, watching Pandora retrieve her Beretta from the drawer, stuffing it in her purse. "What's going on?"

Pandora strutted back over to her desk. "Can you get me a name and a background check of whoever lives there?" She jotted down the address Quinn had given her.

Without question, Bruce opened up a secured database on her computer to begin his search.

Pandora reached for her cellphone and dialed Jackson's number. "Hey, it's me," she walked back to the other side of her office, filling Jackson in on everything Quinn told her. One of Jackson's recent clients owned a slew of helicopters and private jets. She had him pull a few strings to get her a flight to Chicago within the next couple of hours.

"Great, thanks, I'll be home in twenty minutes," Pandora hung up the phone before blowing out a deep sigh. "We're coming, Eden," she whispered.

"Soo," Bruce stared at the computer screen in confusion, "this property belongs to a Travis Rutherford from Chicago."

Pandora walked back over to her computer. "Okay, can you get me a background on him?"

"I did. He's clean as a whistle. Twenty-seven-year-old, college student, no criminal record."

Pandora stared at the screen with her arms folded.

"But that's because he's using an alias. Look at this," Bruce typed in some information on the keyboard, as a profile a mile-long popped up on the screen. "Jeremiah Davis, from Atlanta, Georgia, remember him?" Bruce pointed at the mug shot.

Pandora stared at the screen in confusion, searching her memory. Suddenly, her face distorted into a look of horror. "Wait a minute. Wasn't he the one—"

"Yes…that's him," Bruce cut her off, "you'd better get whoever is near him away from him," he got up from the chair.

"Shoot," Pandora whispered, racing for the door.

"Do you need my hel—"

Before he could finish his sentence, Pandora was gone.

Twenty-Three

Lights out!

Cold water caused Eden to come to. Through
puffy eyes, she scanned her surroundings as best as she
could. She looked around at the dark grey walls and dim
lighting, blinking to help clear her vision. It never
dawned on her how bleak and depressing the home she
shared with Travis actually looked. Laying in a puddle
of her own blood, squishing sounds could be heard
underneath her as she desperately tried to move her legs.

With every ounce of strength she had left Eden
rolled onto her stomach. Slowly, she slid her body
across the floor, bypassing teeth and patches of hair. It
wasn't until her tongue swiped across her gums that she
realized they were *her* teeth. The bitter, salty taste of
blood conquered her mouth. Using the bridge of the
bottom steps, she was able to pull herself over to the
wall. Using the wall for support, Eden slowly stood up.
Her vision faded in and out and her head spun like a tire
on a highway. If she didn't have a concussion before, she
certainly had one now. She heard a swift noise to her left
and before she could fully turn her head to look, a steel
fist rammed into her stomach. Eden hunched over in
pain just as a knee lifted into her mouth, knocking out
what was left of her front teeth.

"I can't believe I really tried to change for you,"
Travis demonically spat. "I promised to get help and it
still wasn't good enough for you!" He swiftly pulled a

nine-millimeter from his pocket and cocked it.

Eden's eyes widened in fear. Raising his hand, Travis forcefully cascaded into her head with the butt of the gun, pistol-whipping her over and over again.

She tried shielding her body from it, but she wasn't fast enough...Eden opened her mouth to scream, yet nothing came out. Travis planted one hand around her small neck. "I told you this wouldn't end well for you. All you had to do was love me the way I deserved to be loved." He barked. "Since you ruined lunch for us, why don't you go to the kitchen and warm me up some of that nasty food you cooked the other night. I'm hungry. I should never be hungry in my own house!" He yelled, beads of spit flying from his mouth.

Eden didn't mutter a word. She stepped out of his grip as quickly as the law of gravity would allow, forcing her body into the kitchen.

"Why are you walking so slow? Are you trying to be smart?" He bellowed, snatching his belt off. "Do you need me to put some pep in your step? Is that what it is?" He laughed, evil laced his voice.

"Raising his brown leather belt, Travis struck Eden across her back nearly twelve times, slicing her skin like a sharp knife. She felt like someone had just dumped a bucket of scalding hot water on top of it. Biting down on her lip to keep from screaming, Eden continued walking toward the kitchen. Maybe if she could just get to the refrigerator, he would stop.

"It makes me sick how much I love you, Eden," Travis shook his head, trailing behind her as she staggered, "why can't you see that I do these things to help make you a better woman?"

Eden could feel herself getting nauseated with

each word Travis spoke. A passionate hatred for him ran through her veins like poison, and if she could just turn around and grab that gun from him, she would splatter his brains all across their living room. Using what ounce of energy she had left Eden sped up her strides. The second she reached the kitchen, she dropped to her knees and vomited everywhere. Travis jumped back, making sure she didn't get any on his new sneakers.

"Baby, are you alright? You're not pregnant again are you?" A glimmer of hope filled his voice.

This man was sick...

Eden threw up until her insides felt like they too, would come out. Travis patted Eden's back until she was finished, and then helped her off the floor. Grabbing a paper towel from the towel rack, Travis helped Eden lean against the wall to keep her balance as he cleaned her face off. Tears rolled down her face, and her swollen eyes were bloodshot red.

"No, you can't be pregnant. We haven't done anything."

Eden tried to push him away with all of her might. "You are *sick!"* She blurted without thinking. Travis's eyes stretched open, looking at her as if he were the devil reincarnated.

"Shut up!" Travis shoved her into the wall. He listened to her begging and crying for him to leave her alone, and his anger only worsened, "or better yet, *I'm* gonna shut you up *for good*!"

Travis wrapped both hands around her neck and choked nearly every ounce of air out of Eden's body until she was purple in the face. With her eyes gaped open, she scratched and clawed at his grasp. Just as her eyes began to slither in their sockets, Eden prayed, asking God for help. She couldn't fight anymore. *She had taken enough.*

Suddenly, a piercing pain hit Travis in his side. Startled, he let Eden go, as she collapsed to the floor. He gripped his side, just as another sharp sting hit his gut, causing him to stumble against the wall with a blunt force. Travis grunted loudly as he looked down at his midsection. His shirt was covered in blood. When he looked back up towards the door his eyes gaped open, being met face to face with Pandora and Quinn. They stood at the backdoor entrance, each of them protected on both sides by their husbands.

Pandora's Beretta was aimed straight at Travis's head, ready to splatter his brains against the wall.

"How did you get in here?" Travis heaved, muttering profanity through his clenched teeth.

Pandora released another bullet from her chamber, ripping into his knee cap. "I knocked," she spat. "But you were so busy whooping her behind I figured I'd let myself in." Her words turned into a painful gasp the second she spotted Eden's pitiless body propped upright against the wall. She wasn't moving, and her limp limbs were all spread out on the floor.

"Eden?" Pandora called for her. When she didn't get a response, panic cascaded through Pandora's subconscious. It clawed up her body and wrapped itself around her throat.

Andre and Jackson rushed over to Travis to make sure he didn't move. Quinn clutched her chest with both hands, rushing over to Eden. She kept trying to catch her breath, but it wouldn't come quick enough. Tears flooded Quinn's eyes as she knelt down and looked at the battered mess Travis had made of her friend.

Emotionally, Eden was unreachable at this point. She didn't even twitch. Quinn wasn't sure she even realized they'd come to her rescue. Seeing her friend in such a catastrophic state caused Quinn to wince. Intense, blazing pain etched itself so deep into her soul she thought she'd never be able to escape it.

"So, you like to beat on women, huh?" A hard kick from the back of Jackson's boot went straight into Travis's face.

Andre turned just in time to see Pandora's gun locked and loaded, aimed straight for Travis's head. Her eyes pierced at him, vengeful and relentless. Andre rushed over and wrestled the gun out of her hands before she pulled the trigger.

"Let go of me, Andre," she threatened, tears soaring down her face.

"*Don't* turn into the very thing you're trying to destroy," he warned, "we've done our part. Let God do the rest."

Pandora shook her head quickly, not wanting to hear anything he had to say. She walked up to Travis and kicked him as hard as she could in the groin with her heels.

Travis yelped in pain.

"I hope you burn in *the deepest, hottest* parts of hell for this," Pandora wiped her tears.

"Get her up and to the car," Andre motioned, pulling out his cellphone, "I'm calling the police and an ambulance."

"Go ahead," Pandora confirmed, refusing to take her eyes off of Travis, "be sure to let the police know you've found Jeremiah Davis. I'm pretty sure they'll be here within fifteen seconds," she sneered.

Travis snapped his head up at her, wincing through his pain. "That *is* your real name, isn't it? I *remember* you," she pointed at him, "your fiancé got pregnant while you were at a junior college, and you tried to bargain with her to get an abortion because you were planning to enter into the NBA draft that next semester."

"You got the wrong person, lady," Travis cringed in pain, squirming on the floor.

"No, I think I've got it right," she assured him. "When your fiancé refused to get rid of her baby, you gave her an old-fashioned abortion...*Just beat the hell out of her*. As if that weren't enough, you set the house on fire, making sure she was in it when it all went up in flames, but you didn't know your own mother was in the house with her. Three lives...*gone*," Pandora squatted down until she was eye level with him, "yup...I remember you, now. I was the one you called to get you out of hot water. I guess it was my luck I didn't have time to take on your case. You managed to get away, but the thing is, sick-minded people like you can never go too long before they slip up again. I could kill you right now if I wanted too, and I *certainly* want too but I'd rather you rot in misery, spending the rest of your life getting beaten and tortured in prison. *Just like you did to my friend."*

"Police are on their way," Andre walked over to Eden. He shook his head in remorse, kneeling down to help lift her up. Jackson quickly rushed over to help. Quinn got up and stepped back, watching Jackson and Andre lift Eden off the floor. Pandora stood up and looked at Eden for a second before quickly turning away. She couldn't stand to see her like that. She walked over to Quinn and they both hugged one another, relieved that it was finally over. They'd gotten Eden to safety.

Tears fell from Eden's face. Finally, she was saved, but was she really? As Jackson and Andre carried Eden toward the door, she looked over at Travis one last time. She wanted to see all of the mistakes she'd made. She wanted to etch his face into her memory in hopes that she'd never run into someone like him again.

Little did she know, Travis had found a way to sit up and was staring right back at her with eyes full of hate. Eden's eyes grew wide with terror when she saw him reach for his gun and point it in her face. She screamed out as loud as she could, causing Andre and

Jackson to stop walking, and Quinn and Pandora to snap their head in Travis's direction.

Pow!

"Till death do us part," was the last words she heard before he unloaded his gun, sending a bullet straight into Eden's head. Everything after that seemed to move in slow motion. At a glance, Eden saw the terror etched into Quinn and Pandora's face as they shrieked in horror. She felt herself falling, as Andre tried to dodge her out of harm's way a half-second too late. She saw Jackson snatching his gun from his hip, unloading two bullets into Travis's head, killing him in an instant. Blood splattered everywhere.

"No!" She heard Quinn cry out just before her hearing grew faint. Eden's eyes rolled to the back of her head, permanently turning out her lights.

Eden and Ruby watched as Eden's lifeless body was placed into the ambulance by paramedics. Through feverish, over bright eyes, she cupped her mouth with her hands and cried. "I'm sorry...I'm so-so-so sorry. None of this should've happened."

"I'm sorry, too," Ruby rubbed her back, "such a beautiful, young life. *Wasted."*

"I don't have any more excuses to give you. You were right, mom. I messed up my life," she sobbed in distress. "I deserved everything that happened to me. There were so many missed opportunities and chances I had that I didn't take. I got into my feelings, and it led me down a horrible path."

"I've always told you growing up, that you have to be careful of three things; the choices you make, the stones you throw, and the company you keep."

"This must be a dream," Eden looked around the brightly lit area, giving herself the benefit of the doubt. Maybe she would wake up and everything would go back to the way things used to be.

"I think they're all wishing for the same thing too," Ruby said, just as their surroundings changed and they were standing in the middle of a large empty train station platform. Everything around them was dreary. There was a small light hovering above Ruby and Eden, constantly flickering between contrasts of pale light and pitch darkness. Eden heard a loud conductor's whistle from afar and turned her head to see a humongous black train proceeding down the tracks, stopping directly in front of them. The train was filled to capacity from the front to the rear with wailing, screaming, pleading souls.

"What's going on? Where's that train going?" Eden widened her eyes in fear.

"To hell," Ruby raised an eyebrow, pointing to a dark, snake-like figure in the conductor's seat.

"Hell?" Eden jerked her head back in fear, "not with those innocent women and teenagers on board," Eden pointed out. "And look, there's an elderly woman with a cane over there, and a man on crutches amongst the crew."

"And there's a deacon, church members, and ministers too," Ruby laughed

"All aboard!" A deep voice bellowed out from the front of the train, preparing to take off.

Eden jumped back in fright, listening to the souls as they pleaded for mercy. Eden grabbed on to Ruby's arm. She had never heard a more heartbreaking sound in her life.

Ruby looked at her watch. "The engineer is waiting for you...time is wasting."

Eden's eyes nearly popped out of their sockets. "Waiting for what?" she replied, taken aback, "I don't have to get on there, do I?"

"You tell me, sweetheart," Ruby responded softly, turning to face her daughter. "Is there a ticket and a seat reserved with your name on it?"

Eden stared at her mother through tear-filled, regretful eyes. "There's probably a front-row seat," Eden muttered, lowering her head.

Ruby studied her daughter for a long time, taking in her energy.

"I wish there was some way I could go back and fix every mistake I made," she crossed her arms, shaking her head.

"Unfortunately, that's not how life works. What's done, cannot be undone. The past cannot be changed. The future, however can be."

Eden slowly looked up at Ruby.

"If you were given a second chance, what would you do with it?"

"I'd cherish every moment," Eden gasped, "I'd fix my relationship with my friends, make better choices, and get the help I needed to emotionally heal. I'd do whatever else it takes to become a success instead of a statistic."

The train revved its engine and took off down the tracks, leaving a puff of smoke behind.

"Well…we serve a merciful, forgiving God who loves to give second chances," Ruby smiled, "I think he's heard you."

Eden's hand went flying into her chest, "So I'm not gonna die?"

"Not this time. You've been placed amongst the ranks of people like Peter, Jonah, Mark, Samson, and David, all trophies of God's grace. However, just like God has been merciful, patient and forgiving to you, you must be merciful, patient, and forgiving to others," Ruby darted her eyes at Eden.

"Of course I will, I promise," Eden answered. She gazed at Ruby for a long time, soaking up her aura as if she'd never have a moment like this again.

"Well, then I guess my work here is done," Ruby nodded approvingly, breaking the silence. "I have one last thing to show you and then I have to go."

"Will I remember any of this? Will I remember our time here? Wherever we are…" Eden looked around.

"Whatever is meant for you to remember, you will remember," Ruby turned, standing face-to-face with Eden. She gently placed her hands into hers. "Clothe yourself with compassion, kindness, humility, and patience and you'll be just fine. *Vengeance is mine*, saith the Lord. God has forgiven you and given you a second chance, now it's time for you to extend a second chance to someone else."

"Mom," Eden shut her eyes and shook her head, "Why do you keep saying—"

When she opened her eyes, she was standing in front of her mother's old condominium elevator. Eden looked to her left and to her right, but Ruby was gone.

Twenty-Four

One year ago...

"Anyway, I was halfway up here and realized I forgot the papers in my car, so I'm going home," Pandora laughed, "I will not walk back up ten flights."

Ruby and Eden laughed, "so you came all the way up here just to tell us you'll see us later?" Eden asked.

"If the elevator works, I'll be back in a minute. If it doesn't...see you next week," she laughed and left the condo.

As Pandora made her way down the hall, her phone vibrated in her purse. Pulling it out, she accepted the call.

"Joanna," She said, politely. "Oh, hello Mr. Washington, I spoke to your lawyer the other day. I planned on calling you to set up an appointment as soon as I got back to the office."

She walked up to the elevator and pressed the button. She was relieved when the downward arrow lit up.

"Sure. I'll give you a call back before the day is out. No problem. Talk to you soon." She ended the call and put her phone back into her purse just as the elevator door opened. She proceeded to walk inside but collided with someone getting off.

"Oh, I'm sor—" Pandora ran right into Jackson, who was now face-to-face with her. It was the closest they'd been in a while.

"Pandora," his eyebrows raised.

She gasped, immediately stepping back. Nervously looking away, she replied, "excuse me," before moving around him and quickly got on the elevator.

"It's nice to see you," Jackson followed her with his eyes.

He wanted so badly for her to say something…anything, but she refused. She stared down at the elevator buttons and ignored him, rapidly pressing for the first floor. Backing out of the elevator, Jackson nodded, embarrassed and crushed. Even though Pandora refused to look at him, he couldn't take his eyes off of her. Her beauty was a work of art that he wished he could hang on the walls of his heart. He'd originally come over to return all of the money Ruby spent on the baby furniture, but now he felt directionless— unsure if he was coming or going.

Lowering his head, he slowly turned away. Just as the elevator door began to shut, Jackson spun back around and stopped it from closing. He had so much to say to the woman of his dreams, and he needed to get it out. He wasn't sure what would happen, but he owed it to himself to give it one last try.

Pandora's small frame pressed against the wall, as she swiped away the onset of tears from her eyes. Jackson's presence was a reminder of the man she loved, and the sting of betrayal. Catching wind of her tears, he hurried into the elevator.

"Stay away from me," she darted, angrily, her hand stretched out in front of her.

"We need to talk," he ignored her demand.

Pandora stepped to the side, attempting to pass him, but Jackson used his body to block her path.

"Get out of my way before I shoot you again," she hissed, "*this* time, I won't miss."

Jackson wasn't budging…not this time. "Please, stop fighting me and just listen."

"Nothing you have to say is worth listening to," she scolded, trying to push him away.

"I miss you, Anna," he softly lifted her chin to face him, "I can't sleep, I can't ea—"

Yanking away from his touch, she slapped his hand away. Jackson snatched her hands and pinned them to the elevator wall above her head.

"Stop. Stop being so mad and let me say what I need to say!"

"Get off of me!" She scolded, finally looking up at him. His eyes bore into hers with such intensity, her anger melted away like candle wax.

"I never meant to hurt you," he continued, "I meant to lie, I meant to manipulate, but it was all to be with you in the end. I'm sorry this is happening, but I will go crazy if you continue to hate me."

His dominate stare sucked her in like a vacuum. She wanted to hate Jackson for everything he had caused, she had every right. He wrecked her friend's life and made a fool out of her heart, but as they stood toe-to-toe sharing a moment in the moving elevator, her heart wouldn't allow her to.

He released her hands as the elevator continued to travel down. Reaching over to the panel of buttons, Jackson hit the emergency stop button, causing the elevator to come to a halt.

He faced his ex-lover, staring at her intensely. Pandora wanted to protest but locking eyes with him took her strength away. Her pulse began to elevate, as butterfly's swarmed around in her stomach.

Moving into her, Jackson pressed his lips against hers. The familiar touch of love sent electricity running through her veins. He wrapped his hands around her waist and pulled her into him, catching wind of her Clive Christian perfume. It drove him crazy. Nothing was more arousing than her scent in his arms. Her lips were so soft beneath his as she slowly opened them, allowing his tongue to creep inside. That was the flare that set fire to every nerve. Jackson nibbled and teased on her lower lip, tugging at it between his teeth.

Pandora's eyes slowly widened, remembering where she was. She couldn't do this to Eden, not in her own home. She was a loyal friend, and this was betrayal in its purest form. Her mind wanted to stop, but as Jackson reached down and massaged her neck with his lips, she couldn't do anything but clutch his waist and hope she didn't fall.

"Wait," she panted, pushing him away, "we have to stop. I can't do this."

Jackson looked up. "Why would I stop if it makes you feel good?" He kissed her again until his passion consumed her thoughts, and her inner protests were silenced. The more he aroused her, the more she wanted to be touched. The intense, earth-shattering promiscuity in the small elevator came crashing to a halt as they both reached the point of no return, tearing away from their kiss. They took what they wanted, ravenously, passionately, leaving no stone left unturned. Ten minutes later, Pandora found herself quickly buttoning her blouse and adjusting her skirt. Her seven minutes in heaven had worn off, and the reality of where she was and what she'd just done, settled in.

"I have to go," she adjusted her collar, "I told Eden I'd come back up to help her, but I think your presence is more important at this point. I'll call her later."

"Let's go to dinner tonight and talk," Jackson suggested, "we can find a way to fix th-"

"No-no," she proclaimed, finally looking up at him with a pained expression. "We can't do dinner, we can't talk, and we can't do…this... anymore, ever. This was a mistake," she reached past him and released the emergency button on the elevator, as it started back up and made its way to the ground floor.

"Our love is a mistake?" He furrowed.

"Yes…no...I mean…" Pandora grew silent for a second, trying to gather her thoughts. "I've forgiven you so many times in the past for your mistakes. I felt like a fool in love, but I was content with that. We were flawed, but it made me feel human," her heart sank. "I would do anything to make us work," she swallowed, taking a step back," but I won't do this."

Jackson lowered his head and stuck his hands in his pockets.

Pandora walked over to him and picked his face up to meet hers. "My career forces me to be cold-hearted, ruthless, and emotionless at times, but when I leave my office and go home, I'm just a regular woman. I have a heart," she used one hand to pat her chest. "I have feelings, Jackson. I'm a good person, and I have good friends. Eden is one of them."

"But what about me? What about love?" He grimaced, "What about Puerto Rico? Everything is set for our wedding. We're supposed to leave tomorrow. I didn't flake this time."

Pandora's heart fluttered and shattered thinking about what could've been just as the elevator reached the ground floor.

"Will we ever have our chance?" He asked.

Pandora shrugged. "Maybe in our next lifetime," she muttered. The door slid open. "Goodbye, Jackson."

Jackson cringed, watching her walk away from him as the elevator door closed. Forcefully clicking the elevator button up, Jackson fixed his jeans and secured his belt buckle. He punched the elevator wall in a rage before slamming his body against it.

"I've gotta get rid of that girl," he muttered out loud, rubbing a hand down his face. All week long, Jackson couldn't sleep because Pandora was on his mind. He stayed up night after night, chastising himself about all the things he'd done wrong to lose her for good. Her beauty intoxicated him, and Jackson couldn't stop thinking about her. Pretty soon, he'd lost control of his feelings and it turned into an overwhelming, unbalanced, delirious, all-consuming boundless *obsession*. He thought their euphoric lovemaking in the elevator could get her back, but he was wrong. Eden was standing in his way and he needed to get rid of her. Jackson *did* want to become a father however, Pandora's love had taken precedence over everything and he was willing to risk it *all to get it back.* Jackson got off the elevator and proceeded down to Ruby's home. The second he got to the door, it swung open and Ruby appeared in the doorway with an attitude.

"I *thought* that was your trifling self, pulling in my parking lot. You have *some* nerve showing up here," she sneered.

"It's nice to see you, Miss Ruby," Jackson replied humbly, ignoring her rude comments.

"Nice to put my foot up your a-" Eden grabbed her door and opened it wider, holding a cup of apple juice in her hand, quickly stepping in front of Ruby.

"I got it mom, *please*," Eden insisted.

"Listen, I didn't come here to fight or to make anyone else upset. I just wanted to give Miss Ruby back all of the money she spent on the baby furniture," Jackson stepped back, stuffing his hands into his pockets, "I also wanted to talk to you about some things, Eden," he looked up, eyeing Ruby, "*alone*." Ruby almost jumped out of her skin.

"I don't want your pitiful money," Ruby hissed with an attitude, "and how dare you have the audacity to come to my home and think my daughter is just gonna accept your lousy apology and talk." Eden didn't want anything to do with Jackson, nor did she want to hear anything she had to say, but with the birth of their baby coming up in a couple of weeks, she needed some type of closure.

"Mom," Eden spun around to face Ruby, "Just give us a few minutes okay? He doesn't have to come inside, we'll stand right in the doorway," she promised.

"Agreed," Jackson nodded, pulling out a wad of cash from his pocket and handing it to Ruby. An angry Ruby slapped Jackson's hand away as all the money flew into the air.

"I *said* I don't want anything from your sorry behind!" Jackson stepped back and sighed, biting his lip to hold in his anger and remain humble.

"And just look at that smug grin on his devious

face," Ruby sneered. Ruby tried to move past Eden. If only she could get her hands around his neck, she could choke all the hell out of him that he put their family through over the years. Eden turned around, practically tossing her cup of juice to Jackson,

"Hold this," she said quickly, "I'll be right back," Eden spun herself and her big belly around to face her angry mother a second time, urging her into the house. After a few seconds of trying to move around Eden, Ruby gave up and allowed Eden to force her in the house. Jackson shook his head just as the door closed behind him. Staring down at Eden's juice, Jackson realized his plan was going smoother than he'd expected thanks to Ruby's antics. He reached into his pocket, pulled out a bottle of Prolixin, and laced Eden's drink with it. Prolixin is an odorless, tasteless serum used to treat the symptoms of schizophrenia. When used properly, it diminishes the hallucinations and lessens their obsessive compulsivity. With a lethal dose however, it could kill a person within twenty-four hours without it even being detectable in their bloodstream, appearing as if the person died from natural causes. Jackson was no murderer, but sometimes the game of love could turn *deadly*. Putting the cap back onto the bottle, Jackson placed it back into his pocket just as Eden opened the door and entered into the doorway.

"I'm sorry," she replied, reaching for her cup. She guzzled down the remainder of her apple juice and let Jackson say what he had to say, parting with a slight hug when they'd finished talking. Jackson turned his back and walked away with a devious smile across his face in hopes that it would be the final time he'd *ever* see Eden. As he walked down the hall, his cellphone rang. He reached into his pocket and answered on the second ring,

"Yeah…"

"Jackson, baby, what's taking you so long?" A female voice responded.

"Ashley?" Jackson looked at the caller ID on his phone. He didn't recognize the number.

"Yes, it's me," Ashley replied impatiently, "the guard let me hold his cellphone to call you. Our little deal is *off*." Jackson froze in his tracks.

"Excuse me? Why?" He whispered into the phone.

"You think you're *slick*. I murdered my entire family to be with you, and you promised me that lawyer *bitch* you heard about could get me off with a clean slate. How ironic it is though, that the day she lost my case, I hear it through the grapevine that you two were leaving the courthouse bathroom together," Ashley fussed, "I *also* heard from a wandering eye that you two have been spotted together on *several* occasions. Are you sleeping with her, Jackson? Are you trying to play—"

"Baby, no," Jackson lied, "I don't know where you're getting this crazy information from but it's inaccurate. I love you, Ashley, you're the only woman for me. You can't call our deal off. I can't live another *day* without you." A brief silence sounded on the other · end of the phone followed by a long sigh.

"Fine, but are you *sure* this is gonna work?" Ashley responded with an attitude.

"Baby, it's foolproof, I promise. I've already paid the prison guards off. At eight forty-five AM exactly, they're gonna open the gate, and leave the door cracked for you. The minute they let you out of your cell for breakfast, I need you to run out," Jackson walked down the hall, speaking as low as possible. "The prison van will be right there waiting, and the guard left the key inside. Eden and her mother are going to lunch at noon, but Ruby has to stop by the Babies-R-Us. *That's* where I need you to be. Kill Ruby. Make *sure* of it, and then snatch her car and meet me at the top of the warehouse by one o'clock. I'll meet you there with a chopper and we'll be out of this county in no time."

"I can't wait to see you," Ashley pressed her ear into the phone, taking in all of Jackson's promises, "I miss you *so* much."

"I miss you too, baby. Tomorrow, we'll be together forever," he lied, rolling his eyes to the back of his head. "I have to go. Get some sleep, okay?"

"I will see you tomorrow," Ashley whispered before ending the call.

Jackson placed his phone back into his pocket. *Got all my chips in place,* he thought. *If my persistence works, I'll be in Mexico saying I do to the love of my life, Eden will be dead, that baby will be dead, her annoying mother will be dead, and Ashley will get caught by the police and get sent straight back to prison,* Jackson grinned excitedly before bursting through the stairwell of Ruby's complex, heading down the steps. The following day, everything went according to Jackson's plan, except one thing. The drink he poisoned Eden with, put her body into labor and killed their baby, but it *didn't* kill her.

*****

Travis's birthday...

Travis sat in the driver's seat of his Mercedes in a drunken stupor. Jade's thick juicy lips painted with her favorite candy apple red lipstick were face down in his crotch.

Ten minutes later, she sat up in the passenger seat with a devious smile planted across her face, wiping the corner of her mouth. "Happy birthday, Baby."

"Thank you," he grunted, resting his head on the back of the headrest.

"I know you're probably still upset with me, but I had to see you again and apologize," Jade responded with a somber glow.

Travis fixed his boxers and zipped his jeans. "Thank you for the blow job, but you can't apologize for what you did," he shook his head.

"So, you're gonna hold this over my head for the rest of my life?" She winced.

"You killed my baby, Jade," Travis turned to sneer at her, "you can't apologize for that."

"Correction, I crumpled the hallway rug up. It was your clumsy wife that tripped over it and fell," she folded her arms.

"Whatever. You knew what you were doing," Travis shook his head.

"I don't care!" she fussed, "you told me we were going to Virginia to do a job and make some money. You told me this Jackson guy paid you a lot of money to make this Eden girl disappear. You did *not* say you were going to marry her and get her pregnant!"

"That wasn't my plan, okay?" He shot back. "I just, I-"

"You what?" Jade leaned in and pursed her lips, "you fell in love with that skank, and you married her!"

"Yes, I did. I love her. I'm sorry! But you know how much I wanted a baby and you took that from me."

"And you know how much I wanted you," Jade began to cry, "and you took that from me and gave it to her."

Travis sighed, rubbing his temples. "Listen, this will all be over soon. The job is getting ready to be finished, I just have to muster up the courage to kill her. We'll have our six hundred thousand, move away somewhere and start our lives together," he lifted Jade's chin to face him, "I promise."

Suddenly, everything around Eden faded to black. The crying voices echoing in the background grew louder, as surges of aching pain shot through her entire body. Eden tried to grab her head, but she couldn't move her arms. Loud beeping sounds filled her ears. Eden had no idea what was going on, but she couldn't move no matter how hard she tried.

"Oh my gosh," Quinn's voice filled her ears, "is she trying to wake up?"

Eden could hear heels scraping the floor, growing closer to her.

"I think so," Pandora gasped, "somebody get in here, something's happening!"

Within seconds, Eden could hear a hurdle of footsteps that sounded more like a stampede of elephants running in her direction. Eden's squeezed her eyes out of entropy, doing her best to open them. With every ounce of strength she had, she twitched her eye muscles until a brightness blinded her vision.

"Eden," Quinn's anxious voice cried out.

Eden's eyes twitched until finally, her eyes were fully open. Things were fuzzy at first, but the more she blinked, the clearer things became.

"Get Dr. Barnes in here, ASAP!" One nurse said, checking Eden's pulse.

"Oh, baby, I knew you would come out of this alive," tears of joy flooded from Pandora's eyes as she looked on in awe, "I didn't care what those stupid Doctors said."

Like waves in a strong current, Eden began to remember everything, bit by bit. Her eyes slowly scanned her surroundings. She remembered her accident and everything leading up to it. Her eyes danced around the room, locking themselves on Jade the minute she recognized her hovering over her hospital bed with a face full of tears. Her eyes shifted to the left, slowly forming into a glare the second they landed on Jackson. Eden remembered every single thing Ruby had shown her.

"*Vengeance is mine, saith the Lord,*" Eden could hear Ruby's voice in the back of her mind.

But, *to hell with that...*

To   be   continued...

Made in the USA
Columbia, SC
01 December 2020